WHAT LIES BENEATH

WHAT LIES BENEATH

MAUREEN MYANT

This edition produced in Great Britain in 2024

by Hobeck Books Limited, 24 Brookside Business Park, Stone, Staffordshire
ST15 0RZ

www.hobeck.net

A CIP catalogue for this book is available from the British Library.

ISBN 978-1-915-817-63-1 (ebook)

ISBN 978-1-915-817-64-8 (paperback)

Cover design by Jayne Mapp Design

Printed and bound in Great Britain

Are you a thriller seeker?

Hobeck Books is an independent publisher of crime, thrillers and suspense fiction and we have one aim – to bring you the books you want to read.

For more details about our books, our authors and our plans, plus the chance to download free novellas, sign up for our newsletter at **www.hobeck.net**.

You can also find us on Twitter **@hobeckbooks** or on Facebook **www.facebook.com/hobeckbooks10**.

To my grandchildren

Prologue

IMAGINE A GLOBE. *Made of glass. One with snow that falls when you shake it. Inside the globe is a village, a Christmas card scene, perhaps, with a church at its centre.* Here is the church, here is the steeple, open the doors and here are the people. *Look closer. There is no church, only a house in the snow, all alone. It invites you into the living room with its shabby, yet comfortable furniture. The log fire burns brightly and spits out the occasional spark that dies on the hearth. Sitting round it are four people. A happy family scene. Or is it?*

Lisa, the mother of the house, is laughing. She wants you to believe she hasn't a care in the world. Her cheeks are flushed from the heat of the fire. Her eyes sparkle but the deep line between her eyebrows is a giveaway. She's worried. A work problem? Difficulties with one of her children?

She's been with David, her husband, forever. David is reliable, you'd turn to him in a crisis. Head of town planning in a large local authority. Well paid, not that you'd know from the suits he wears. His depute wears Armani but David is happy

1

with Marks & Spencer. He's not wearing a suit now of course, not on holiday. His face is flushed, too, but not from the heat of the fire. High blood pressure? Nope, he's hacked off with Ollie.

Oliver next. The spoilt, youngest child. Lisa denies having indulged him, but we all know what mothers are like with their youngest child, their baby, clinging on to them as a reminder of their youth. Ollie's not that bad. His easy-going nature is difficult to ruin. His parents have had their ups and downs with him. Of course they have. But he's twenty now and past all that. You'd hope.

Huddled into a corner of the larger sofa is Emilia. Beautiful, waif-like Emilia with her long red hair. Turn back the clock thirty years and it could be Lisa sitting there. She clutches a glass of wine to her chest, sipping occasionally. It's not yet evening and already she's drunk. She listens to the banter between her parents and Oliver but doesn't join in. It's not only the drink making her pissed. She's found out something about her mother and resentment oozes from her.

The conversation winds down. Lisa yawns. She's thinking about chores: unpacking and cleaning the kitchen of mouse droppings before starting to prepare the evening meal. David looks at his watch and frowns. His favourite child should be here by now. He goes to the window and looks out at the snow dancing down. Not a sedate waltz but a frenzied Strip the Willow. We need to step back outside, into the cold. It's time to meet Ros.

Chapter One

THE SNOW CAME EARLIER than forecast. Ros was on the A1 when it started, and it didn't seem too bad then, but now she was on a minor road with no other cars and for the last hour it had snowed nonstop. She leaned forward, hands taut on the steering wheel, her eyes screwed up and focused on the road ahead. Only the hedges hinted at where the road was, and the relentless blizzard was devouring them. She was exhausted; the snowflakes were mesmerising as they swirled around the car. More than once in the past ten minutes, her eyelids had drooped. A fox ran out from the hedgerow; she stamped on the brake. Despite not going fast, the car skidded, and she fought to control it before it slid to a halt and stalled. The fox stared at her; its eyes gleaming in the car's headlights. Ros pressed hard on the horn until it moved, slinking away in the sly way they have.

Ros closed her eyes for a few seconds, safe in the knowledge that cars rarely came this way. It was a one-track road leading to a few houses and ended at the Warren. Literally, the road to nowhere. She opened her eyes hoping the snow would have lessened. If anything, it was worse. There was nothing for it but to carry on. She turned the key. Rusty, her ancient Fiat Punto, was temperamental but he rarely let her down. She released the clutch, but the wheels spun, unable to grip the icy road. Fuck! She hit the steering wheel. The snow was falling faster than ever. Why hadn't she stayed in Glasgow? At the best of times, her parents' second home in Northumberland was far from her favourite place. Yes, the countryside was pretty enough but there wasn't a pub within walking distance, and it smelled, oh how it smelled, no matter how long the windows stayed open. The smell was pervasive, a mustiness that never went away. *And* there were mice who left their horrid droppings everywhere. It was less than hygienic. And now, the icing on the cake; she was caught in a snowstorm. She pulled her jacket close and shivered.

What a horrible day she'd had. First, the fight with her mother when she said Ian couldn't come. Ros hadn't been going to phone her – she was all set to turn up without saying anything – but Ian had insisted. Her jaw clenched as she remembered the conversation.

'Everything all right, Mum? I didn't wake you up, did I?'

Her mother's voice was thick with sleep. 'Of course not. I've got a bit of a cold.'

Liar. She'd slept in. Mum was always a late riser. 'Oh, right. Mum, I'm going to bring someone with me, is that OK?'

'Dan? Yes, of course. That'll be lovely. It's been ages since we saw him.'

Shit. Surely, she'd told her. Ros lowered her voice. 'I finished with him over a month ago. Don't you remember?'

'No, you didn't tell me.' Her mother's voice was sharp. 'Who's this then?'

'Someone special. You'll like him,' Ros twirled a lock of

4

hair as she spoke, a sure sign she was nervous. She didn't dare look at Ian.

'Right.'

'What do you mean?'

'You say the same thing every time, *someone special*. I'm fed up with it. We all are.'

Ros's heart beat faster. 'Is that a no?'

'Yes, I believe it is.'

There was a pause, neither of them wanting to give in. Her mother caved first. 'So, what time do you think you'll get there? You should set off by one if you want to be sure of getting there before dark. Oh, and there's snow forecast too.'

'Actually, Mum, if I can't bring Ian then I don't think I'll come.' It was petulant and unworthy of her. Her mother had been looking forward to this family reunion, their first Christmas all together for three years, but the words spilled out anyway.

'Suit yourself.' Her mother cut her off.

Ros stared at her phone in disbelief. That hadn't gone well.

Then there was the argument with Ian. He was dismissive when she suggested they should defy her mother and go to Northumberland.

'I'm not going where I'm not wanted.' His face was closed, his mouth tight.

'OK, then. Why don't we go somewhere together? I'll book us into a hotel.' She sat down beside him, but he stood up and put on his coat.

'I don't think so.'

'Why not? You said you wanted to spend Christmas together.'

'Did I?' He'd stared at her until she turned away.

'Fine, do what you like,' she muttered. 'I've got a lot to do, so if you don't mind...'

He'd let himself out, shutting the door so quietly she wasn't sure he'd gone. She held herself together until she looked out of the window and saw him in the street below. He didn't look up at her but sauntered down the street, stopping only to pat a dog and speak to what looked like its attractive owner. They chatted like old friends, their faces too close together. Only then did she throw her mug at the door where it shattered. She was fuming. Not only had she broken her favourite mug but what option did she have other than to go to Northumberland? She'd never survive Christmas on her own and now Ian was gone, there was no alternative.

Ros thumped the steering wheel again. If Mum had agreed to Ian coming, she wouldn't be in this predicament. She grabbed her handbag from the back seat and rummaged through it for her mobile phone. No signal. Of course not. There was never a signal in this dump. It was a good sign, though. She must be close to the Warren. Maybe near enough to walk. She looked at the mileage indicator. She reset it before every journey, no matter how short. It read 121.7 miles. Now all she had to do was remember the distance to the Warren. Was it 123 miles or 132 miles from Glasgow? Please, she prayed, please let it be 123 miles. She looked out of the window, hoping for a glimpse of something familiar. There was nothing but snow and the faint outlines of trees. Wait! Was that the old, dilapidated cottage in the distance? A grey smudge of a shape. She was sure that the ruin wasn't far from the Warren.

God, it was cold. The little heat there had been in the car

had disappeared now the engine was off. Her father's advice about driving in winter came to mind: 'Always have a shovel, a piece of carpet, a blanket and some provisions in the boot. They won't take up much room and they're life-savers.'

She was fine for food. Mum had asked her to bring snacks as her contribution to the family reunion; she had two carrier bags full of nuts, crisps and other treats, in the boot. No chance she'd starve. No cosy blanket unfortunately, but a suitcase full of clothes; she'd wear them all if she had to. That left the shovel and piece of carpet. If only she'd taken Dad's advice. But she hadn't – well, in her defence, no-one listened to their parents' advice after the age of ten, did they?

Five minutes to three. She pictured her family sitting in front of the fire, drinking tea, laughing and joking. They wouldn't be concerned about her; she was always late. And of course there was the row with her mother. Maybe they'd never be worried. They'd think she was in Glasgow, sulking. She'd been so adamant, too quick to say she wasn't going to come. Damn her stupid temper. Surely, they'd phone. Although there was little chance of them getting through to her here with no signal. Her spirits slumped. She turned on the radio to hear what the BBC had to say about the weather.

Four minutes later, Ros switched it off. As much use as a chocolate fireguard, as Great Aunt Mae used to say. Why did they persist in telling people to stay at home if it snowed? Surely, the more people out on the roads the better? More cars would churn up the snow and help make the roads passable. Not that it would make much difference here on this road to nowhere. Her parents loved it; the desolate, isolated beauty of Northumberland. Ros, on the other hand, found the barrenness eerie and disquieting. Especially now.

She reached into the glove compartment for the tin of travel sweets, a habit from childhood. There had always been one in the family car. They were pretty disgusting but were a welcome treat when they'd been on the road for hours and needed something to perk them up. She smiled as she remembered the games she and her siblings had played. The obvious one, of course: who could make a sweet last the longest. Em always won. She was *such* a control freak. She tucked them away in a cheek in the way a hamster stored food. Em's sweets lasted for hours while she and Ollie would give in after a few minutes and crunch their way through them. Then there was the prediction game. What flavours would Dad buy this year? Fruits of the forest were best; they all hated the citron mix. Grapefruit – ugh. And the daftest game of all, getting a sticky sweet in their hand that they then had to put in their mouth without looking at it and guess what it was from the taste. Dad said it would improve their palates and claimed Ollie's was excellent because he always got it right. No one had the heart to tell him Ollie always peeked, his long lashes hiding the fact that he opened his eyes ever so slightly as he put the sweet in his mouth. All Ros ever tasted was the sickly icing sugar that coated them. Her father persisted in the custom long after childhood. Once they'd learned to drive, they each got a tin in their Christmas stocking.

She brought out the tin– it had been there since she got the car – and used her fingernail to slice through the Sellotape around it. When she opened it, she found that the sweets had merged into a glutinous mass in the summer. She prised one out and slid it into her mouth, surprised to find it was still palatable. She wasn't sure which fruit of the forest it was, but at least it wasn't grapefruit.

She closed her eyes and weighed up her options. Stay here, do what the radio had told her to do, and wait for help? No chance. The possibility of any help coming soon was nil.

What about getting the car moving? There was no shovel, but maybe she could use her hands to dig a way forward. If she got it moving, she'd be fine. But a quick glance at the windscreen told her that wasn't going to happen. The snow was falling thick and fast. As quickly as she could clear it away, it would cover up her efforts. She doubted a shovel would help. There was only one thing to do: leave the car and walk to the Warren. It wasn't an appealing option. Cold as it was inside the car, it would be much worse outside. But when she thought about it, it was obvious she'd have to try. It would be dark in under an hour.

First, though, she had to get out of the car. While she had been deliberating over what to do, the snow had been building up even more. She switched on the wipers but they didn't move. She put her gloves on ready to leave the car and tried to push open the door, but it stayed closed. God, she'd been buried. Her breathing quickened, and she forced herself to slow it down. What an idiot she was, the snow hadn't been falling for long enough to bury her. She wound down the window a little, leaned forward and poked at the snow. It fell away. Sitting back in the driver's seat she let out a long sigh. Any remaining doubts she had about leaving the car, disappeared. She pushed harder against the door grabbing on to the steering wheel when she lurched sideways as it opened.

The cold hit her hard. Her nose stung as she breathed in the icy air. The snowflakes falling on her cheeks were like pinpricks. Her forehead tightened; her eyes watered. She needed a hat and hoped she'd remembered to bring one. She felt her way round to the back of the car and cleared the snow from the rear screen, using her arm to sweep it off, cursing as ice-cold snow slid inside the sleeve of her jacket. Never mind, she'd change into her waterproof, a much more sensible option. She'd brought walking shoes with her, and they'd be better than the fashionable leather boots she was currently wearing. She removed her boots and put on her walking shoes. Hat, now. Where was it? She opened her suitcase and hunted for it. There it was, at the bottom. She shoved it on. Two minutes later she was ready. She locked the car, laughing at her caution. There was zero chance of there being anyone around to steal from it. As she was about to start off, she remembered there was a torch in the glove compartment. She hoped she wouldn't need it. Surely, she'd be home before dark? She retrieved it and switched it on to test it. The snow was disorientating, and she paused before setting off, looking round to check she was heading in the right direction.

To begin with, she tested the snow with each step, fearing she'd sink into a ditch. After a few steps she felt safe enough to stride out. The snow was three or four inches deep except where it had drifted. The hedgerow on each side of the road would keep her on the right track. Nonetheless it was slow work and tiring. She fingered the bag of nuts in her pocket wondering if she should have brought more but she hoped she had only a mile to walk; she'd be fine. Snow nipped at her face. How could something so soft have such a bite?

She was now walking too fast and not paying attention, she tripped. The snow cushioned her landing, but she banged her wrist on the ground and cried out in pain. Shit. She got to her feet and brushed the snow off. By now she'd been walking for twenty minutes and there was no sign of the Warren. She screwed up her eyes and tried to focus. The ruined cottage was not far away she thought, though it was hard to judge distances with all the snow swirling round. The old building had always scared her. When they were young teenagers, Em told her a murder had taken place there. Apparently, the owner had taken in a traveller and stabbed him to death, soaking his clothes in his own blood. When they were much older, Em confessed she'd made up the story, inspired by Northumberland folklore and an illicit viewing of *Psycho*. Ros put the memory out of her mind. Nothing for it but to carry on.

Each step was difficult. The snow was soft, which made it a little easier to negotiate, but it was tiring. She'd slowed down after the fall, scared she might slip again. There might be rocks lying underneath the perfect white sheet of snow. If anything, the snow was now falling faster. When she looked behind her, she noticed it was covering her footsteps. A little stab of fear pierced her. She had two possible outcomes to her predicament: firstly – the one she hoped for – in two minutes she'd come to the top of this hill and see the lights of the Warren. If she saw nothing, her next option would be to retrace her steps and spend the night in the car. If there were any steps to retrace; the snow was covering them fast. She stopped, careful to keep facing the same way. She was scared to turn in case she lost her sense of direction completely. It had happened to her once on the Whangie, north of Glasgow. A walk she'd done dozens of times. One minute she'd been striding along only fifty yards behind the group she was with, the next the smirr had thickened into an impenetrable wall of mist. Bewildered, she'd stopped, turned around to see if anyone was behind her and, somehow, she'd wandered off the path. Her calls to her friends had been swallowed up by the dense fog. Terrified by the prospect of wandering into a bog, she hadn't known what to do, so she'd stayed where she was for the longest few minutes of her life until the cloud lifted, and she saw another group of walkers who she latched onto. Until then, she would have sworn she knew the

Whangie well. Turned out she was wrong. It had been a frightening experience and a sobering one, but it was nothing compared to this. The Whangie was a popular walk and there were always other people around. Not like here.

'I will not cry,' she whispered to herself. 'Everything will be fine. The hedgerow isn't going anywhere. I'll get to the top of the hill and see the house.' She resumed walking, trying to go a little faster than before. She kept her head down to avoid the stinging snow in her eyes and every hundred steps she stopped and took her bearings. The third time she did this, she saw a figure in the distance, near the ruined cottage. Her heart thumped as she thought of Em's silly story. Don't be stupid. It must be one of her parents. They'd come looking for her after all.

'Hello, Dad, Mum? Her voice was weak; they wouldn't hear her if she didn't increase the volume. She tried again but only a croak came out. Surely, she wasn't getting a cold. 'Dad!' she yelled with all her might. But there was no reply. She squinted into the distance, but it was hopeless. The more she stared the more it seemed she'd been imagining things. A peep at her watch told her she'd been walking for thirty minutes. Fifteen more, then she'd turn back. With her head down she slogged forward, looking up every hundred steps. The wind grew stronger, against her, pushing her back. Fuck, it was cold. Her body told her to rest but she traipsed on. This was England for fuck's sake, not Antarctica. She wasn't going to die in a little bit of snow. A nasty little voice whispered, *people die in summertime, too, out walking in the hills.* Another, more comforting voice, reminded her she was in low-lying Northumberland, not in Scotland, high up in the mountains. She was concentrating so hard she didn't notice the figure watching her from the trees until she was no more than six metres away. Without thinking, she called out,

'Hello, can you help me? Do you know this area? Do you know where we are?'

What an idiot. The last thing she ought to do was draw attention to herself, a lone female far from the safety of other people. Walking past this figure was the best option. They stood there, staring. Ros stared back. In the swirling snow the shape was indistinct. Whoever it was they were taller than her mother but smaller and more squat than Dad or Oliver. He – she was now sure it was a man – he was wrapped up against the cold, a scarf across the bottom half of his face and a red hat pulled down over his eyebrows so no features were visible. They stood there looking at each other until he raised something and pointed it at her. It looked like a rifle. Now she felt what it was like to be an animal trapped in head-lights, unable to move. All she could think of was the book of Northumberland lore she'd read as a child with its tales of Red Caps, shapeshifters and other supernatural beings. Red Caps were squat, goblin-like creatures who preyed on lone travellers. They took their name from the hats they wore, soaked in the blood of their victims. Her heart was pounding. He was several feet away she'd have a head start on him if she ran. But her legs wouldn't move. She was doomed. After two or three seconds he turned away, walking further into the copse until the snow swallowed him up. Ros bit her lip. What a fool she was, letting her imagination take over. She watched him disappear, the walk was definitely a man's, perhaps he was one of the local farmers. But why hadn't he answered her? And had he been holding a rifle? She must have been hallucinating, disoriented by the blizzard. Red Caps didn't exist anymore than fairies or kelpies or elves.

Her nose was running; she delved into the pocket of her coat for a tissue. 'Onwards and upwards', she muttered, 'it's only one of the farmers. And it wasn't a rifle. Nothing to worry about. And it certainly wasn't a Red Cap. There's no such thing.' She walked on, determined not to fret about something she had no power over. She'd been walking for forty minutes; it was time to turn back. But she didn't want to go past the woodland again. Five more minutes would do it.

The snowflakes were smaller, falling more slowly. She prayed she hadn't left the road, but she wasn't sure. The countryside was more open now and there was no hedgerow to guide her. The light was fading fast. She pulled the torch out of her pocket and switched it on. If she were on the right path, she should see the lights of the house soon. If not, then she had completely lost her bearings. More than anything she longed for her family. Especially her mother. She wanted to be in front of the fire with a glass of wine in one hand and a cheese sandwich, no, a bowl of soup in the other. She imagined the smoke from the fire and the warm, comforting smell of Mum's chicken soup. Upstairs her bed waiting for her, hot water bottle tucked inside. She'd have a nap before dinner. There was a rock sticking out of the snow a few yards ahead, a dark blob amidst the white. I'll rest for a moment, she said to herself, forgetting her resolutions about keeping going. A minute or two will do it, then I'll walk on. There were weights on her eyelids, pulling them down; she had to close them, if only for a second...

Chapter Two

It was hard to avoid staring at Em. Lisa hadn't seen her looking so grim since she'd been in hospital after her breakdown a few years ago. Her hair was unwashed and greasy. She'd lost weight, too. She wasn't quite as thin as when she'd had anorexia. It was best not to comment but the effort was costing her. Lisa's face was no longer soft and welcoming but screwed up, like a discarded tissue.

'Spit it out, Mum.'

'What?'

'Your face would turn milk. Aren't you pleased to see me?'

Drunk, thought Lisa. Three in the afternoon and she's pissed. There had been a smell of alcohol when she and Oliver had arrived an hour ago. Stupidly, she'd offered them a glass of wine. Oliver had refused but Em had all but leapt on the bottle. It was already half empty.

'I am pleased to see you, of course I am.'

Em rolled her eyes and turned away from her mother.

She grabbed the wine bottle and poured another large glass, some of it spilling on the side table.

'You've probably had enough,' said Lisa removing the glass from her hand. She tried but failed to keep a censorious note from her voice.

'What the fuck do you think you're doing? I haven't finished.'

Lisa sat back in her chair, stunned by the venom in Em's words. She'd never spoken to her like that before. She had no idea what to say or do. Fortunately, David intervened.

'Apologise to your mother right now.' A tic under his right eye showed he was angry though you wouldn't know from his quiet, calm voice.

'Why should I? She's nothing but a liar and a hypocrite.' Emilia jumped up and stomped out of the room, slamming the door hard behind her.

'What the hell's got into her?' asked David.

Lisa shook her head. 'God knows. Do you know anything, Oliver?'

Ollie shook his head. 'Nope, she was very quiet on the way here. At a guess I'd say she was hungover.'

'Humph. Well, we'll leave her to it. She can sleep it off. I'd better get on with cleaning the kitchen. Lisa hesitated then added, 'It doesn't look as though Ros is coming. She'd be here by now if she were, you know how she hates driving in the dark.'

'What are you not telling me?' said David.

It was scary how he could read her. She told him about their argument, watching his mouth tighten in the way it always did when he was annoyed. He'd never admit it, but Ros was his favourite. In his eyes she could do no wrong. Once, Lisa had tried to explain to him how worried she was about Ros's attitude to men, how she moved seamlessly from one boyfriend to the next. Always had done, from the age of fifteen. He'd dismissed her concerns with an airy, 'You're worrying about nothing. She's too young to settle.'

'I'll give her a ring,' said David, picking up the phone and leaving the room.

If he managed to speak to her, he'd smooth things over and persuade her to come if the weather improved tomorrow. He had a way with her, always did. Lisa should have told him before, got him to go round to her flat. She walked over to the window to close the curtains taking a moment to stare into the darkening evening. She gasped. When she'd last looked, the snow had been a flurry at most. But now, it was a blizzard. Their footprints from earlier had disappeared and both cars were undefined mounds. She hugged herself, hoping Ros wasn't on her way, praying she was safe at home.

David came back into the room.

'Anything?' asked Lisa.

He put the phone back into its stand and shook his head. 'Nothing. No answer from her landline and nothing from her mobile phone.'

'Maybe...'

'What?'

'I don't know. Maybe she's not answering because she's annoyed with me or...'

'Could be, anyway, I've left messages on both phones, asked her to ring us to let us know she's safe. If she gets the m—Just then, the phone started to trill. 'That'll be her now.' He picked up the receiver. 'Ros! Hi. Are you on your way?' He waited for a second, then looked at the display, puzzled. 'It says withheld number. There's nobody there.'

'It'll be an automated call, David. Some scammer trying it on.'

'Oh, right.' He put the phone down. 'Idiots. Ros could have been trying to get through.'

He was about to go into one of his rants. Lisa diverted him. 'Mm. Do you want a cup of tea before I start on the kitchen?'

'No, I'm fine, thanks, I'll help you with the mouse droppings and set a couple of traps.'

They went through into the kitchen, which was warm now the ancient Aga had had time to heat up. Lisa grabbed a disinfectant spray and started on the task of cleaning up the mouse droppings. David stood by and watched.

'Here,' she grabbed another spray and cloth and passed it to him. 'You can check the bathroom and the bedrooms. And once you've finished, bring down the sheets and duvets and we'll air them in front of the fire.'

Twenty minutes later he was back, tasks completed. 'I've spread the bed linen out in the living room. Shouldn't take long to air them.' He was restless, jumpy. He'd never relax until he found out what was what with Ros.

Lisa smiled at him. 'Why don't you give Ros another ring.'

This wasn't the relaxing, happy evening she had planned. Em upstairs drunk, Ros at home in a huff, David fed up because Ros wasn't coming. She herself was as tightly strung as strings about to snap on a violin. She sighed. She'd forgotten how stressful family life was.

Her thoughts were interrupted by David crashing through the door. 'I've spoken to Ros's flatmate. Ros left the flat at twelve o'clock to come here. I'm going out to try to find her.'

'Hang on a second. What did Gemma say, exactly?'

'I've told you. Ros left the flat at twelve o'clock. She said to Gemma she hoped to get here around three. That was four hours ago.' His voice rose.

'Yes, I know. But it doesn't mean anything terrible has happened to her.' David had a tendency to take the smallest mishap and transform it into a great catastrophe.

'It doesn't take four hours to get here.'

'No, but it's been snowing. I know...' She carried on before he had a chance to interrupt. 'I know that makes it worse, but most likely she's in a service station somewhere, waiting until the worst of the snow passes. Why don't we check things out on the internet, see if there's any news on there and decide what to do then?'

David took a deep breath. 'You're right. Yes, that's what we should do.' He got up from his chair. He looked tired and Lisa got a sense of how he might look ten years from now.

The internet didn't tell them much more than they already knew or had guessed: it had snowed heavily in the Borders and the North of England; main roads were passable but only with difficulty and motorists were advised not to travel unless absolutely necessary. The lack of information was frustrating.

'I wish they'd tell us when they'd started to warn people to stay at home,' said Lisa. 'Was it as soon as the snow started? When did it start, anyway?'

'About half past one,' said David. 'You remember; it was snowing lightly as we were unloading the car. I can't be sure, but I think the ground was completely covered by two. It wasn't deep, though.'

'Have you looked outside?'

David went to the window. 'Shit,' he said. 'It's pretty bad out there.'

'OK, let's think this through,' said Lisa. 'She left Glasgow at twelve?'

'It's what I was told.'

'She would have hit the border as it began to snow.' Lisa's voice slowed as she realised the implications of this. Ros would most likely have been off the main road by then and onto minor roads. It would have been much better if she'd been on the A1. 'You're right, we should go out and look for her. We won't be able to drive in this, but we can walk up the road for a bit in case her car's stuck somewhere.' She didn't care to think about what they'd do if there was no sign of her.

Lisa ran upstairs to tell Oliver what they were going to do. He wasn't in his room, he was in Em's, talking to her. The intensity of the murmuring made her pause. Unable to stop herself, she pressed her ear against the door.

'What on earth's wrong with you, Em? You've been in a right mood since we got here. You were well out of order with what you said to Mum.'

'It's nothing. I've had a bit too much to drink, s'all.'

'Come off it. There's something not right with you. Are you eating properly? You look terrible.'

Lisa's mouth filled with saliva. Oh God, not this again. When Em was a teenager, they'd almost lost her to anorexia. Were they going to have to go through it again? What had triggered it this time, when everything was going well? A first-class degree in Film and Media Studies, followed by a distinction in her journalism masters. True, she hadn't reached her goal of hosting a review show dedicated to films, but she was only twenty-four and had already been commissioned to write reviews for the *Herald* and the *Scotsman*. She had also written a few features about contemporary life: scathing little pieces about the hold social media had on their lives. If she weren't eating again, Lisa didn't think she could take it.

'Lisa? Are you coming?'

She jumped at the sound of David's voice and moved back to the top of the stairs. 'I'm going to tell the others what we're doing,' she called before knocking on the door. When she walked in, Oliver was sitting on the edge of Em's bed while she hid underneath the covers.

'Dad and I are a bit worried about Ros. We're going to walk up the road a bit to see if there's any sign of her.'

'Wouldn't it be better to take the car?'

'I don't think we'd be able to get it moving. It's pretty bad out there.'

Oliver stood up. 'I'll come with you.'

'No, it's fine. You stay here in case she phones. I'm sure everything's all right but you know what a worrier Dad is.' She forced herself to look at Em. 'You OK?'

Emilia's voice was muffled. 'I'm fine. Didn't sleep well last night and now I've drunk too much. I'll take a nap now.'

Lisa had learned from experience not to fuss so she smiled and said, 'That's probably best,' before leaving the room.

'Mum?'

'Yes?' She didn't turn round.

'I'm sorry... you know... about what I said earlier.'

'OK, pet. We'll see you later.'

David had already been outside by the time she got back downstairs. 'It's hard to see anything out there,' he said.

'We'll have to give it a shot, anyway.' She and David put on their thickest jackets and hiking boots. Lisa gulped when David opened the door. It was impossible to see more than a few metres as the snow was falling so thickly. She looked up at David. 'You warm enough?'

He nodded. 'Let's get on with it.'

They walked down the driveway. When they reached the road, Lisa looked down it hoping to see Ros's car. Futile.

There was no car pootling along, bringing their daughter to them. Lisa set off up the hill.

After ten minutes when they were a few metres from the top, a walk that normally took about three minutes, David stopped. 'This is madness. She won't have come out in this. You were right; she'll be at a service station with hundreds of other motorists, waiting it out.'

Lisa struggled on a few steps, closing her eyes against the stinging snow. 'I know, but we'd never forgive ourselves if she were out here, alone. Does your mobile have a signal?'

David fumbled in his pocket and brought out his phone. 'No,' he said after a few seconds. 'Yours?'

She shook her head. 'No, I checked a minute ago. We can look again at the top of the hill. Sometimes there's a signal there.'

Another minute and they were there. The road in front was hidden beneath the snow. Lisa stared into the whirling whiteness willing Ros to appear. Her knees jiggled up and down as she scanned the desolate scene. She tugged at David's sleeve and pointed. 'Look, over there, do you see it?'

David looked but shook his head. 'What? I can't see anything.'

She stared into the spiralling snow, but she too saw nothing. Had she imagined it? The flicker of light she'd seen had gone. Yet something niggled, and then it dawned on her; it had looked like torchlight. She set off, trying to run. 'It's Ros, I know it is,' she called over her shoulder. Not looking where she was going, she tripped and fell, feeling her ankle twist as she went down.

David caught up with her and pulled her up. 'You OK?'

Lisa nodded. Her ankle was sore, but it wasn't serious. 'Look, down there.' She pointed to where there was something dark in the snow.

Lisa half ran, half slid down the hill, David panting at her side. She gasped as she got near to the light. There *was* a torch, its light dim. It lay about five metres from Rosalind's slumped figure.

She was too scared to touch her, couldn't bear to think she might not be alive. Then with a huge effort she pulled herself together. Ros couldn't have been there long and she was young and healthy. She'd be fine. Lisa turned to David, her eyes pleading.

'I'll see if she's all right,' he said.

There are times in life when seconds stretch into hours, and this was one of them. Everything slowed down as Lisa stood there helpless. David reached past her, knelt down and shook Ros. He looked back up at Lisa. 'She's waking up. Look.'

Chapter Three

Ros HAD NEVER BEEN so glad to be at home with her parents and siblings around her. 'Thanks,' she said as Mum passed her a cup of tea.

'What on earth happened to you?' asked Oliver.

Ros rolled her eyes. 'Work it out, brainiac. It's snowing and the car got stuck. Doesn't take a genius.' She smiled to take the sting out of her words.

'But didn't you see how heavy the snow was?'

'It was fine when I left Glasgow at noon. Cold but no snow, not a hint of it. There was nothing until I got to Berwick and then, wow. Ice storm.'

'Surely, you should have stopped then?'

Ros glared at him. Christ, he was annoying at times. 'Well, I didn't.'

'But—'

'Enough, Oliver. Can't you see how tired she is?'

Ros smiled in gratitude at her mother, forgetting in an instant how mad she still was with her. 'I'm fine, Mum. He can't help it; he was born a pest.'

The door opened and her sister came in. Ros brought her drink up to her face to hide her shock at Emilia's appearance. She'd seen her two weeks ago, maybe three. She'd looked OK then – a bit thin as usual – but now, fuck, there was no other way to put it: ghastly. The words 'heroin chic' came to mind. Surely, she would have noticed if her sister had been taking drugs.

She waved a hand. 'Hi, sis. You OK?'

Em sat down beside her. 'I've been better. Drank too much earlier on. Now in desperate need of some tea. Any going?'

'Give me five minutes,' said Mum. She disappeared into the kitchen and reappeared with a tray carrying a pot and more cups as well as a plate of scones. 'Here, get stuck in. It'll be a while until dinner.'

The scones disappeared in minutes. Ros hadn't realised how hungry she was and Em, too, had one, she was reassured to see.

'More anyone?'

'Yes, please,' said Em.

———

Lisa went through to the kitchen to get more food. What a relief to find Ros safe and sound. She refused to think what might have happened if they'd decided not to go looking for her. They had done the right thing, and their daughter was fine. No point in 'what ifs'. She went into the larder and brought out a cake tin. She'd spent the previous week baking. Em had followed her into the kitchen and was making more hot drinks. Lisa risked a glance; she looked better now she had some food in her.

'I'm starving,' said Em. 'But not for sugar. Is there anything else to eat?'

'Make yourself a sandwich if you don't want cake. There's plenty of ham and cheese in the fridge.'

Em took two slices of bread and packed her sandwich with cheese and tomato. Lisa left the kitchen reassured; her daughter was eating normally after all. What was going on with her? She'd been drunk when she turned up with Oliver. Em had gone down to visit him in Newcastle for a couple of days. They must have had a late night. She shouldn't have offered them wine. What had she been thinking? It was far too early to be drinking. Never mind, all was better now. The air of hostility had vanished from her daughter.

Back in the sitting room, Lisa sat in her favourite position on the old but comfortable red sofa, legs curled up underneath her. This was what she wanted: all the family under the same roof, safe and happy. She'd give it half an hour and then start on dinner. It was going to be a good Christmas after all.

At half-past eight they sat down to dinner, a beef casserole. To begin with, conversation was easy, as if they had never been apart. After her bad start, Emilia was funny and charming, talking non-stop about the latest film releases. Ros was quiet, probably shaken by her experience in the snow. Oliver was in good form; now fully recovered from his disastrous time at Cambridge. He had been too young and immature to take advantage of the opportunity offered to him. He'd won a scholarship to study English, but it had strict conditions attached, none of which mentioned getting blind drunk, calling your tutor a 'fucking wanker' and threatening to kill him. They'd never got to the bottom of that. There must have been more to it than what Oliver told them. It was the tutor's word against Ollie's, and he was sent down after his second term. It didn't help that he'd failed all his essays up to then. It took David and Lisa two years before they persuaded him to have another shot at university, Newcastle this time. He wanted to go to a more 'authentic' university with no 'fucking posh dickheads'. No university is completely toff free, and Lisa told him so, but he got his way in the end and was doing well from what he'd told them over dinner.

'I got 80 percent for my last essay,' he said, helping himself to more vegetables.

'Pretty good,' said David.

'Yeah, best in class. You see, it *was* the right thing to do to go to Newcastle after all.'

David laughed. 'Did we ever say anything different?'

Stupid idiot. Lisa held her breath. Oliver said nothing but continued to eat.

When Oliver finished, he crossed his knife and fork on the plate and looked at David. 'Actually, Dad. Yes. You did say different. Many times. Don't you remember? You told me I was throwing away a golden opportunity. A bit clichéd but better than, what was it now? Oh yes, you said I'd wasted my life. I was eighteen, Dad. Eighteen.'

David looked down at his unfinished meal and pushed his plate away. 'I'm sorry, Oliver. I was...'

'...so disappointed,' finished Oliver for him. 'I hated Cambridge. Hated it. I never wanted to go there. It was what you and Mum wanted, not me.'

'And your school,' added Lisa, trying to take the heat away from them. 'They were keen, too. They were the ones who suggested you try for a scholarship. And to be fair, Oliver, you never said anything at the time about not wanting to go.'

'Like that was going to happen. With Em in the state she was in.'

Em blushed. 'Let's forget it, shall we?'

'Sorry,' said Oliver, not sounding the least bit remorseful. 'But you have to admit, you did take up all the energy at that time. Ros and me never got a look in.'

Lisa said nothing. That had been a dark time, and she didn't want to go back there. Not at Christmas, her perfect family Christmas, not at any time. She reached across to Oliver and took his hand.

'Oliver, let's not fight. We're delighted you're doing well. Newcastle suits you in a way that Cambridge never did. You were right and we were wrong. I'm sorry.'

Oliver looked down at his plate.

'Please, Ollie. I've wanted this for a long time, all of us together and now...' She broke off, aware of tears near the surface. It had been a hell of a day. They'd all been happy once, hadn't they? Or was she kidding herself? But holidays hadn't always been like this with everyone on edge, tiptoeing round each other, in case they said something to offend. They had toured France in an ancient Peugeot, camping *à la ferme*, buying cheap food at local markets, kicking a ball round fields, organising penalty shootouts between all the different nationalities in the campsites. Or at Christmas, leaving out carrots for Rudolph, a whisky for Santa, the children's faces red with pleasure and expectation. How had it come to this? All three of their grown-up children at odds with them. Whether it was because they were upset over something that had happened earlier or something else. At least she knew what set Oliver off. As to why Em had arrived drunk and looking, if she were honest, fucking awful, what was going on there? Ros, too, with a new boyfriend every three months. Why? By giving her children a stable home life, she'd hoped to see them settled and happy. Instead, they all had problems. She grimaced as she thought of how her friends envied her 'perfect family'. What was it Anne had asked? 'You have three wonderful children who've never given you a moment's worry. What's your secret?' Christ. If only. Lisa had tried to open up once, but someone had interrupted her, and the moment passed. Tears threatened, she blinked them away and smiled at Oliver hoping he'd leave it. And bless him, he did.

'Is there anything for pudding?' David said when the silence became too deep to ignore.

'Apple crumble and cream,' she said. 'In the oven. The crumble, not the cream. The cream's in the fridge.' Her tongue was too big for her mouth; she spoke slowly, enunciating every word.

David poured them all another drink ignoring Lisa's warning look. Three bottles, including the one Em had drunk most of this afternoon, finished already. At least Em had laid off the booze this evening. Unlike Lisa. She had drunk too much, and her head felt full of cotton wool. Sleep was what she wanted. More than anything.

Ros got there before her. 'I'm going to bed,' she announced. 'I'm totally exhausted. There's nothing like a walk in the snow to wear you out.' Lisa laughed too loudly at the joke. God, how much had she drunk?

'Isn't it a bit early for bed?' said David.

'I'm knackered, Dad.'

'Me too,' said Em. She got up from her chair and before anyone could say anything else, they'd both left.

Lisa longed to leave too but the look on Oliver's face stopped her. He needed her to make things all right between him and his father. She resigned herself to a late night. 'I'll get pudding,' she said.

Two hours later they were still at the table; the earlier awkwardness had disappeared along with the wine from yet another bottle opened by David. She'd rue this in the morning, but it was worth it to see David and Oliver getting on so well.

Later, in bed, Lisa went through the evening's events, trying to make sense of them. Why had she been so concerned about Emilia? Her terrible mood had disappeared once she'd got shot of her hangover and she'd been in great form: chatty, making jokes. True, she was thinner than usual, but there had been nothing to worry about in the amount of food she'd devoured tonight. No, there was nothing more to it than Em being a little tired and emotional earlier on and, as a result, she hadn't looked her best. No one did when they were drunk. But... no matter how hard she tried to suppress it she couldn't shake the disquiet she felt – even Oliver was worried, and he wasn't known for his observational skills. What the hell was wrong with her? Had her anorexia returned, had she lost her job, was she using drugs, was she pregnant? Her eyes opened wide. Emilia was pregnant and frightened to tell them, or, more likely, she hadn't decided whether or not to have the baby. Lisa lay in bed trying to take this in, desperate to wake David but he was sound asleep, his breathing deep and regular. He wouldn't be too pleased to be woken up to discuss Em and a possible pregnancy. She turned over trying to find a cool spot in the sheets and thought about the implications. She could be a grandmother in a few months. A grandmother – shit. She'd barely got used to being a parent.

An hour later, Lisa was trying to sleep. David was

snoring in the annoying way he had. Not a regular, predictable snore but one which caught you unawares. It had a habit of disappearing for ten minutes only to return just as you were dropping off. For Lisa, it was torture. She looked at the alarm clock, 03:54. Enough. She slipped out of bed, shivering in the cold. Over the past year she'd learned there was nothing to be gained from lying awake in bed. With any luck, the fire would still be burning downstairs, down to its dying embers. She'd soon revive it. As she crept downstairs, avoiding the squeaky stair near the bottom, she heard a scurry coming from the direction of the kitchen. Damn mice.

Downstairs, she added another log to the fire then wandered into the kitchen to make a cup of tea, careful to make enough noise as she approached, to scare away any mice. When she opened the door and put on the light, she saw the kitchen was in a mess. What the hell? She'd put a quiche in the fridge for lunch tomorrow. What was left of it was on the kitchen table, with crumbs from a loaf of bread scattered all round. They'd go through all their food in no time if they continued to eat at this pace. She'd hoped there would be some casserole left but it had been devoured. That was annoying but the mess was worse. David had taken the glasses through from the living room and left them by the side of the sink. He could at least have washed them. Lisa sighed and started to clear up. She'd told them all so often about the need to leave the kitchen clean because of the never-ending problem with mice. It had gone on for years. It was so bad that Oliver had given the Warren the name of Mae's Mousetrap when he was little. Mae was David's aunt from whom he'd inherited the house. However, it only took a few minutes to clear up, so there was no harm done, and, more to the point, no mouse droppings amongst the crumbs.

She put the kettle on the Aga and waited for the water to

boil. While she was waiting, she looked out of the window. At least it had stopped snowing. With luck the snow would lie until Christmas Day. It would be lovely to have a white Christmas, as long as the snow stopped, of course, and they were able to get out for walks. The kettle whistled and she made some tea. Back in the living room, she sank into the old comfortable red sofa they'd had for the best part of thirty years. Lisa had refused to buy new furniture for this house, telling everyone it wasn't economical, but, if she were honest, she wanted an excuse to hang on to some of their old stuff. She was sick of houses filled with identikit furniture and resisted Ros's attempts to make her shop in popular furniture stores.

Lisa looked round at the eclectic mix in the room. Each piece had its story. The nest of tables had come from a skip. They were unfashionable mahogany, but she'd painted them a chalky white and distressed them long before it was fashionable to reclaim things. Visitors often asked where she'd got them. Then, there was the coffee table that was made by Ercol and had belonged to David's parents. Thank goodness she'd stopped him from taking it to the dump. But the sofa was her favourite. They'd bought it in an expensive furniture shop in Glasgow after a visitor had thumped herself down onto the cheap piece they'd had at the time and the frame had cracked. Lisa didn't know who'd been more embarrassed, her or the Terminator, as her friend was now known within the family. She decided there and then to make sure their next sofa would last for more than five years, and it had. It was enormous, solidly built and would outlive them all. At the time they bought it, it was big enough for all five of them to sit together to watch TV. As the children grew older, they'd scorned it, nicknamed it the Beast and talked about their friends' parents who renewed their furniture every two or three years. All of which made Lisa more determined to hang on to it. She'd had it re-upholstered for more than it would cost to buy a new one and shipped it down here last summer. Although its replacement looked smart and fitted in well to their home in Glasgow, she preferred this one and every time she sat on it, it was like settling down for a gossip with an old friend.

Tonight, though, she couldn't relax. There was Em with her skinny, androgynous body and Ros with her moods, as well as the tension between David and Ollie. David was preoccupied with something – or someone. For weeks now he had too often sat in silence in the evening, staring ahead, his face set and grim as if he didn't like what he saw ahead. It could be work, she conceded. His job at the planning department in the council was stressful, people all too ready to complain if they didn't get what they wanted. Lisa told herself that's what it was, but what if she were wrong? What if he'd found someone else? No, she wouldn't go there. It was impossible. They'd been together for the best part of forty years, since they were at school together. He'd never be unfaithful.

She sat by the fire enjoying its warmth, pushing her thoughts away until at last, she was sleepy enough to risk going to bed again.

Back in bed, she snuggled up against David's back, relishing the warmth from his body. Everything was going to be fine.

Chapter Four

Ros LAY in bed and listened to the sounds of a night in the countryside, so different from the city noises she was accustomed to. An owl hooted in the distance, faint but distinctive, out on the hunt. A fox screamed, sounding for all the world like a baby. Nearby, mice scuttled behind the skirting board. The house was old, late eighteenth century, they'd been told, and it had all the ailments of the elderly. Pipes rattled like a pneumonic chest, timbers groaned like an old woman with crumbling bones. She'd fallen asleep that night immediately but had woken not long after, disturbed by footsteps on the stairs. Mum, doing her midnight wanderings; she'd always been a light sleeper. Ros considered going downstairs to talk to her. But the comments made earlier about the number of men she'd brought home were festering in her head, and she wasn't ready for a heart to heart. Instead, her thoughts turned to Ian.

He'd been a customer at the café where she often did shifts when she didn't have temporary work with one of the orchestras. Although she'd thrived at the Conservatoire, it was hard to get a permanent position as a violinist. She didn't want to give up her dream of being a musician and become a teacher instead. Mum never spoke about how she'd wanted to be an actress, but Dad had mentioned it once, how she'd decided to teach because her acting jobs had taken her away from home and her three young children. Ros didn't know what was worse, three young children or giving up your dream in order to teach. Both possibilities were appalling: children were uncivilised and boring. She was only twenty-four, plenty of time to make a career in music.

She wondered how her mother felt about giving up her acting career. Perhaps she resented her children but if she did, she never showed it. Of course, Ros had no way of knowing how good her mother had been. She fully respected Ros's desire to be a musician. 'Don't give up on your dreams,' she'd said. Ros hadn't thought much about it at the time but now she guessed her mother had been loath to go into teaching. She never complained. Looking back on it now, Ros felt guilty at how she'd reacted to her mother's words. A scornful *as if.* Followed by *only losers give up on their dreams.* Why had she been so crass? She was only seventeen at the time. But was that an excuse? No. She'd make time to talk to Mum properly, find out how she felt about giving up on acting. After all, if Ros didn't get a permanent orchestra post soon... No, she wasn't going to consider that.

Her thoughts returned to Ian. When she'd told him why she was working in a restaurant, he'd been so interested. He was musical too, he said, though he'd never had the opportunity to learn to play an instrument. He claimed to love classical music but when she tried to talk to him about her favourite pieces, his responses had been unexpected.

'What's your favourite Mozart opera?' she'd asked one evening not long after they'd met.

'I don't know. Madam Butterfly?'

What a dilemma. Should she point out his mistake, risk embarrassing him? She kept her peace. Perhaps he'd said he liked classical music in order to have something in common with her. Ros liked this hypothesis. It suggested he was interested. She needed reassurance about this. Her self-esteem had been dealt a blow by him, for sure. She knew she was attractive; she'd had to fend off many men. Again, she raged inside at her mother for her comments, for fuck's sake, she was practically a virgin she'd turned down so many offers. Ian, on the other hand, was oblivious to her charms. Ill at ease at times and yet... he was the one who'd asked her out and he'd definitely hinted about coming here at Christmas. She'd swear it. When it had fallen through, he hadn't been impressed with her suggestion that he should turn up, drop in while passing.

'Your mother clearly doesn't want me there,' he'd said, his voice icy. Ros had been taken aback. It sounded as if he were taking the rejection personally, which to be fair to her mother, certainly wasn't the case. She could have said she was bringing Brad Pitt (a heart throb according to Mum but an old man to Ros) home and got exactly the same response. On the whole, maybe it was best he wasn't coming. Ian Murray was an enigma. Someone she wanted to know better, but definitely mysterious, which wouldn't go down well in her family. Mum always made such a big deal about how they shouldn't keep secrets. She always told them they could tell her anything, they should be open and honest with each other.

Restless, she twisted round in bed, trying to find a cool spot on the sheet. Sleep would never come if she kept thinking about him. She heard someone on the stairs; the second from the bottom always creaked. It was probably

Mum going back to bed. She had problems sleeping at times. Most likely, she was worried about Emilia. What was Em thinking, turning up pissed and looking like she was on drugs? Mum would be frantic. Emilia, God, she was a pain at times. The past few weeks were a case in point. Em's reaction to Ian had been bizarre, no, not bizarre, worrying. She'd met him once, two or three weeks ago, but had taken an instant dislike to him, throwing many sharp comments his way. She mentioned the age difference between him and Ros, which admittedly was steep, but it was Em's remark about unmarried men in their late thirties that got to him: *Can't tear yourself away from Mummy?* He'd flinched then. She and Em had a huge argument about it after he'd left. It had rankled for days.

Fifteen minutes later, and she wasn't asleep. Worse, she was thirsty. Her watch said five past six. In spite of her exhaustion, she hadn't slept well. Best get up, go downstairs and make some hot chocolate to help her relax. She ran downstairs, as quietly as she could, which in this house meant only every other stair creaked. To her surprise, Emilia was already there, sitting by the fire. She looked up as Ros came into the room.

'You're up early,' Emilia said.

'Can't sleep. What about you?'

'Same thing. There's some hot chocolate in a pan in the kitchen if you want it. I made it a minute ago.'

'You mind reader,' Ros went through to the kitchen, poured the remains of what was in the pan into a mug and took it back through to the sitting room. She sat down opposite her twin sister. 'Have you spoken to Mum?'

'No. I heard her moving about downstairs, but I waited until she'd gone back to bed before coming down.'

'Couldn't face a tête-à-tête, eh?'

Emilia bridled. 'What do you mean?'

Ros shrugged. 'Have you looked at yourself in a mirror recently?'

'We're not all as conceited as you, you know.' Em sounded bitter.

Time to lighten things up. 'Can I help it if I'm gorgeous?'

Em shook her head. 'What are you like?'

They sat for some time in silence, sipping their hot chocolate. Ros wanted to say more but she was frightened she'd drive Em away. Her twin was always so touchy about everything. She sighed; Em looked up.

'The dirty old man not with you then?'

'Nope.'

Em raised her eyebrows. 'Why not?'

'Mum said no.'

Em muttered something that sounded suspiciously like *good for her*. Ros didn't rise to it; she wasn't up to a fight so early in the morning. 'Seriously Em, are you OK? You look a bit rough.'

'Don't change the subject. Well, well, well. Mum said no. I told you there was something not right with that bloke. She's got a sixth sense, our mother, or did you tell her he was twenty years older than you?'

'OK, I admit it. There is a bit of an age gap, but it's thirteen years not twenty,' said Ros. 'And, no, I didn't get a chance to tell her. I suppose you've already done the deed for me.'

Em looked indignant. 'Certainly not.'

Ros wasn't convinced but she let it go.

'He's practically a different generation from you,' said Em.

'Oh, for heaven's sake, what is it with you and age? He is not a different generation. We're both millennials.'

'Changed your tune, haven't you. Last time we spoke about millennials you swore we were Gen Z.'

'Give it a rest, twinnie.'

'You know I'm right.'

Neither of them spoke for a few moments then Em said, 'So, you haven't told me how you met him?'

'You didn't ask.' Ros was irritated at how her sister had behaved when she met him for the first time. Her rudeness towards Ian had been excruciating.

'I'm asking now.'

She shouldn't answer but, oh, a chance to talk about him. At last. 'He was a customer at Farfalle. Came in one day and we started talking about opera, and then, a few days later, he appeared with tickets for *Apollo et Hyacinthus*.'

'Oh, love's young dream!' laughed Em.

'Give over, you.' Ros pushed her. 'You know I love opera.'

'Yeah, comfortable things like *The Marriage of Figaro* and *La Traviata*, not a boring old thing in Latin.'

'It was good,' protested Ros. 'A most interesting production.'

'Interesting? That good? Go on then, tell me about it.'

Her bluff had been called. She grinned at Em. 'I slept through half of it and yawned through the rest. So did he.'

'I bet he got the tickets cheap.'

'No! They were front stalls. Pretty damn good seats, actually.'

'Reduced to a fiver because they didn't want the theatre to be empty.'

'Don't talk rubbish,' said Ros, rattled. The theatre had only been half full.

'Believe me, I know. Someone at the *Herald* told me. They couldn't give the tickets away.'

Ros laughed, trying to lighten the mood. Emilia's tone was aggressive. But her sister wasn't going to be fobbed off.

'What exactly do you know about this man anyway? What does he do? Who are his family?' The questions came out like machine gun fire: rapid and merciless.

Ros gaped at her. 'What is this? Are you my mother now?'

'Come on, tell me. What exactly do you know about him?'

Ros shifted in her seat. Ian had told her little about himself, dodging questions and instead getting her to talk about herself and her family. She'd googled him, feeling a bit like a stalker, but his name was a common one and she'd ended up with well over 300,000 hits. Adding in Glasgow to her search terms had reduced it to about 65,000. She'd given up after a few pages. She'd found only a 192.com reference that gave part of his address. He wasn't on Facebook, nor was he on LinkedIn. She tried looking at images, but that hadn't helped either. There were hundreds of photos but no-one who looked remotely like *her* Ian. How could someone be over thirty and have no trace on the internet? It worried her a little, and now Em was making her more anxious. What did she know about him after all? He had parents who might or might not want him with them at Christmas depending on when you asked him. No siblings. He'd told her early on, one of the few questions he had answered. He'd muttered something about shifts when she'd pressed him about why he was often free during the day but avoided saying exactly what he did. It wasn't much. Maybe Em was on to something; she was a journalist after all, maybe she'd found something out about him, something unsavoury. But attack was the best form of defence.

'What's all this about, Emilia? Why are you so interested in my love life? Not getting any?'

Em's eyes opened wide. 'Some of us don't need a man to define us.'

For once in her life, Ros stopped to think before speaking but only for a second; she said it anyway, the words sounding judgemental. 'Are you telling me you're gay?'

'For fuck's sake! You think I'm gay because I don't see the need to have a man hanging round? And if I was, so what?'

'I didn't mean—'

Emilia interrupted her before she finished. 'Look, Rosalind. We're not all like you. When were you last single?' She narrowed her eyes. 'Actually, now I think about it, you haven't been single since your first boyfriend when you were fifteen. It looks to me as though you're too frightened to be without a man, ever. Why, Ros? What are you trying to prove?'

Ros opened her mouth to deny what her sister had said but no words came. Was Em right? Was she trying to prove a point? She tried to laugh it off though in truth Em had upset her. 'Can I help it if I'm in demand?' she asked. But this tactic wasn't going to work. Emilia stared at her, one eyebrow raised, the picture of scepticism. *You can't fool me* was the subtext. For whatever reason, Emilia was keen to make an issue of this.

Ros stood up without looking at her sister, mumbling something about getting something to eat and went through to the kitchen to try to control herself. Who did Emilia think she was? Better than everyone else with her celibacy and her rigid diets and controlling behaviour over food. Tiny portions, disapproving looks – that eyebrow again – when Ros was eating. Ros adored food. Couldn't get enough of it. A little voice told her now and again that she mustn't let her appetite get out of control, but she was a sensual person, and she loved the smell and taste of good food. It was surprising she and Em were sisters. If they didn't look so alike, she'd swear there had been a mix up at the hospital when they were born. She poured herself a glass of water and drank it slowly.

Emilia had struck a nerve. Since she was fifteen, Ros hadn't been single for more than a month. This past month had been the longest she'd been without a boyfriend. She'd chucked Dan thinking Ian wouldn't need much persuasion to step into his shoes. How wrong she'd been. But he must like her. He had asked her out after all. Em was right; it hadn't turned out to be much of a date. A lengthy opera followed by a quick coffee in the bar across the road from the Theatre Royal and then home. Not as much as a peck on the cheek at the end of the night. She squirmed as she remembered coyly looking up at him saying, 'How about a coffee then?' And his desultory reply, 'No thanks, I've had one,' as if that was what she was offering. However, they'd moved on since then. She now got a continental greeting of a kiss on both cheeks when they met. Baby steps. She was going to have to be patient.

She put Ian out of her mind. It was more important to find out what was going on in Em's life to make her look the way she did. She was way too thin. Was anorexia butting in on their lives again? If it was, what had triggered it? When Em was seventeen it had been exams, her need for perfect marks, the unspoken pressure from school and their parents to get five As in her Highers. It went on for years, all through university. But now? People always assumed you have a special connection with a twin, but it was years since they'd been close. She'd never been able to 'read' Em. Although they were identical, their personalities were different. Someone once told her twins were often polar opposites and it was certainly the case with them. Emilia was quiet, thoughtful, worked hard. She wasn't musical like Ros. She played the clarinet but not to a professional standard. Her strength lay in words. She wrote beautiful prose, using words as if they were a precious resource, disdainful of cliché and overwriting. In contrast, Ros was outgoing, musical and rarely stopped to think before she spoke, something that led her into many difficult situations. How many times had she been forced to backtrack after saying something crass? She cringed remembering how she'd once responded to a vegan who invited her to a bring-your-own-buffet party with: *I'll bring some bacon butties, shall I?* That relationship never got off the ground.

Her sister baffled her with her devotion to causes: campaigning for Amnesty International was her latest. Emilia's Facebook page was hugely political: reposts of campaigns led by Amnesty; someone in Sudan imprisoned for changing her religion; a journalist who might be executed for writing an article against the government in some obscure African country which, if she were pressed, Ros would have to admit she'd never heard of. It was all very worthy, but Ros couldn't get excited about someone who lived thousands of miles away. *Her* Facebook page was full of the here and now: pictures of nights out, selfies of her and her latest beau (although there were none of Ian as he refused to have his picture taken, with or without her) and maybe the occasional reposting of a story nearer to home, something heartrending, an autistic child who wanted to swim with dolphins perhaps, or a missing teenager.

Veganism had been the first of Emilia's campaigns. When she was fourteen, she had stopped eating meat, then, a few months later, fish. The following year she eschewed all animal products, and her diet became more limited. It took months for her parents to realise how little she was eating. Emilia wore baggy clothes to cover up how much weight she'd lost. By the time they grasped how bad the problem was, Emilia weighed less than 45 kg. Dad hadn't coped well to begin with. He'd thought it was just Em being difficult. Mum had been more understanding, more clued in and she had insisted on a referral to CAMHS, the child and adolescent mental health team who diagnosed Em with an eating disorder. Ros, knew of course that veganism wasn't to blame, her twin's problems were more wide-ranging than that. Em was a perfectionist, had issues with anxiety and yes, she was a bit of a control freak. She'd ranted for hours about the ethics of using animal products and although Ros had tuned out, some of her views must have rubbed off on Ollie because he was now a vegetarian although Em had long since given it up.

But now she'd turned up looking half-dead, not unlike how she'd appeared in the days before she'd been hospitalised. It wasn't good. The parents were sure to start fussing and Em would react by withdrawing into her shell, which would be an invitation for them to prod and poke at her as if she were a winkle. It didn't bode well for a happy Christmas. She put the glass into the sink and went back through to the sitting room, ready for battle. Ros wanted to get away from the subject of herself and men.

'Enough about me. What about you?' She took a breath before her next sentence knowing it was likely to cause an uproar. 'As I was saying before you cunningly diverted the attention away from yourself onto my love life, you look fucking terrible. What's going on? You don't look like that because you're a bit drunk or tired or whatever excuse it was I heard you making to Mum.'

Emilia was holding her head up with one hand. She looked very similar to their mother, in a pose Mum often used. Her blue eyes gazed at Ros, a stare so intense that after a second or two she looked away.

'What's going on?' she said. 'Are you sure you want to know?'

The temperature had dropped. Ros shivered. 'Yes, I do want to know.'

'What do you want to know?' Oliver entered the room, his hair standing up on end as it always did when he had been asleep. He looked at his sisters. 'You two been fighting?'

'Maybe,' said Ros. 'I want to know what's made her look like this, the bride of Dracula.'

Oliver stared at Em. 'Yes, Em. What is going on with you?'

'You see it, too?' said Ros.

'Hard to miss it. And why were you so rude to Mum?'

'What's this?' Ros's face lit up. She liked nothing better than a fight between one of her siblings and a parent. Except perhaps a fight between Oliver and Emilia.

Emilia's face was pink. 'It was nothing. I was tired and had too much to drink. I've apologised already.'

Oliver swept his hair off his forehead. He was enjoying this. 'She told Mum she was a fucking hypocrite, and a liar then told her to fuck off and stomped out of the room.'

'What?' exclaimed Ros.

Oliver shushed her. 'You'll wake the parents.'

Ros lowered her voice. 'What were you thinking?'

Emilia shook her head. 'You don't want to know.'

'I fucking do. Have you gone mad or what? Mum's not a liar or a hypocrite. And as for telling her to fuck off? Out of order.' She paused to take breath. 'Are you on drugs?'

'Typical,' said Emilia. 'You can't see past your own problems.'

Ros frowned. 'What exactly do you mean?'

'Oh, we all know about your little coke habit. I turn up looking ill and you immediately assume I'm taking drugs because you don't have the imagination to think it might be anything else.' She huddled further into the sofa looking worse by the second.

The words spluttered from Ros. '*My* coke habit? My coke habit? I tried it once and it was you who offered it to me. Is it any wonder I think you're on drugs when you're the pusher!'

Em laughed. 'Oh, Ros. I've never touched drugs. It was a bet between me and one of my friends. She told me I'd never get you to take coke. She remembered how snooty you'd been about it at school. All moral high ground and *only an idiot would contaminate their body with that crap*. But I knew if I pretended to take some then you'd do it, too. You couldn't bear thinking I might have an experience you didn't. I won fifty quid, thank you.'

'What? But you...'

'I sniffed up some sherbet. Remember how it made me sneeze? Frothy snot coming out of my nose. You were so stressed about it.'

Ros didn't know whether to laugh or cry. She had thought Em was having a fit when the froth came out her nose. It had given her a terrible fright and strengthened her resolve against drugs but fuck... why had Em not admitted what she'd done? 'You're changing the subject again,' she said. 'What is wrong with you?'

'Call it a personality defect,' Em said with a shrug.

'Seriously, what's going on?'

Emilia looked down at her hands. 'Nothing,' she whispered. Oliver gave an exasperated sigh.

'For heaven's sake, tell us.'

'Believe me, you don't want to know.'

Ros glared at her. She was not going to beg but she tried

one last time. 'Em, I can see things aren't right with you. I'm sorry I said it was drugs. And I won't run to Mum and Dad with whatever it is going on in your life.'

Emilia glared back at her. 'I don't believe you. You'll run tittle tattling as you always do and anyway all of this is a diversion. You brought up my alleged "illness" in order to get me off the subject of your precious Ian. You ought to be careful of him, you know.'

This was getting them nowhere. 'Look, whatever it is you've found out about him, spit it out. It's going to be bad enough here over the next few days without you hinting about some deep dark secret you've unearthed about Ian. Frankly, I don't think you know anything. I think you're jealous.' As she said this, Ros realised it was possibly true. Her sister's antagonism to Ian had all the features of someone who was attracted to him against her will. She watched Emilia closely to see her reaction, but her face had closed up. There was no chance of her divulging anything now.

'I've had enough of this. I'm going to bed.' Ros left the room without looking back and went upstairs. As she did, she picked up the murmur of their voices. No doubt Em was telling Oliver what she had found out about Ian, if anything. She was relieved Em wasn't doing drugs but furious she refused to confide in her.

Once she was back in bed, she felt herself close to tears, all the trials of the previous day flooding into her mind. She wished she'd stayed at home; her family always wound her up, especially her mother and her sister. It made her laugh to think how some of her friends had envied her when she'd been at school. *You're so lucky with your family, your mum's so cool, and your dad, too, and you have an identical twin sister.* So many people were fascinated by identical twins. *Do you ever swop places?* One of her first boyfriends thought there would be nothing better than having both of them. *I wouldn't mind if Em snuck into bed with me.* She'd sent him packing with an earful of insults. What were he and his tiny penis doing now? The tiny penis that had never done much for her. She put him out of her mind.

Mum hadn't been cool about Ian, had she? It would have been better to ask Dad if Ian could come here for Christmas; he never denied her anything. Too late now. She'd played it all wrong. She should have stuck to her guns and refused to come. Yes, it would have been boring and lonely in the flat on her own, but she would have saved face. Now her mother would know she didn't keep her word. She had one over Ros now. She would also have avoided that hellish journey. Another half hour in the snow and she might have frozen to death. How terrifying. She was tired, her eyelids were growing heavy. As she closed her eyes she saw the white blankness of the countryside in front of her, the snowflakes whirling round in a dizzying blur. Her last thought before she gave into the sleep, which was overwhelming her, was to wonder who the figure was, standing amongst the trees in the copse.

Chapter Five

WHERE IN GOD'S name was she? The mattress was too
lumpy to be her own bed, and there was a strange smell, not
unlike mushrooms. It was cold, too, her feet were numb and
for a horrible few seconds Lisa imagined she was sleeping
outside, something she'd avoided since a damp camping trip
to Wales many years ago. Her head hurt, too. Someone had
placed a vice round her forehead and was tightening it slowly
with malevolent intent. She forced her eyes open. The wall
was only a few inches away and was covered with a rose
patterned wallpaper that told her where she was. The
Warren.

David's Aunt Mae had used that wallpaper to decorate
every bedroom. She'd bought too much in a sale one January
in the early seventies. She had miscalculated the number of
rolls needed for one bedroom thinking each drop of wallpaper meant a roll. The decorator had told her the bedroom
had about thirty drops. To be on the safe side she'd bought
thirty-two rolls. He had been merciless in his teasing, *the
obnoxious little man* as she described him. Not wanting to

lose face, she pretended she liked the pattern so much she wanted every bedroom done the same. His eyes lit up – extra work. *So I told him, David, how you'd insisted you'd paper the other rooms.* Lisa's lips twitched as she remembered David's face when Mae said this. But somehow, he'd managed. At least the ceilings weren't too high like they were in the house in Glasgow. Lisa longed to paint over it – she hated the wallpaper – but as it was good quality and in excellent condition; it wasn't a priority. In any case, she would never manage to persuade David to decorate again and, sooner or later, it would come back into fashion. She hoped.

Lisa looked at her watch and sighed: three minutes to nine. More than anything she wanted to go back to sleep. Her head hurt, her stomach churned in the way it always did when she had too much red wine, but, above all, the worries of the previous day – especially those about Emilia – were flooding into her mind. Now she'd slept on it the idea of Em being pregnant was ludicrous – she'd never mentioned a boyfriend – but if she got the chance, she'd sound her out later.

God, she was so tired. Less than four hours sleep. She found it hard to function on eight hours. Four was a joke. And there was so much to do: stuffing to be prepared, mince pies to be made, as well as the mulled wine they always drank on Christmas Eve. Shit. She'd promised to make truffles, too. Hopefully, the cream hadn't turned to ice overnight in the ancient fridge. She should have bought the box of chocolates on special offer in Marks & Spencer.

Lisa turned over and tried to ignore the pressure on her bladder. The other half of the bed was empty; no wonder she was cold. Maybe David was making a cup of tea. Doubtful, but it would be wonderful if he did. No, it was no good, she had to pee. She reached over to where she had dropped her dressing gown in the early hours and put it on before getting out of bed, shivering as she threw back the duvet. The room wasn't as cold as she had feared. The range offered a central heating of sorts, not as efficient as at home but it took the intense chill off the air. After visiting the toilet, which thankfully was deserted – one of the few things she disliked about the Warren was its lack of an additional bathroom – Lisa dressed in the strange half-light coming from the snow lying outside and set off downstairs with the aim of killing her headache with as many painkillers as she could stomach.

The kitchen was empty; everyone must be in bed apart from her and David. It had been a tense evening and although it might have been worse, much worse if she were honest, it hadn't been the happy reunion she'd planned. A quiet cup of coffee was exactly what was needed, if only she knew where the painkillers were. Lisa rummaged through the drawer on the old pine kitchen table where there was usually an emergency supply until she found an old packet of paracetamol. They were past their best by date but would have to do. She ground some beans and made coffee in the cafetière. A few moments later and with a large cup of coffee in her hand, she wandered through to the sitting room. The fire had gone out, which was a shame, but the room wasn't yet cold enough to make her think about making up another one. David was nowhere to be seen. She looked outside. It was barely light, the sky was weighed down with thick yellow-grey clouds, but she managed to make out footprints in the snow leading away from the house. He must have gone for a walk. God knows why; it was cold enough to discourage anyone, let alone David, who loved his home comforts. Well, he was free to do what he wanted, there was no time to worry about it; too much to do.

The old sofa shifted around her body, enclosing her,

making her feel safe. Her headache started to lift; her limbs were relaxed. She went through the day in her head: mince pies first, then the stuffing. No, she'd do the stuffing first; it was the least pleasurable of the jobs, kneading greasy sausage meat. After the pies she'd make the mulled wine, ready for this evening, or maybe she'd make some soup for lunch. There were plenty of carrots in the box of vegetables Oliver had brought with him; she'd make carrot and lentil soup, everyone's favourite. She told herself she'd get going in a minute, before they all started getting up and wanting breakfast. With any luck, no one would get up before ten and she'd have made the soup and stuffing by then. For the time being, she was happy to sit here in perfect contentment at having her family all around her. But it wasn't perfect, not with Em behaving as she'd done yesterday. No, she wasn't going to think about it, the way her daughter had spoken to her.

By the time she finished her coffee, any warmth left in the remains of the fire had long since disappeared. Her ankle ached as she went through to the kitchen to start on the preparations for tomorrow. She must have hurt it more than she realised when she fell last night. She ought to relight the fire for her family getting up. Bugger it; she'd let one of the others do it for a change.

When she got into the kitchen, she remembered she hadn't charged her phone. She'd better do so now. Lisa rummaged through her handbag and took it out to check the battery. Only ten percent remaining. She checked her emails. There were several in her inbox, rubbish, mainly, but one was from the new deputy head teacher who she'd met briefly on the last day of term. What did she want? Her finger hovered over the message. She wasn't sure she should open it. What if it was work related? This was her holiday. Last term had been hellish, especially the last day. She groaned as she remembered it.

She'd been smiling as she approached the school entrance, eager to start her holiday. Cold air blasted through the open doors, and she stopped to put on her gloves. A mistake. She sensed the head teacher's presence before he spoke. He'd stepped in front of her and asked in a low voice if he could 'have a word'. Everything about him screamed bad news: from the slight twitch of his upper lip to the glint he'd been unable to hide as he lowered his eyes from Lisa's. *And* he'd waited until the end of the session on the last day of term; a nice touch that. A group of S1 pupils gawped as he ushered her into his room, and he shooed them away with a brusque *move along there*. Her friend, Anne, passed them on her way out. She lifted a cupped hand and mouthed *drink*. Lisa shrugged. There was no knowing when she'd get away.

Once in his room, he offered her coffee, a delaying tactic. Lisa looked at her watch. 'Not for me, thanks.'

'Sit down, Lisa,' he indicated a chair on the other side of his desk. 'How are you?'

She remained standing and looked him in the eye. 'I'm fine, but in a bit of a hurry as it happens.'

'Mm, we should catch up properly sometime when we're both less busy,' he shuffled some papers and looked up, making eye contact for the briefest possible moment. 'Sarah Whitehorn.' He picked up a pen and twirled it round in his fingers.

'S5 pupil, yes. What about her?'

'Anything you want to tell me?'

'Her file is fully up to date on SEEMIS.' The staff all joked about how he never looked at the electronic database that contained all relevant information about pupils. He was a master of delegation. Some claimed he'd forgotten his password and didn't want to admit it, but it wouldn't surprise Lisa if he'd never bothered to get one.

'Of course it is, I'd expect nothing less from you, from any of my staff, but if you wouldn't mind summarising your latest dealings with her, it would save us both time,' he paused. 'Seeing as I, too, am in a hurry.'

Touché. Lisa sat down opposite him, on the edge of the chair. 'Sarah came to me last week, after the prelim results. I thought she wanted to talk about her English mark; she scraped a B when she was expected to get an A. But it was a more personal problem.'

'Go on.' He tapped the pen on the table.

'She's worried she's gay. There's a girl she likes...'

He raised an eyebrow. 'Who?'

'She didn't say.' It was a lie. Sarah had spoken at length about the attractions of Jasmine Ferguson, a beautiful girl, fancied by most of the school, boys and girls alike. But it wasn't relevant to this discussion.

'And your response?'

'I said what I would say to anyone in this situation: feelings towards members of the same sex are common at her age, there's nothing wrong with this and yes, she might be gay. I gave her the addresses of various groups and advised her to tell her parents, to talk to them about it.'

His eyes narrowed. 'I see.' The pen tapping increased. 'And how did she react?'

Lisa closed her eyes and tried to picture her interview with Sarah. 'She was quiet for a few moments then said they wouldn't understand. I offered to meet with them and her together, but she refused. We talked a bit more and she agreed to think about it. She's coming to see me again after the holidays.'

He pushed the papers in front of him towards her. 'No,

you won't be seeing her again. Sarah's been allocated to another pastoral care teacher at her parents' request. I received an email from them this morning, accusing you of professional negligence by not telling them about this. Sarah's been self-harming and when they found out, she told them she was gay.'

'She's over sixteen.' Lisa spoke calmly in spite of the fact that her heart had been replaced by a hammer in her chest. She saw Sarah as clearly as if she were in front of her; the cuffs of her school jumper pulled down over her wrists, her hands restless. The signs were there but she hadn't picked them up. 'She's sixteen. You know how strict we have to be about confidentiality. There was nothing to suggest she was a danger to herself or anyone else.' There was a defensive note in her voice, and she stopped herself from saying more.

'Yes.' He drew out the word, giving a strong impression of disapproval. He probably thought teenagers were not entitled to privacy, especially if they were the sons or daughters of articulate, middle-class parents with easy access to a lawyer. 'Well, her parents are not happy – see for yourself.'

He placed two pages of closely typed text in front of her. Only letters of complaint were lengthy in Lisa's experience. Praise comes in small packages. A brief note with *thanks for all your kindness* or a thank you card, an occasional bunch of flowers, once or twice a bottle of wine. Nobody goes into detail about the good things and what they mean to them. She picked up the paper. She sensed the head teacher's eyes on her as she read. It was hard to concentrate but some phrases jumped out. Stinging, wounding words: *professional negligence* in the first paragraph, followed by *very disappointed in Mrs Truett*. It was like being a child again, a reminder of her parents who always found her lacking. A list of things other teachers had done wrong in the past took up over a page. At least she wasn't the only one under attack. Lisa shook her head as she read on. The complaints were both trivial and inconsistent: Mr Harris never gave homework, Miss Young gave too much, Mrs Sharif wasn't strict enough, Mr Taylor shouted at Sarah in first year, a supply teacher gave her lines for blowing her nose in class. By the time she reached the last paragraph, her eyes had glazed over. But the final sentence woke her up. *Given the amount of professional negligence shown by your staff over the years, in particular Mrs Truett's lack of duty of care, we have no option but to seek legal advice.* It was no surprise, but it needled her nonetheless. True, the buck stopped with the head teacher, and the email mentioned many other teachers but why had they used that damning phrase *in particular Mrs Truett's lack of duty of care?* Lisa pushed the papers towards him, noting the whites of his eyes were tinged with yellow. A drinker. No surprise there. Teaching is stressful and a head teacher is, more often than not, alone at the top. 'Have you spoken to the other teachers named in the email?'

'No. I'm afraid it's your actions or lack of them that have incited this threat. The letter makes it clear. I don't want to bother anyone else with these trivial complaints. Might spoil their Christmas break.'

Lisa stiffened. 'Are you implying I've been negligent?'

He put the papers into a file, avoiding eye contact. 'No, no...'

'Because as I've already said, Sarah is over sixteen and I'm bound by confidentiality, so I don't feel my "actions or lack of them" are to blame. Have you replied to her parents? Perhaps a meeting with them would calm things down. I'm free until break on the first day back.'

He looked at his watch. 'They're coming in today. And no,' he held up a hand to stop her speaking. 'I don't think it's a good idea for you to meet them. Might inflame things. Leave it to me and Charlie. We'll sort something out.'

Charlie Simpson, the Depute in charge of S5 and S6 was a nice bloke, ten times more competent than Phil but what might he say behind her back? Lisa took a deep breath and said, 'I'm not happy.'

He shrugged and stood up.

The heat in her chest spread to her neck, rose onto her cheeks. 'I hope you intend to support me. You'll have to emphasize confidentiality. If I had gone against Sarah's wishes and spoken to her parents, she would have been perfectly within her rights to sue me. She's not a child, for f ... for goodness' sake!'

He smirked. She'd let him rattle her. Damn. 'No need to shout. Now off you go and have a good holiday. Any plans?' Someone knocked on the door before she could answer, 'Come in,' he called.

'We're going to Northumberland, to our cottage there,' she muttered.

'Good for you,' he turned to the person who had come in. 'Jo, come in. This is Lisa Truett. One of our Pastoral Care team. Lisa, this is Joanne Marshall, our new Depute Head, here to look round. She was appointed yesterday. She'll be in charge of Pastoral Care. Starts in February. She leaves behind a heartbroken head teacher at Sandhill High.'

Lisa wondered if Anne had been told she hadn't got the job. Putting on her best professional smile, she held out her hand. 'No, I haven't had the pleasure.'

'Delighted to meet you. Did I hear you saying you're going to Northumberland for Christmas? My husband and I bought a place there, a couple of months ago. Maybe we'll bump into each other.'

The last thing Lisa wanted was to meet a colleague on

57

holiday, especially one she didn't know. She demurred. 'It's a big place, and we're in the middle of nowhere.'

'So are we. About sixteen miles inland from Bamburgh.'

Lisa's smile didn't waver. 'Lovely,' she said. She moved towards the door.

'So, where exactly are you?'

Lisa rummaged inside her handbag for car keys. 'It's hard to explain. It's in the national park, a bit out of the way. I'm sorry, I must go. Have a lovely holiday.'

'You too,' Jo said to Lisa's back. 'I'll look out for you.'

And now there was an email from her. For a moment Lisa considered deleting it without reading it but she reconsidered as her finger hovered over the trash can icon. It might be about Sarah or something else of importance. She opened it.

Hi Lisa! Hope you don't mind. I got your email from Phil. Great to meet you yesterday. I bumped into your friend, Anne, in the pub yesterday afternoon (my goodness, she can drink!) and she told me the whereabouts of your cottage. We're neighbours! We must meet up. Hope to see you soon, Jo.

Lisa wished she'd never mentioned the cottage to Phil. She should have said something bland like: 'We're having a quiet day at home.' But no, she'd opened her big mouth and Jo had overheard. Shit. And Anne, hell's teeth. She must have been drowning her sorrows at not getting the DHT job. It wasn't like her to be so indiscreet. Damn, damn, damn. Nothing against Jo but Lisa didn't want to socialise with her or her family. She decided to ignore the message. The only people she wanted contact with were here in the cottage with her. She switched off her phone and put it back in her handbag. Out of sight out of mind.

. . .

Rosalind lay in bed, playing Candy Crush on her iPad, trying not to check WhatsApp every minute. With the lack of mobile coverage there was no chance of a text but surely Ian would message her to find out if she'd arrived safely. She'd been too harsh yesterday and she regretted throwing her favourite mug at the door after he'd left the flat. Not cool. But it had been his idea to come with her. What did it mean? He was always asking her about her and her family, yet he hadn't made a move on her. Maybe he didn't fancy her after all. No, not possible. Any man she set her sights on was fair game and they usually succumbed within days, if not hours. If anything, the difficulty she had was holding men off. She wasn't being vain, but she only had to look in the mirror to see her attractions. Her hair, like her sister's, was long and red. Not a fiery, gingery, carroty red but a dark copper. When she'd travelled in India, little children had run after her in the street asking to touch it. She'd been horrified and flattered at the same time. The colour wouldn't last; after all she'd seen her mother go white when she was in her early forties, but she'd make the most of it while she was young. What was the famous quotation again? *Better an hour of glory than a life without fame?* Or something like that. Em would know. She'd ask her later. Ros planned to hold on to her glory for as long as possible. A girl's hairdresser was her best friend and Ros tipped hers well, knowing she'd be relying on her in a few years' time.

Her complexion, too, was a bonus. True, she had to use factor fifty in the sun; her creamy, virtually translucent skin went pink after only a few minutes. Not a good combination with her hair. Any desire for bronzed skin had vanished when she was fifteen. Friends tried to tempt her with bottles of fake tan. One went as far as giving her a voucher for a tanning session at a local salon, but their orange faces were off-putting, and she and Em remained pale and interesting. Lastly, and this gave her the edge on Em, her figure was perfect. She was a little over five foot six, a size ten with a tiny waist, rounded hips and breasts that were neither too big nor too small. Em on the other hand, was as flat chested as a boy. She was now officially a healthy weight, but she was a stone lighter than Ros and it showed. Her skin had suffered from the poor nutrition she'd had as a teenager and dry patches appeared from time to time on her face and arms. Ros was a bit smug about this, but it was the truth after all.

Thinking about it brought her back to the subject of Em's behaviour earlier. Weird. She'd swear Em had been about to confide in her before their stupid brother had charged in. She could go and see if Em was awake, but it was only nine o'clock. Chances were, she was still asleep. She liked her bed, always had. Waking her would piss her off. Never mind, there was always later.

Ros turned over in the narrow bed. She'd begged her parents to change it to a double, but they'd never got round to it. God knows why they'd kept this place. It had been fun when they were younger. Well, maybe not fun, exactly; she was fourteen when her father inherited it, beginning to go into the difficult teenage stage, as her parents had insisted on telling her, and she had only enjoyed the first two or three visits there. Later, it was something to boast about, 'her parents' country cottage', and briefly it had taken her into the most elite of the school cliques with some of the most popular girls in school vying for invitations. That stopped after she stupidly asked Olivia Anderson Brown to come for a long weekend. Olivia had turned up her nose at everything: the furniture was shabby, there was nothing to do but walk, the smell of damp was 'disgusting'. When she'd found a mouse in her bed, well, that had been the end of the friendship. Ros always suspected Ollie was behind this, but he'd denied it. Anyway, it put paid to her popularity. Olivia was merciless in her condemnation of the Warren to all the others in her small-minded coterie. Ros could hear her now, her voice high with indignation as she'd told everyone how, 'It was absolutely filthy, I mean, like, gross. There was an actual mouse in my bed'. After that denouncement, no-one wanted to come for the weekend. The sting of rejection hurt. No, she wasn't going to waste time thinking about those losers. They were hateful, each and every one of them. What had been worse though was Em's scorn at her being taken in. Her condemnation of Ros and her gullibility was scathing. It struck her that perhaps it hadn't been Ollie who put the dead mouse in Olivia's bed after all. Em was equally capable of having done it. Good for her. She smiled as she turned over and went back to sleep.

Chapter Six

Iᴛ ᴡᴀꜱ ten thirty and David hadn't returned from his walk or whatever it was he was doing. Typical of him to disappear when there was work to be done. But the soup was made and, with luck, and the addition of some more stock as needed, it would last for two days. The stuffing was in a bowl in the fridge and the mince pies were in trays waiting for the temperamental oven to heat up. Lisa never played the martyr – no one who'd had a mother like hers would ever do that – but honestly! Not another person around to make her a cup of coffee, let alone light the fire. She'd imagined them all together in the kitchen, laughing and joking as the mince pies were made, passing cups of coffee around. An idyllic picture that she'd never managed to live up to. Delia's Christmas cookbooks didn't help, with their descriptions of mince pies being made on Christmas Eve to a background of the King's College Choir singing carols on the radio. Who on earth left making mince pies to the last minute? She shook herself out of incipient martyrdom. It was an impossible dream. And she was playing right into it with her homemade everything.

What the fuck was wrong with shop bought stuffing anyway? Marks & Spencer had lots of different flavours and fuck, oh fuck, oh fucking hell, she'd forgotten the turkey. No! Lisa banged her head against the wall. What an idiot. She'd bought it well in advance and squeezed it into the chest freezer in the garage, thinking it would save time. Now, here she was, in Northumberland, miles from anywhere, in the midst of the worst snowstorm she'd ever seen, with five people to feed and nothing to cook.

The irony was, she'd dreamt of this for years. Anxiety about Christmas always brought it on. The same dream each time. It was Christmas Day and she had forgotten to send any cards or had missed out on buying a present for one of the children, or the turkey was in the freezer with a big note stuck to it saying THIS TURKEY NEEDS TO BE DEFROSTED THOROUGHLY FOR 24 HOURS. She pinched her arm in case she was indeed asleep, but this was no nightmare, this was real. Lisa sat down on the nearest kitchen chair, put her head in her hands and willed herself to stay calm. For several minutes she sat there working out how much food they had. Trouble was, she had counted on the turkey providing not only Christmas dinner but at least two more meals. So that left at least three main meals to provide. With a sigh she got up from the seat and walked over to look out of the window. It had several inches of snow around its edges like the fake stuff used as decoration. It had started snowing again, the flakes large and plentiful. The cars were completely covered. There was no point in trying to move either of them. The roads would be more blocked than ever. There was Ros's car to get past for a start. The nearest town of any size was seven miles away, which was too far to walk in these conditions. A fourteen-mile round trip in search of a turkey? No, she needed another plan.

She crossed over to the window and stood gazing out. Think, think. There was plenty of bacon and eggs for breakfast treats. Spaghetti carbonara for one meal and, at a push, a fry up, and there were plenty of vegetables for making soup. She'd make them into a hearty winter stew with the addition of some cannellini beans. Lisa was lost in thought and didn't register the figures walking towards the house until they were only a few yards away. There were three of them... David was one of them, thank goodness. One less thing to worry about. He'd been away for hours. But who were the others? Shit, no. It was Jo – and presumably her husband. Damn. There was too much to do, more now she'd realised there was no turkey. Lisa glanced round the kitchen. It looked messy but welcoming. At least there would be freshly made mince pies to go with the coffee. She put on her best hostess smile and went to the door.

The three of them were chatting animatedly and didn't see her. Their progress through the snow was slow and David looked worn out. Lisa wished she'd lit the fire, it had been petty not to and now David was coming back, covered in snow and, no doubt, with cold gnawing at his bones. At least the kitchen was warm and there was a hot bowl of soup to heat them up if necessary. As they got nearer, she noticed exactly how cold David was. His lips were tinged with blue, and an unsightly drip dangled from the end of his nose. When he came into the house his glasses steamed up and he took out his hanky to clean them. Joanne and her husband hovered on the doorstep. Lisa went to the door to welcome them. Her heart thumped uncomfortably when she saw them properly. Fuck. It couldn't be! She recognised Jo's husband immediately. She put on her best poker face.

'Come in, come in,' she said. 'Let's not lose what little heat there is.' She took their coats and indicated the kitchen table. 'Sit down and I'll put some coffee on. Or would you prefer soup?'

'Bit early for soup. Coffee would be lovely though, thanks,' said Jo, handing Lisa her Barbour jacket. 'This is my husband, by the way. George.'

Lisa shook his hand briskly, not looking him in the eye. 'Lisa, I'm looking forward to working with your wife.'

'Mm. It's nice to have one of Jo's new colleagues nearby. She can't wait to start her new job.'

Lisa turned away. 'I'm about to put some mince pies in the oven. Would you like one, or would you prefer a scone?'

Jo shook her head. 'Neither thanks, must watch the waistline.'

Lisa forced a smile. Another middle-aged woman obsessed with her weight. She was a size ten at most. Jo was dressed immaculately in a cream, cashmere jumper Lisa recognised as being from Reiss and what looked like designer jeans. Lisa regretted the worn-out leggings and hoodie she'd flung on earlier. She turned to George. 'And what about you, Geoff?'

'It's George, Lisa.' His voice was amused. Her ears rang with the unspoken *as you well know*. 'Whatever's easiest, I don't want to put you to any trouble.'

'Sorry, my mistake, George. Actually, both are a bit of a nuisance. We'll have biscuits instead.' David frowned at her abrupt tone. She put the mince pies in the oven and relented. 'We can have one of these when they're ready.'

'What, between us?' smirked George. 'Something to look forward to.'

Prick. Lisa ignored him and made the coffee. David was hovering around her, and she took the opportunity to ask where he'd been. His evasive reply of *I fancied a walk* made her suspicious. David wasn't one for lone walks. He'd happily walk for miles with someone by his side, but it was the company he enjoyed not the exercise. Yet again she wondered about his recent behaviour, worried there might be someone else. Had he been trying to find a mobile phone signal? She put her concerns aside. First, she had to break the bad news about the turkey. 'Now, don't worry,' she started. 'There's plenty of food. But no turkey, I'm afraid.'

'Why, what's happened?'

'Well, the turkey is in the freezer at home.' She steeled herself for his reaction. David was a big fan of Christmas dinner.

He laughed. 'No, it's not. I wondered when you'd notice. It's in the boot of the car. Yes, you might have forgotten to take it out of the freezer, but I didn't. I bunged it in the boot and left it there because there was no room in the fridge. Don't know how you missed it.'

'Thank goodness. You'd better bring it in. It'll never defrost out there.'

'No, you bring it in. I'm too cold to go back out there.' He lunged towards her and managed to get a freezing hand under her hoodie. Lisa yelped and tried to get away, but he had a firm grasp.

'OK, I'll do it after we've had our coffee.' She was only too aware of Jo and George watching them. Judging them.

'Don't mind us,' Jo said when Lisa caught her eye. 'By the way, did you get my email?'

Lisa forced herself to look blank. 'Sorry, what?'

'Oh, never mind. We're here now. Are you going to be in Northumberland for the entire break. It would be great to meet up. Maybe Boxing Day for drinks? Our place?'

'Brilliant,' said David before she had a chance to make an excuse. Not that she had a plausible one to hand. It was highly unlikely they'd have anything else to do.

The next half hour dragged. Jo talked about plans she had for reorganising pastoral care. Lisa smirked when she caught David hiding a yawn behind his hand. She rolled her eyes and he half smiled. When Jo paused for breath, Lisa interrupted.

'Well, this has been lovely, but I have to get on with making lunch. Do stay if you want.' This latter sentence said in her most unwelcoming tone. They took the hint and rose.

George struggled into his jacket. 'So, Boxing Day then. Come for lunch. You have children, don't you? Bring them, too. The more, the merri—' He stopped as the door opened and Emilia walked in, her hair freshly washed and falling in shining waves over her shoulders. Everyone's eyes were drawn to her.

'Oh, sorry,' she said. 'I didn't know we had visitors.'

'They're about to leave,' said Lisa. 'Emilia, this is Joanne who is the new depute head at my school, and this is her husband, George. They've bought the Old Mill. You know, the Lumley's old place.'

They shook hands, George holding on to Emilia's a fraction too long. 'She reminds me of someone,' he said. He didn't take his eyes off her.

Lisa's mouth was dry. 'I always think the twins resemble one of those models the Pre-Raphaelites used, the one who modelled for Ophelia, what was her name again? Lizzy Siddal, wasn't it?'

'Mum! No way. She's got such a long face.'

'It's the hair, I think. Everyone with long red hair looks like a Pre-Raphaelite.'

'I can see the resemblance, but your daughter's right, Lisa,' said Jo. 'The face shape is entirely different. Your daughter looks like you, not Lizzy Siddal.'

'Poor you, Emilia,' she joked.

'Twins, eh?' said George. He directed his next comment at Em. 'Is your twin as beautiful as you?' David frowned and Jo looked put out. Lisa stepped in before anything else was said. As for Em, she was mortified, her face bright pink.

'Well, goodbye, then, and maybe we'll see you in the next couple of days.' Lisa opened the door, willing them to take the hint and go.

'See you soon,' said Jo and they were off.

Em turned to Lisa as soon as they were out of earshot. 'What the fuck was all that about?'

'Language,' Lisa said automatically. 'God knows.'

'He was a bit of a perv.'

'Can't you take a compliment?' David said. His smile didn't reach his eyes. He was ruminating about what had happened.

'Well, yeah. But not from some old geezer like him. He makes you look young in comparison.'

'Is that meant to be a compliment?' Lisa flicked the dish-cloth at her. 'Right, there's lots to do. Can you go and make sure the others are awake, Em? And David, we need more logs for the range. Oh, and the fire needs to be lit.'

Alone at last in the kitchen, Lisa allowed herself to breathe again and told herself to relax. Then, a knock on the window made her jump. George. He gestured to her to open the door. She had no choice and he stepped inside. 'I've told Jo I've forgotten something. Are we alone?'

Lisa wished someone would come into the kitchen. She nodded.

He stared at her, his eyes searching her face. 'Well, well. Elizabeth Paterson. After all this time. I've been thinking about you a lot recently.'

'Well, I haven't given you a—'

'Yeah? Doesn't matter. We need to have a little chat.'

'I haven't anything to say to you.'

'I think you do. You've a lot of explaining to do. About why you disappeared the way you did. Although I can make a good guess why. Meet me later, halfway between here and my house, about 2.30. No,' he raised his hand as she started to protest. 'You'll find a way, or we have this conversation in front of your family.' He slipped outside before David came back into the kitchen.

'Was that George? What did he want? He was a bit off with Emilia, wasn't he? Maybe she's right and he's a bit of a perv.' He didn't wait for an answer but picked up a mince pie and stuffed it into his mouth. 'Oh yes, these are good. Do you want – actually Lisa, you're very pale, are you OK?'

Lisa stammered an answer, mumbling about lack of sleep and too much wine.

'Early night tonight, I think.' He took himself off out of the room.

Once she was sure he'd gone, Lisa sat down at the kitchen table and stared at the wall as if it held answers. What the hell was she going to do?

Chapter Seven

Ros PICKED up her bow and stroked the strings of her violin. Despite trying to play the Beethoven sonata they'd requested, what came out was a ribald, rugby song. The whole orchestra started to chant, substituting Rosie for the Dinah of the song. They were all staring at her, laughing. Sweat trickled down her back. The percussionist leered at her, his tongue hanging out while he banged on the bass drum.

Rosalind woke with a start. She had been standing naked at an audition. What a relief to find there was no orchestra and no percussionist and the drumming was only someone hammering at her door. Em shouted through to her, 'Mum says it's time to get up.'

Ros looked at her watch. Ten minutes to twelve. She was starving. Her stomach twisted in protest at the lack of food and her mouth was as fusty as a hamster's cage that hadn't been cleaned out for weeks. She needed to brush her teeth. She wasn't ready for the day ahead, didn't want to face her mother. Last night she'd been let off lightly because of the scare she'd given her parents, but Ros knew what would happen now. Mum would get her on her own and start hassling her about Dan who, she had made it clear, was exactly the sort of young man *who was most suitable.* And no doubt she'd want to know about Ian, and the last thing Ros needed was an inquisition that showed how little she knew him. Her mother's voice rang in her ear as clear as if she were standing beside her. *You don't know if he has brothers or sisters, what his parents do, where he was brought up and yet you wanted to bring him home for Christmas?* The most annoying thing was, she was right. What did Ros know about him?

At least the others were up by now. Safety in numbers. She heard Em going into her room, she'd drag her downstairs so she didn't have to face Mum on her own. Resigned, Ros jumped out of bed and got dressed. She met Ollie coming out of the bathroom, unshaven and looking as though he'd been up all night. 'I want to know what's up with Em,' she hissed as he passed her. He held his hands up in submission. 'Don't we all. If you want my advice, let her be. She'll tell us in her own good time.'

Mum appeared at the top of the stairs. 'Tell you what?' she asked. Oliver squeezed past them on the landing. 'You'll have to ask Em,' he said, disappearing into his room.

'Do you know what's going on?'

Ros wished she did; it would be one way to win Mum round. But she had no idea. 'I asked her, but she wouldn't tell me.'

Her mother's gaze was penetrating. 'I hope you're telling the truth, Rosalind.'

Full name, not a good sign. Ros tried a smile but there was no placating her. 'Get yourself washed,' said her mother as if Ros was five years old. 'There's work to be done.'

It was pointless to dwell on George. Lisa had too many other things to think about. Emilia for one. She counted to ten before knocking again, and when there was no response, she called out to say she was coming in. Em was sitting in front of her dressing table, twisting her hair into a messy bun. Lisa sat down on her bed and tried to catch her eye in the mirror. 'Emilia, sweetheart. I know there's something wrong. Tell me about it, please.' The tone of her voice was needy. She made a face and tried again. 'Are you eating well?' Looking after yourself?'

Em whirled round. 'It's all right, Mother. Don't worry. I'm not anorexic. I'd eat my own hand before I'd go back to that place.'

Lisa willed herself not to react. It had almost killed her to see Em in a psychiatric ward and she never wanted it to happen again. Calmly, she said, 'I'm glad you're eating but there's obviously something wrong. You know you can tell me. Anything, anything at all.'

A long-drawn out sigh. 'Oh, please! Leave me alone.'

Lisa stood up. One day, she thought, one day you'll know how impossible it is to leave you alone. Worrying and caring about your children is like a scab you can't help picking at. She should leave it, but she had to know. 'Are you pregnant?' The words came out in a rush. 'Because if you are, we'll support you, your dad and I, no matter what you want to do. If you want to keep it, or if—'

Em held up her right hand, palm forward. Bloody American films, they had a lot to answer for. 'Stop right there. You are the absolute limit, Mother. Of course I'm not pregnant. How could I be? I've never had sex with a man.'

It took Lisa a moment or two to digest this. 'OK, good.

Fine.' Damn it, she was an idiot. She turned to leave. But then it struck her what Em had said and she stopped with her hand on the brass door handle, looked down at it, noting how tarnished it was. She'd get the Brasso out later. 'Do you mean you're gay?' The words came out before she could stop them. 'I mean, if you are, please don't worry—'

'Jesus wept! No, I'm not fucking gay! Too bad. That would be right up your street. I can see you now, playing the understanding parent, joining support groups, *Parents for Homosexuality*.' She flung herself down on the bed and glared at Lisa.

Lisa rubbed her forehead, trying to ease away the worry lines. 'I'm sorry to have upset you but a girl in my pastoral care group was self-harming because she felt she couldn't speak to her parents about possibly being gay and I...' Lisa tailed off. She was making a complete hash of this. So much for her counselling skills. She tried again. 'It's not good to have secrets, they can eat us up and I want you to know you can tell me anything.'

Emilia had turned her back on Lisa again. 'Secrets? Huh. Eating you up? Well, you'd know all about that, wouldn't you, Mother?'

Lisa stood at the door, fiddling with the brass knob. She made her voice strong. 'What on earth do you mean?'

Emilia hit the side of her head with her hand. 'Everyone has secrets, Mum.'

'I don't.' Her voice was less sure now.

Em pulled on a pair of jeans. 'You know what they called us at school: the *Too Good to be Truetts*. Everyone envied me and Ros. Our cool parents who were so liberal and hip they'd allow their own son to smoke dope in the house.'

It had come back to haunt her, no surprise there. She and David had argued for hours what to do when they found out

Ollie was using weed. Lisa wanted to take a hard line, but David persuaded her it was a phase and that playing the heavy parents wouldn't work. 'We felt it was better to know where he was...'

'Oh, yeah. And where did it lead him? Did you ever ask yourself? Sometimes, Mother, if you're a parent you have to lay down the law. It's illegal to smoke dope and yet you allowed it in your house. Ollie was under such pressure at school to smoke, it would have helped if you had given him proper guidance instead of being all soppy and liberal. See where it's got him now.'

A cold fist closed round Lisa's heart, squeezing it tight. Her breathing was uneven. 'Is Oliver in trouble?'

Em shook her head. 'I'm saying nothing.'

'Emilia, please. If you know something you must tell me.'

For a brief moment she hesitated as if she were about to say something, then she laughed. 'You should see your face, Mum. I was joking. You take everything so seriously.' She pushed past Lisa onto the landing outside. 'We are all fine. It's Christmas. We're here to eat, drink and be merry. And here am I being Queen Bitch. Let's start again.' She gazed into Lisa's eyes; Lisa wasn't fooled. She was hiding something. Before she had a chance to answer, Em scampered downstairs, jumping from the third from bottom step as she always did. Lisa stood at the top of the stairs looking down. More than anything she wanted to believe her, but Em was lying. Something was going on. Not wanting to follow her downstairs when she was upset, Lisa remained where she was for a moment then walked back towards the shelter of her bedroom. She'd give it half an hour.

When she'd calmed down, she went into the bathroom, washed her face and took a deep breath. This wasn't the family Christmas she so desired. It was so long since they'd all been together for more than a couple of hours, she'd forgotten how difficult family dynamics were at times. The shifting nature of alliances baffled her. One minute, two of the siblings would be screaming at each other, the next, they'd be best friends.

She smiled at the memory of an evening out when the twins were about seventeen. As they left the house, Ros screamed at Emilia. 'Why don't you go outside and slip down a drain hole?' Em was out of hospital for the weekend, on her way to recovery and Ros had been jealous at the attention she'd got.

'We can't go out and leave them,' Lisa said to David, 'they'll kill each other.' He'd dragged her out of the house, telling her not to be melodramatic. She took in little of the play they'd seen. She hadn't truly believed that they'd kill each other. That was her over-reacting. But she was frightened one of them might run away, Em especially. Instead, when they opened the door to the sitting room, they'd found the girls on the sofa huddled together watching *It's a Wonderful Life*, Ros sobbing into her handkerchief.

'Why did you never tell us what a fantastic film this was?' David was right all along when he claimed they quarrelled because it was what their parents expected.

When Lisa went into the kitchen, the scene there was as she had imagined for weeks. A family idyll. All her children in the one place and at peace with each other. Ros and Ollie sitting at the table while Em heated up the soup.

'I'm assuming this is for today, Mum?' she said.

Lisa smiled.

'Can we eat it now? We're all starving.'

'Yes, of course, that's what it's there for. I'll leave you to serve up, shall I?' Lisa sat down at the table that Ros was busy setting, placing cutlery, plates and a basket of bread on to the wooden surface. 'Listen, everyone. I feel we didn't get off to the best of starts for this holiday.'

'It's OK, Mum. We're all cool,' said Oliver.

She wasn't convinced. There was a tight look to Ros's face, but out of the blue, she smiled at Lisa.

'Sorry, Mum. I shouldn't have asked to bring Ian along. It was a daft thing to do.'

For once Lisa was speechless. Ros never admitted to being wrong. As a child, she had stubbornly stuck to what she wanted, however absurd it was: a baby giraffe for Christmas, a trip to Antarctica to watch the penguins swim, an adventure like those the Famous Five had. The denial of all of these had led to major tantrums. At last, she managed, 'That's OK, sweetheart. Maybe we can meet him sometime in the new year.'

Ros grimaced. 'Yeah, maybe.'

Lisa raised her eyebrows.

'Oh alright, you've rumbled me. Thank goodness I didn't bring him here. Em talked some sense into me. There is something a bit strange about him. I guess I don't know him that well and it's a bit off to expect you to put up with a complete stranger.'

'Oh, OK. Well, if you change your mind...' Lisa tailed off, not sure of what to say to this suddenly mature daughter of hers. She changed the subject, aware of Ros's discomfort as if she knew how out of character she was behaving and was terrified someone would notice and comment. Lisa started to fuss about the lunch knowing this would put everyone off the track. As she was eating her soup, she told them about how she'd forgotten the turkey.

'Oh God,' said David. 'Do you remember the venison disaster? When you got stewing meat by mistake and tried to roast it?'

'I'll never be allowed to forget, will I? Thousands of meals I've cooked and yet what's the one that always comes up?'

'That was what finally made me turn vegetarian,' said Emilia. 'Don't you remember, there was a DVD of Bambi in my stocking? I watched it before Christmas dinner and then when we were in the middle of the meal, Dad told a story... What was it again, Dad?'

David laughed. 'God, yes. I was out for a meal with friends. It was years ago, long before venison was popular, and Jim McEwan asked the waiter what it was. 'It's deer, sir.' And Jim replied: 'Aye, I can see it's dear; it's two quid more than the steak. I want to know what animal it's from.'

'And I didn't get the joke, so you had to explain it to me,' said Em. 'I couldn't believe it, you'd made me eat Bambi's mummy. I was heartbroken for days.'

'Oh, so it had nothing to do with the fact that it was inedible?' asked Ros.

'Well, there was that, too.'

'It wasn't one of my finest moments. Though, to be fair, you'd never shown much sentiment before about eating animals. Do you remember when you twigged what lamb was?'

Em nodded. 'Oh yes. We were eating a leg of lamb. It was delicious and I asked what it was, and when you told me, I said: Is that like the lambs we saw in the field? And you said yes.'

'And you went quiet for a few seconds, and I thought: Oh dear, we've got tears coming for the poor, wee lambs. But not a bit of it. You started eating again and looked up and said, very seriously: "I'm glad they taked the wool off. I wouldn't like to eat wool."'

Lunchtime passed in a wonderful haze of memories. It

was going to be fine. The rough edges had been worn down and they had all settled back into doing what they did best: laughing and joking. George's threat was at the back of her mind, a constant menace. There was nothing she could do about it. She wasn't going to give in by going to meet him, and if he turned up, as promised, she'd deny everything.

After lunch, David suggested going out. It had stopped snowing an hour previously, but the sky looked yellow and forbidding.

'A walk?' asked Ollie. 'Don't fancy it.'

'We can't stay indoors all holiday.' Although Lisa loved the cottage, it was claustrophobic at times with its small, dark rooms and she needed to be outside. Ollie was right, it looked as if there was another blizzard on the way. And anyway, she didn't want to go anywhere where they might run into George.

'Sledging!' announced Ros. 'It was all I thought about last night when I was driving through the snow.'

'No sledge,' said David. 'Though there are plenty of bin bags.'

'But you brought one of our old ones down a couple of years ago.'

'No, it's in the cellar at home. Sorry.'

'Shit. Bin bags it is then.'

No one else was keen on this idea. They'd rip through them in seconds and end up soaked. The energy was draining from the room. They had cabin fever already and they'd been there for less than a day.

'I know,' said Em. 'We'll build a snowman. Come on! You know you all want to.' She looked round expectantly.

It didn't take long for everyone to agree and minutes later they were outside muffled in scarves and gloves and ready to go.

'A snow sculpture, I think,' said David. 'Life size and anatomically correct.'

'Man or woman?' asked Oliver.

'Why not do both?'

'Great idea. Mum and the girls can do the man and we'll do the woman.'

The women moved a few feet away. The snow was firm and held together well making it easy to mould. They started by building up a bank of snow to a height of five feet, patting and shaping it into a rectangle. Ros worked on the legs, carefully carving them out and Lisa did the body. The head was left to Em, who was the most artistic. As they worked, Lisa wondered why snowmen were usually shapeless. It wasn't difficult to make a little bit of effort and have it look more realistic. She and Ros finished first and turned to watch Em.

'He's going to be one handsome snowman,' said Ros. He fitted the description of the hero of a romantic novel: square chin, straight nose and large, oval eyes. Em shouted over to David, 'You've got competition!'

He came over to look. 'Not bad, not bad.'

'He's bloody magnificent.'

'Wait till you see ours,' said Ollie. 'She's a goddess.'

Lisa looked at what they were doing. It looked a bit shapeless. 'Are you sure?'

David was helping Em put the head on top of the body. 'Nope, you ain't seen nothing yet.'

Their snowman was finished; they all stood back to admire him.

'Not bad,' said Ros. 'Not bad at all. A heart of ice, of

course, so not much good for the long run but I wouldn't kick him out of bed.'

'Something missing,' said Em and ran off into the house returning with a small carrot and two walnuts in their shells.

'What are those for?' asked Lisa.

Em waggled the carrot at her in a suggestive way. 'Dad said it had to be anatomically correct,' she said as she strategically placed the carrot and walnuts between the snowman's legs. 'Perfect!'

David and Ollie went back to their task while everyone else watched the metamorphosis of their snow woman. Within a few minutes, the transformation was complete: a fertility goddess with huge breasts and massive hips.

'Good heavens. She'll eat our wee man alive,' said Lisa. The face looked uncannily like hers. 'Did you make her look like me on purpose?' she asked.

'Any resemblance to persons alive or dead is coincidental,' said Oliver. 'No, it turned out that way. Anyway, the rest of her is nothing like you.'

'No, thank goodness.' Lisa shivered. The temperature had dropped, and the sky was darkening, the clouds ballooning with the weight of snow. 'Time for tea, I think but we need to get a photo first. This needs to be saved for posterity. David – camera.'

Ten minutes later, the photos were taken, after a lot of fuss reading instructions about how to manage the time setting so the whole family was in the picture. They trailed into the house, freezing cold but laughing. Her family, all together, happy; all Lisa ever wanted. George could go to hell. It was past two thirty. He'd know by now she wasn't coming. Would he carry out his threat? She doubted it. He had too much to lose.

Emilia put the kettle on the range to boil and made some

tea. She brought it through on a tray with cups and a plate of mince pies. The pies were meant for later, but Lisa said nothing. She'd make more if they needed them. There was plenty of mincemeat. She sat curled up on the sofa and listened to the chatter around her. The fire was burning brightly, the flames nibbling into the logs. The room was so dark she found it hard to make the others out. It was time to switch on some lights, but she was so sleepy, it was hard to get the energy. Her near sleepless night was catching up on her and her eyelids began to droop. Five minutes would be so pleasant, maybe ten. She'd ask Oliver to make the mince pies; he'd always liked to bake, and truth to tell, his pastry was better than hers. 'Put the lamps on, will you?' she murmured as sleep started to overtake her.

'They're not working,' said Em after a few seconds.

'Push the plug in fully.'

Em pushed but nothing happened. Lisa was wide awake now, with a horrible suspicion of what had happened. She went over to the main light switch and turned it on. Nothing. Shit. A power cut.

'Don't panic,' said David. 'We have food, heating and hundreds of candles. I brought loads down here last year. We'll be fine, don't worry.'

He was right, there was nothing to worry about. Any food that might go off could be taken out of the fridge and put in a box in the snow; there was food for at least two, maybe three days. They had the range to keep the house warm and cook the food. The only thing missing was light – but they did have plenty of candles, although Lisa doubted there were 'hundreds' – and entertainment. No TV. Well, maybe that was a good thing. Although already Ollie was grumbling about a film he'd wanted to watch tonight. No, it would work out fine.

'Can anyone get a signal on their mobile so we can find out from the internet what's going on?' Lisa switched on her phone, but the battery was pretty much done. She should have charged it when she had the chance.

They lit some candles, setting them out all round the room. For a few minutes, they all fiddled with their phones, but to no avail. No surprise. There was rarely a signal. Nothing from the landline either. The telephone lines must be down. The snow had started again, starting as fine snow, which looked like nothing to begin with, rapidly changing into large thick flakes, that soon covered their footprints from earlier. Lisa drew the curtains, going round each window in turn noting as she looked out the back, the footprints going to and from the back door. Had George followed through on his threat after all? Was he about to burst in and ruin her Christmas? Her life?

'David,' she called, 'come and have a look at this? Did you go back outside?'

David shook his head. 'No, that's a bit bizarre, isn't it? We've all been together all day except when I was out this morning, and I used the front gate to get out. No, wait! I think Ollie went to get some logs to give the sculpture a good solid base.'

'That's cheating!' What a relief. The Warren was idyllic in many ways, but its isolation sometimes scared her and at times like this, when there was no electricity and no way of staying in contact with the outside world, she felt especially vulnerable. Forget about George, she told herself. She had to concentrate on what needed to be done. She went into the kitchen to check on their stock of food. The freezer was full, though if the electricity didn't come back on soon, it might defrost. Perhaps she should put some things out in the snow. They'd certainly stay frozen there. There was a bolognaise sauce for tomorrow's dinner as well as a lamb tagine for tonight, bread for several days and a couple of apple pies. There was the turkey, too, of course so they had at least enough food for three, if not four days, and the snow would have stopped by then, wouldn't it?

It was five o'clock now, so she'd make the mulled wine for later and check on how many mince pies were left. She looked in the Tupperware box – only six left. She'd made twenty-four; they couldn't have eaten eighteen, could they? Anything was possible, she supposed. And the pies were small. Eighteen, though? She'd had one, so it meant the others had had around four each. She wouldn't make a fuss. If Em was eating, then, good, and if not, Lisa wasn't going to put her off the idea by having a go at the others.

'Ollie,' she called, 'I'm making more mince pies. Want to help?'

'You bet,' he came into the kitchen and set to it. Lisa smiled as she watched. It was all going to be fine.

Chapter Eight

ROS FIDGETED IN HER CHAIR, bored. Ten minutes ago, her Kindle had died, and it was too dark to read a normal book. How had people managed to do anything before there was electricity? She was well aware of hygge and the comforting effect of candlelight, and indeed, it was all very romantic looking. The flickering flames of the fifteen candles Dad had lit made the shabby room welcoming and cosy, but there was nothing to do except chat. She could play a game on her iPad, but they used up so much battery power and with no way of recharging... She stood up and stretched.

'I think I'll go and see if my car's all right. Anyone want to come with me? There are two carrier bags in the boot, full of crisps and nuts... as well as my suitcase.'

David shook his head. 'I had a walk this morning while you were all in bed. I'll give it a miss, thanks.'

'How far away is it?' asked Em.

'A mile, maybe? Not much more.'

'OK, I'll come with you. I'd like some fresh air. We'll need torches though.'

'Are you sure you'll be alright? It's cold out there.'

Ros stood up to make a move. 'Sake, Mum. Stop fussing. We'll be fine.'

When they were fully wrapped up and armed with torches and some chocolate they'd found in a cupboard, they set off down the road. The snow had stopped, and the clouds had dispersed, leaving a sky sprinkled with stars. The moon was a fingernail short of being full and gave out a good light. After a few yards, Ros switched off her torch leaving Em's to show them the way. Best preserve as much battery power as possible in case it was needed later.

'So, are you going to try to move it, then?'

'What? Oh, no. It's completely stuck. It won't budge until all this is over. I hope no one's tried to get past it and got stuck, too.'

'Unlikely,' said Em. 'No one in their right mind would drive down a minor road in snow like this. Oh, look! Is that it over there?' She pointed to a dark shape in a lane adjacent to the road.

'Hell, no, we've only been walking five minutes. And it's on the road, such as it is, not one of the lanes. It's further away than this.' She stopped. 'It does look like a car though. Funny, I didn't see it last night.'

'Well, it was snowing heavily, and you were focused on getting here.'

They walked over to the car. 'You don't think anyone's inside do you?' asked Ros, remembering how she had toyed with the idea of staying with her car.

Em pulled a face. 'Surely not. But maybe we should have a look anyway.' They scraped at the snow on the windscreen with their gloved hands. Ros's gloves were woollen, and she cursed as the icy snow seeped through to her fingers, numbing them. When they had a small patch cleared, they shone a torch in. There was a blanket on the back seat, but nothing else to be seen.

'Nothing of note,' said Ros with a sigh of relief. She had been afraid they might find a frozen corpse sitting in the driver's seat. Damn her over-active imagination.

'I wonder what they were doing here.' said Ros as they struggled on through snow thirty centimetres deep in places.

'Who knows,' shrugged Em. 'It could be anyone. Someone lost, someone on their way home for Christmas...'

'Well, I hope they're safe inside, now. Safe and warm. Safe from harm.'

'Sounds like a quote?'

'Is it?'

'Like a hymn, oh!' Em stopped; Ros bumped into her.

'What are you doing, you eejit?'

'You were asleep, so you didn't meet them, but some colleague of Mum's called round with her husband this morning. He was a right creep, kept staring at me. Maybe it's their car.'

'What were they doing here?'

'Mum said they'd bought the Lumley's place. You know the cottage up the hill, about half a mile away.'

'I think so,' said Ros. 'Is that the place where the old man died last year. I remember Mum saying something about it.'

'Yeah, that's it. Maybe they got stuck on the way to the house.'

'Mm, except it's not on the way to their house.'

'Oh, well I don't know whose it could be then.'

They walked on in silence for a few minutes. It was hard work trudging through the snow, and it would be harder coming back with the suitcase and the carrier bags. Ros tried to remember how heavy her case was. She hadn't brought too much with her so it should be alright.

'Oh,' she said. 'I've remembered something... from last night. I was round about here, and I saw someone. I called out but they didn't reply. They stared at me for a few seconds and then went on walking. It was unnerving, being alone in the dark.' She laughed. 'Do you remember the book of folklore Great-aunt Mae had?'

'Can't say I do.' Em quickened her pace.

'Oh, you must remember. It had illustrations all the way through it of the various myths and legends of Northumbria.'

'No, sorry.' Em was moving fast now, and Ros scurried to catch up.

'Oh well, never mind. It'll be in the house somewhere. I'll show you later. Anyway, one of the stories in it was about Red Caps.'

'Is that a type of bird?'

'It's a goblin that wears a red hat, hence the name. They lie in wait for unsuspecting travellers. For a second, I believed it was one of them, and I was going to be brutally killed and my blood used to dye his hat red.'

Em stopped and stared at her. 'What on earth are you talking about?'

I'm telling you, the legend of the Red Caps. With snow swirling around it was positively terrifying. The thing is, it looked like a goblin. All low and squat. Apparently, they like to hang around old ruins and I'd not long passed the ruined cottage. You know the one.'

'Jeez, someone's been reading too much Stephen King.'

'You can talk. You told me someone had been murdered there. It terrified me.'

'No, I didn't.' Em's voice rose.

'You did so! Between the memory of that and the story about the Red Caps I was well scared last night.'

'Must you talk like that?'

'Like what?' Ros had no idea what she meant.

'"Well scared." Why not say "petrified", or if you must use a qualifier, use "very"...'

'You're such a language fascist.' Ros bent down and made a snowball. 'I'm going to get you. You'd better look out. I'm well hard.' She threw it and it landed on Em's face.

The ensuing snowball fight lasted a few minutes, until, exhausted, Ros called a truce. She turned the conversation back to what she'd seen.

'It must have been one of the local farmers, out looking for lost sheep, or whatever. Or maybe the driver of the car we saw.'

'Mm, maybe,' said Em. 'Bet they're in front of a fire now, drinking a nice cup of tea, or, better, a glass of full-bodied red wine. Or blood!' She made a face at Ros.

'I wish we were inside,' said Ros. The cold was settling into her bones, making her shiver.

'Are we nearly there yet?' said Em, in a parody of a child's voice.

'Not far now,' said Ros. 'To tell the truth, in spite of the cold, I feel as though I could walk for miles. It's so claustrophobic in that damn cottage.'

'You've never liked it, have you?'

'It's okay. I wish they'd do it up a bit, though.'

'Christ, you haven't got over that ghastly girl who came to stay!'

'Olivia? Well, it was pretty traumatic. Don't you remember?'

'How could I forget? Jeez, she was the pits. Do you know she sent me a friend request on Facebook recently, said she'd read one of my reviews in the *Herald*. She gave me one of those back-handed compliments she was so good at.' She screwed up her face in concentration. 'What was it she said?

Yes, got it. "Hi Emilia, I saw your review of Ian McEwan's latest novel in the *Herald*. It was top notch. Did you get someone to write it for you? Haha, only joking. No seriously, it was totes amazing. Well done, you." Condescending bitch.'

'For fuck's sake. I hope you told her where to shove her friend request?'

Em nibbled at her lower lip.' Um, no. I couldn't resist it. I wanted to know what they all did, all those glittering blondes who made my life a misery at school.'

'I didn't know,' said Ros, taking her arm.

Em looked at her sideways. 'Didn't you?'

'No! I didn't.' Ros managed to stop herself stomping off. Her twin always managed to make her feel guilty. She softened her voice. 'I didn't know. I'd have killed them if I'd known they'd been getting at you. You know I would.'

'Yes, I suppose so. Anyway, when I was, you know, in hospital all those months, they sent me a card. Above the Get Well Soon message they'd scrawled DON'T.'

She ought to have known. That crowd were so self-serving, so bitchy. They'd been the same since they were eight years old. Bitching about each other's clothes, telling each other they were too fat, or had spots. Boasting about how much daddy earned. Subtly turning against each other. It had been a relief to go to the Conservatoire and leave them behind. She'd chosen to study music knowing they'd turn up their noses at this. They'd mostly gone on to study law or medicine, because it was what mummy and daddy wanted. 'So, how are they all doing?'

'Surprisingly badly. Olivia failed her first-year law exams and ended up with a third-class degree in history. Jemma left med school after her third year and, apparently, she's lap dancing in London, and what's her name, you know the one who had the boob job...'

'Um, yeah... let me think... Emma Boyd.'

'That's her. Do you remember the school debate when she said all single mothers should be forced to work in nurseries looking after babies of people who had proper jobs?'

'Hell, yes. She caused a riot in class. Is she—?'

'You bet. Single mother. Twins. No job. Living on benefits. Can you imagine? Bet she could cut her tongue out now.'

'What a shame,' said Ros.

'Don't you dare have sympathy for any of them!'

'I meant for the babies, having a mother like her.'

Em smiled. 'Oh, alright then. Anyway, I accepted Olivia's friend request, and, next thing, two weeks later, she's sent me a personal message asking me to stop posting all these political messages. it was depressing to see horrible things about women being stoned and what was FGM anyway.'

'What is it?'

'For God's sake, Ros. You are the limit. Female genital mutilation.'

'Yes, of course. I've always been hopeless with acronyms.' She'd never heard of such a thing, but it was best not to admit it. It sounded horrible.

'Hmm.' Em looked sceptical. 'Anyway,' she continued, 'It went on in the same vein, who did I think I was, foisting my political views on her, blah, blah, blah.'

'So, what did you do?' Ros had a certain sympathy for Olivia's view: Em's postings were always so serious.

'Well, nothing at first. I resisted blasting her right back and instead mulled it over for a while. Revenge being a dish best served cold...'

Interesting. 'Go on.'

'So, I sent her a DM back—'

'DM?'

'Direct message – you are hopeless with acronyms, aren't you? Anyway, I said I was sorry she found my views unacceptable. But they were my opinions and I felt very strongly that women had the right to hold on to the genitalia they were born with and not to be stoned to death if they slept with someone other than their husband. But I would take her views into account and cut down on my posting.'

'Bit tame for you, isn't it?'

Em held up a hand. 'Wait. So, she sends me a message back saying she hadn't known what FGM was, and, I was right, it didn't sound very nice at all, but she appreciated me taking on her point of view. She ended up with BFF – best—'

'I know what it means, thanks. Fuck, she hasn't moved on since primary school, has she?'

'*And* she'd stuck one of those awful emoticons at the end, a teddy bear with a little pink heart. Enough to make you puke. But I forced myself to reply in a similar vein and then waited for two weeks, carefully not posting anything too political.'

The snow was deeper here and hard to walk on. Em was panting. She paused to get back her breath. 'Then I went in for the kill. I reckoned I could hack into Olivia's email account.'

'What?' Ros stopped. Her sister was law abiding, never did anything wrong. And she'd hatched up something like this? 'You did what? How on earth?'

Em prodded her to get her moving again. 'Well, she's completely self-obsessed, isn't she? And also, a bit of an airhead. So, I reasoned that her password would be something very close to her, not her name because that's too obvious. After a while, I remembered that when she was here, she told us her dad called her princess, and Ollie made puking noises and she burst into tears. So, I tried it.'

'Did it work?'

'Yup. It was Princess with a capital P and a 1 instead of the i. Luckily, I got it on my third try, because they might have shut me out altogether if not. Then I logged into her Facebook account, which of course had the same password, and got to work.'

Ros was both horrified and impressed. 'What did you do?'

'I created mayhem, my sweet Rosalind. Brought into the open what she's been doing for years: talking behind people's backs, bitching about her so-called best friends. First of all, in my role as Queen Bitch Olivia, I sent a DM to several people about Lauren. *Hey guys, have you noticed Lauren's breath? Should we say anything to her? It stinks.* True, by the way. And I copied Lauren into the message, with her name in the middle so most people wouldn't notice. And then I waited for all hell to let loose.'

'And, did it?'

'You bet. That little group snark about each other all the time, so most of them did a "reply all", bitching in return, which of course got sent to Lauren. Then there was the big reply from Lauren that included select quotes from Olivia about what she'd said about others in the group. And it blew wide open from then on.'

'But her email account, why did you hack into that?'

'Oh, to stop Olivia from noticing her Facebook account had been 'accessed from an unknown device'. You know the message you get when you use a different IP address or a different device? I had her email open at the same time as I hacked into Facebook. Allowed me to junk it and then delete it as soon as it came in so there would be no trace of it.'

What the hell was an IP address? 'Gosh, Em. It all sounds a bit dodgy. What if she'd been online at the time?'

'I did it at five in the morning. She's never been an early riser.'

'Yes, well, but you might have been caught.'

'Well, duh. But it was worth it. She deserved it. They all did.'

Ros hit herself on the forehead. 'There's more to this than you're telling me, isn't there? This isn't only about a silly, cruel card sent to you when you were seventeen.'

Emilia stopped in the snow and turned slowly to face her. 'Yes, you're right, but I don't want to talk about it. Maybe one day.' She walked on.

Ros looked at her slight figure receding and wondered what had made her so bitter. She hurried to catch up with her. 'Sorry, I sounded judgemental, I didn't mean to be.' She squeezed Em's arm. 'So, is there any more to tell?'

Em smiled at her, a real smile that only served to remind Ros how little they saw of this. So often, she was distant, immersed in one of her causes. 'Well, when she finally cottoned on to what had happened, she completely freaked out. Her Facebook page was full of apologies: *Guys, guys I've been fraped. I swear it wasn't me who sent that message. Someone's hacked my account.* Of course, everyone knows their own reply to all messages aren't made up, so they've all reached the conclusion that it didn't matter whether she'd been hacked or not. there's a lot of truth right there.'

'At least it's out in the open now, I suppose. Do you think they'll learn anything from it?'

'I doubt it. They're not speaking at the moment but...'

'And did you put in your tuppence worth?'

'Only to express sympathy at the frape, without of course pointing out how much worse real rape is, and as for female genital mutilation, well, it's a shame she won't make the link herself.'

Ros nodded. 'Yes, it is. You never know, it might make a difference. Might make her think twice before bitching.'

Em raised her eyebrows. 'You're kidding, right?' Suddenly she stopped dead. 'Look, that mound over there. Is that your car?' She speeded up.

They were panting by the time they reached the car. 'Now, where exactly are those crisps, I'm starving.' Em started to sweep the snow off the car, swearing as it crept up her sleeve. 'Come on, help me here.'

Ros joined her and set to work. She wanted to know more, what exactly had gone on with that group of girls, but, for the moment, the priority was to rescue those snacks and get back to the house.

Lisa loved watching Oliver make pastry. His long, delicate fingers made short work of it and his pastry was always better than hers. Such a gentle touch. She should have made more of an issue about him continuing with piano lessons. He played well, but then he had been good at cello, too, and one of them had to go. Shame he'd given it up for football.

He sensed her watching and frowned. 'What?'

'Nothing. It's... well, it's good to have you all around me after all this time.'

'Listen to you, mother hen.'

'Oh, give over. Have you done the pastry? We can make the mulled wine while it rests.'

Oliver brought the pastry together and kneaded it gently before putting it into a plastic bag. 'Fridge?' he asked. 'Or outside?'

'Fridge should do, I think. It won't have brought up its

temperature much yet and we don't want the pastry to actually freeze.'

David had vanished, not long after the girls left the house. Probably back to bed. He liked his sleep and he'd been up early this morning. Lisa frowned, thinking how vague he'd been about his whereabouts. His behaviour had been 'off' for a while. Drinking too much. Long silences. Taking himself off for walks at odd times. She'd noticed, of course she had, but had been too tired and preoccupied with work matters to tackle him about it. She shook herself. She was imagining things. He, too, was probably stressed with work. She refused to think it was anything else, though the little voice niggled at her again: *what if*. No, she wasn't going to go there. She turned to Ollie. 'You know, this power cut's a nuisance. There are things I wanted to watch on TV tonight and listen to on the radio, too.'

Oliver stopped measuring out the spices for the mulled wine. 'Wait there!'

Lisa took over from what he'd been doing, baffled by his sudden disappearance. What was he up to now? Two minutes later he came back, brandishing a small radio.

'Oliver, there's no electricity.'

'Ah, but this is battery operated. Don't you remember? Mae always used it. It's been on top of the chest of drawers in my room.'

'Does it work?'

He grimaced. 'Do you know, I've no idea. I never tried it. He pressed the on switch. Nothing. 'Oh, what a shame.'

'Are there batteries in it?'

He fiddled with the back of the radio. 'No, do we have any spare?'

'We always have spare batteries. You know what your father's like.' Lisa went into the larder and brought out a cardboard box full of them. She rummaged for a second. 'Here you are.'

Two seconds later, the sound of rap came flooding into the room. Oliver turned the dial again. 'What do you fancy? Radio Two, Four?'

'Either will do. It's two minutes to six. We'll get the best news on Radio Four.'

The reception wasn't great, but it would at least give an idea of what it was like out there. The weather was the headline news.

Parts of the north of England has been cut off due to heavy snow. Only the main roads are open, and motorists are strongly advised to stay at home. Minor roads are completely blocked, and many other roads are impassable due to the large number of abandoned cars. Many homes are without electricity and are likely to remain so until after Christmas, although Northern Power has cancelled all leave and workers are trying to re-establish power as soon as possible. However, with further heavy snow forecast for the rest of today and tomorrow, they are pessimistic about the chances of all homes having electricity for the next two days. There will be an extended weather forecast at the end of this news.

'Doesn't sound good, does it?' said Oliver as the newsreader went on to a story about another failed ceasefire in the Middle East.

'At least we have heating and a way of cooking food. Anyway, let's listen to the news for now.' Lisa concentrated on listening while Oliver carried on with the preparations for the mulled wine. He was not at all interested in what went on in the world, the polar opposite of Emilia who was aware of every outrage against human rights that was going on at any time. She was staggeringly well informed whereas Oliver and Rosalind could be surrounded by bubble wrap and hidden in a cellar somewhere so little did they know of what was going on. The news went on as it always did: fighting in the Middle East, war in Ukraine, a mass shooting in the United States. God, it was depressing, like so often these days, Lisa fought back tears. Bloody menopause. It had turned her into an emotional wreck.

And now, the local news. The body of a young man has been found in Jesmond, Newcastle. Police are regarding his death as suspicious and the house in Kennystone Avenue, where he was found, has been cordoned off. He has not yet been identified and police are asking anyone with any information to contact them on 0845 676 0000.

'Oh God, isn't that near where you live?' Lisa asked as she opened two bottles of red wine and poured them into a pan.

'What?' said Oliver who had been trying his phone yet again for a signal.

'Jesmond. Kenny something Avenue. A man's been found dead there.' She handed him an orange. Can you stud this with cloves, please?'

'Did they give his name?'

'No, he hasn't been identified. Hey, watch what you're doing with that orange.' Oliver had dropped the orange on the floor. Lisa bent to pick it up and took it over to the sink to wash it. She dried it with a paper towel and handed it back to Oliver. 'I think we'll need another one as well. Imparts a nice flavour, the orange. Are you OK? You look a bit pale.'

'Yeah, I'm fine. I'm a bit hungry. Seems like hours since lunch.'

Typical Oliver, ruled by his blood sugar. 'There's some quiche in the fridge. But anyway, you must have had about five mince pies. Surely, you're not hungry?'

His head was in the fridge. 'Nope, I only had two. Where's this quiche?'

She nudged him aside. 'On the top shelf I think.' She peered inside. 'That's odd. I'm sure I put it in there this morning.'

'It's OK, I'll have a banana.'

'Are you sure you only had two mince pies?'

'Deffo. Why?'

'I made twenty-four this morning and there's only six left. We ate three between us, which means Ros, Em and your dad must have eaten fifteen between them. It doesn't seem likely.'

'Maybe they're somewhere else?'

'No, I definitely put them all in a Tupperware box to keep them fresh. Oh well, we can ask the others when they get back.'

Oliver frowned. 'You don't think anyone's been in the cottage, do you?'

'What, a mince pie eating burglar? With a penchant for quiche? Who takes food and leaves everything else?'

'Well, if you put it like that. It doesn't sound likely.'

'Come on, the pastry should have rested by now. You roll it out and make the mince pies. I want to get them done before starting on the evening meal. I'll finish off the wine. And when you're done, put a lock on the oven door to stop anyone else getting at them!' She turned off the radio. 'Let's get those mince pies made.'

When they opened the door to the cottage, an aroma of dried fruit and spices wafted towards them.

'What's that smell? It's delicious,' Em said. Her cheeks were pink with the cold as were Ros's and they looked about fifteen. 'When can we have some?'

'Not yet, it's too early. You could chop up the vegetables, one of you,' Lisa said without much hope. Ros was, frankly, too self-obsessed to be much help and Em had a bit of a thing about food. Although she'd eat it, she rarely offered to help with its preparation. It didn't matter, Lisa loved cooking, but it was nice to have the camaraderie that comes with a shared purpose. However, Ros went to the knife block and picked out a small sharp knife. Lisa hid a smile.

'Do we know what the weather forecast is?' said Emilia.

'Don't be daft, we're cut off—'

'Not anymore, Ros, thanks to your great aunt Mae. Remember this?' Lisa pointed to the radio.

Emilia picked it up. 'Wow! Who would have thought this piece of old junk would have come in useful?'

'We used to have one like it at home,' said Ros. 'But we got rid of it years ago. What's the point when we can stream everything?'

'Except we can't now, can we?'

'Ah right. What's new, then?'

'Electricity lines down all over North of England, more snow expected. Don't take a trip unless it's absolutely necessary, the usual shutdown when it snows.'

'Ugh. Well, let's coorie doon this evening and tell each other ghost stories.'

'I don't think so,' said Lisa. 'I hate to remind you but last time we did that we had three terrified children and one wet bed the next day.'

'I was only nine!' protested Oliver. 'I couldn't help it.'

They all laughed at his outrage. 'I know, but I don't think we'll take the risk. Anyway, I hate ghost stories and anything frightening.'

'Ooh,' said Ros. 'Who knows, maybe there's a killer out there at this very moment, stalking us, looking in through our windows, wondering which one of us to take out first.'

'Shut up, won't you!' said Oliver.

Ros looked at him. 'What's up with you? Gosh, you always were a scaredy cat, weren't you? You haven't changed.'

This was out of character for Oliver. He never picked a fight with anyone, never spoke harshly to a single soul. If anything, he was far too gentle for his own good. And now here he was, glaring at his sister as if he wanted to kill her.

'Oliver,' she said. 'It was a joke. Not a particularly good one, but a joke.'

He stared at her. 'Well, I don't find it funny.'

'Oh, for heaven's sake,' cried Ros. 'Lighten up. Jesus. Next, we won't be able to make jokes about your other favourite subject – vegetarianism.'

'Meat is murder,' he said, but without much conviction.

'Yeah, well. What about all the fish you eat?'

'Ros, I'm not going to get into an argument about vegetarianism with you. I know you're a carnivore. You've made it perfectly clear you have no soul. So, let's leave it, shall we?' He put the last tray of mince pies into the oven and left the kitchen, slamming the door behind him.

'Oops,' said Ros. 'I'd forgotten how touchy he is about certain subjects. Should I go after him, do you think?'

'I'd leave it,' said Em. 'He's probably hungover.'

The door opened and Lisa swung round, expecting to see Oliver but it was David, wiping sleep from his eyes. 'What's up with Ollie?'

'It was my fault,' said Lisa. 'I brought up the time he wet the bed after we told ghost stories. It was tactless of me. I'd forgotten how sensitive he is.'

Ros frowned. 'No, Mum, it wasn't that. He went off on one when Em made a stupid joke about an axe murderer on the loose. It was a total over-reaction.'

'I suppose so. Although there's been a suspicious death in Newcastle. Near to where he lived.'

'So what? There must be suspicious deaths there all the time. Where're you off to, Em?'

'Oh, there's something I wanted to check in a book. What time is dinner?'

'About eight.'

'OK, I shouldn't be long. I'll be down in half an hour to set the table, drink some wine, stuff myself with food.' She smiled as she said this, but it didn't reach her eyes.

Damn it all. It had all been going so well. She should have kept her mouth shut about Oliver's bed wetting. Would she ever learn? Now Oliver had gone off in a strop when the other two were on form for once. She'd forgotten how hard it was to negotiate family life.

Chapter Nine

Ros TOSSED the last pieces of a chopped red pepper into a roasting tray brimming with vegetables. 'Have I done enough?'

'Yes, brilliant thanks. That's a great help.'

'Well, if you don't want me for anything else, I'll go upstairs and lie down.'

As if. Ros was going to find Oliver and torture him if necessary. She had to know what was up with him. He wasn't one to sulk and she didn't buy this story of being upset by a reference to a long-forgotten event in his childhood, for God's sake.

Her mother lifted the tray of vegetables and put it to one side. 'Are you tired?'

'Knackered,' said Ros. She made herself yawn. 'But I'll set my alarm for an hour's time so I don't miss the lamb tagine.'

Upstairs she paused outside Em's room. What had been all that stuff about bullying at school? It sounded awful but Em clearly wasn't ready to talk about it. Imagine being sent a card like that when you were at your most vulnerable. How could they? Horrible people. Em had got them back big style though. Ros would never have thought she was capable of it. It was so appropriate for that little clique, with all their bitching and back biting. Poetic justice. No, she'd leave Em alone for now. There would be other opportunities to talk.

Ros had missed their chats. They'd been inseparable as children. Too bad they'd lost their closeness in their teenage years. It was her fault, no denying it. Obsessed with her looks, with being popular, with fitting in with the in crowd at school, she'd neglected her sister for so long they had grown apart. That would change now they'd started talking again properly instead of the sniping that had been characteristic of their interactions for many years.

She yawned again. Heavens, she was tired after all. How good it would be to snuggle into bed and close her eyes. For a moment she dithered by the door of her room but then she heard the murmur of voices from Oliver's room. For fuck's sake! They were excluding her again. She was always the odd one out, the younger twin, the middle child no one wanted. Tears filled her eyes; she blinked them away. Get a grip. March right in there and find out what's going on. Or it might be better to be more subtle, ask nicely as her mother always said when they were younger. She took a deep breath, knocked on the door and went in.

'Hey, you two, what's up?'

Oliver looked dreadful; his skin ashen. Ros peered at him. 'You OK?'

'Does he look it?' snapped Emilia.

She had to see this out. She sat on the edge of Oliver's bed. 'Why won't you tell me what's going on?'

'Because you'll tell Mum and Dad and Christmas will be spoilt completely,' said Em.

'And you think it isn't already ruined? You turn up looking like something dragged out of an undertaker's, Oliver storms out because someone mentions an incident from years ago and, which frankly, Oliver, get over it! Not to speak of me and my stupid infatuation with a man who clearly isn't interested in me. Honestly, look at us. We're acting like a bunch of daft teenagers.'

Emilia laughed. 'Well, at least you included yourself in the guilty list.'

'So? What the fuck is going on?' She spoke slowly, enunciating every word.

'You mustn't breathe a word of this to Mum and Dad, swear?' said Oliver, his handsome face tense with anxiety.

'Sounds serious,' said Ros, trying to lighten the atmosphere. 'Do you want me to get a witness?'

'Oh, it is. I have seriously messed up this time.'

'What do you mean?'

He looked down at the floor and mumbled something that she didn't catch. He sounded close to tears. Ros shot a look at Em and mouthed: *Is he OK?* Em shook her head, a gesture that said everything.

'I didn't hear what you said.'

He looked up. 'I'm mixed up with some pretty bad things.'

There was a draught in the room; she pulled her cardigan tighter round her. 'What sort of things?'

'Drugs.'

Silence. Ros couldn't believe what she was hearing. 'You're a drug addict?'

Slow shaking of the head. 'No.'

'What then?' Out of the corner of her eye she saw Em roll her eyes. 'What?' she demanded.

'You always were a bit slow on the uptake, sis. He's been dealing.'

The room tilted. She was lightheaded, dizzy. A dealer. He couldn't be. 'Not a real dealer?'

Oliver was silent so Em spoke for him. 'Oh, yes. Mixed up with Newcastle's finest.'

'But how?'

Oliver started to speak. She had to lean forward to hear him. 'The usual way. I smoked a bit of weed at the weekends, got friendly with my dealer. He was an alright bloke.'

Em's face remained impassive. Ros wished she could say the same of her own. She never did have a poker face. She caught a glimpse of herself in the mirror, her expression a stereotype of shock.

'And?'

'Well, one thing led to another. He asked if I wanted to make some money. Who doesn't?' He glared at his sisters defying them to contradict him. Em opened her mouth so Ros intercepted to tell him to go on. 'It didn't seem important, most of my friends wanted to smoke at the weekend. This way I could continue to smoke but I'd earn a bit of money on the side. It was a no brainer. Students prefer to buy from other students. So, I agreed to supply my friends at the university.'

Ros couldn't stop herself. 'You can go to prison for dealing.'

'For fuck's sake, Ros. I'm not daft! Anyway, to begin with it wasn't much. Three or four friends. If the police find you with that amount well, it's small enough to claim for personal use so as far as I could see, there was no risk.'

'Oh fuck, you haven't been caught, have you?'

Oliver reddened. 'Look, Ros, this is hard enough. Can

you please let me tell the story without you interrupting every few seconds?'

Ros fell silent. He continued. 'So, that went on for a few weeks. I made next to nothing, enough to keep me going. Then one night when I went to meet Dillon, my source, he didn't turn up. Some other guy was there. Tougher. A right nasty piece of work. He put the screws on me, told me I needed to sell more. Within a month, I was dealing weed to about fifty or sixty students.'

Ros bit on her lower lip.

'That was bad enough. I was getting worried. Now if I was caught, I would definitely get a prison sentence. I was also behind with my studies.'

'But you said you were getting on well. Eighty per cent for your last essay.'

Oliver shook his head. 'I had to tell the parents something. You know what they're like. I didn't manage to submit it. My tutor gave me an extension but now we've no electricity and my laptop's run out of battery how will I get it done?'

'You'll manage,' said Ros. 'We won't be cut off forever. Anyway, you can take notes, get ready for when the electricity comes back on.'

Oliver's laugh was bitter. 'Yes, I might get this one in, but the next? I doubt it. Dealing takes time. I've been getting calls at all hours of the day, sometimes in the middle of the night. You have no idea how exhausted I am.'

It's your own fault, you stupid bastard, thought Ros. Aloud she said, 'You'll be found out. You can't keep pretending.'

'Ros, do you want to hear this or not?'

She took the hint and Oliver continued.

'As I was saying, I was way behind with my work. All the

interruptions, phone calls and the like, having to constantly check what was my money and what was theirs. Then one night when I was collecting the supply they upped the ante. There wasn't enough weed to go round, they said. Only coke, ketamine and MDMA.'

Em looked up, glowering. 'For fuck's sake, Ollie. You never told me about the other stuff.'

'I wasn't happy about it. But at least it wasn't heroin. They knew their stuff. Heroin isn't the drug of choice of students, but ketamine is. They can't get enough of it.'

'Ketamine?' asked Ros. She'd heard the name but had no real knowledge of what it was and what effects it had.

'It's a sedative. Puts you into your own wee world. Great for listening to music, or so they say.'

Two red spots appeared high on Em's cheeks. 'You reckon it's all right because you weren't dealing in heroin, do you? Well, I can tell you, ketamine is fucking dangerous. It's been used in cases of rape. People who've taken it often find it hard to move so they become sitting targets for sexual predators. It can harm your bladder, too. There are kids of twenty who've had their lives ruined by it.' She spat out the words.

'You seem to know a lot about it,' said Ros. This was getting out of control. She wished she'd never asked.

'A friend of mine took it once. She ended up in a room with three men. I'll leave you to imagine the rest. She'll never get over it.'

'Fuck,' said Ros. 'Fuck.'

Em took a deep breath. 'I'm writing an article on it. I don't think enough people are aware of what it does. And now I find my own brother deals in the stuff. You... you fucking shitbag.'

Oliver swallowed, moistened his lips. 'For fuck's sake,

Em. 'I promise you, I didn't know this stuff! Anyone I've met who's used K hasn't been a rapist—'

'Will you listen to what I'm saying? It makes people vulnerable. I didn't say it made them rape people, but it does make them more likely to be a victim.'

'I'm not making excuses. I was a fucking idiot, but I swear to you I wanted out. In the end I didn't take the deal. You can end up in prison for dealing in Class A drugs—'

'And for dealing in cannabis,' interrupted Em.

'I know, but with Class A, it's a dead cert and I wasn't going to take the risk. I told Dillon – that's the guy who got me into it in the first place – I told him it had to stop. He wanted out, too. He was scared they'd get him to deal heroin. His sister had died from an overdose and if his mother found out he was dealing in the stuff... well, you can imagine. Anyway, the next day I was attacked coming home from the pub, beaten up. It could have been worse, but it was enough to show me they meant business. They didn't break anything, and they were clever enough not to go for my face, but my ribs are bruised...' He lifted up his shirt to reveal a rainbow of bruises on his body.

Ros gasped but Em was far from sympathetic. 'Serves you right.'

'Emilia, shut up. You can see how upset Ollie is. He doesn't need you lecturing him.' Ros turned to her brother. 'You have to get out of Newcastle. You can finish your degree in Glasgow or anywhere for that matter. But you can't stay there and wait either for them to kill you or the police to arrest you.'

Emilia lay back on her bed, arms folded, eyes narrowed. Perhaps she'd never forgive Oliver, but they could discuss that later. For now, Ros was worried about the odd smile on Oliver's face. 'I'm waiting for you to say something, Oliver.'

'I know, I know. They were full of threats. How they'd kill me if I didn't do what they said. I didn't believe them but now...' He gave a short laugh. 'It gets worse...'

What now? Ros said nothing and waited for him to go on.

'Dillon went missing a couple of days ago. I was furious. I thought he was bailing out leaving me to take the pressure.' Ollie stood up and moved across to the window. He looked out into the darkness as if searching for someone or something. 'And now, Dillon has turned up dead.'

'What? How do you know?'

'I found an old radio, battery operated. I didn't hear it, Mum did.'

'Mum knows about this?' Ros's voice rose to a screech.

'No, no. She picked up on the area where his body was found. "Jesmond, isn't that near where you live?" and when I asked whether they'd named him...'

'Oh God, it wasn't Dillon, was it?' said Ros.

'I don't know for sure. They haven't identified him yet.'

A ray of light. 'So, it might not be him.'

'I hope it isn't but... It's too much of a coincidence.'

'Do you think you're in danger?'

'I don't know.' He rubbed the bridge of his nose. 'They threatened us both. They've already beaten me up. I don't know what to think.'

Ros thought she might vomit. 'You need to go to the police. For heaven's sake, Oliver. This is serious.'

He looked away. 'I'd be incriminating myself.'

'But someone's been murdered. You have to tell them what's gone on.'

'And then I end up in prison, a sitting target for some drugs baron? They have people everywhere.'

Ros's head was spinning. She was lightheaded with fatigue and disbelief. She wished she'd stayed downstairs where it was warm and comfortable and she thought her brother was in his final year at university and safe, not a drug dealer who'd got involved with a mad criminal gang who went round murdering people, for fuck's sake. 'Murder, Oliver. You have to go to the police.'

Em nodded in agreement. 'Ollie you'll have to do something, the first thing is to get out of Newcastle. Tell Mum and Dad you want to be closer to home or something. You don't have to mention the drugs.'

'No!'

'What else are you going to do?'

'I don't know.' He scowled. 'Fuck, I wish I'd never said anything to you.'

'Why did you?' asked Ros. 'Why did you tell Em?' The unspoken words *and not me* hung in the air.

Ollie shrugged. 'I don't know. Does it matter?'

It did. It was another way she'd been kept out of things, but this wasn't the time to say so. She shrugged. 'We need a plan. At least they don't know you're here.'

Ollie didn't reply.

'Tell me they don't know about this cottage.'

A deep sigh. 'Dillon knew.'

'Jesus Christ! Do you think he'll have told them?'

'I don't know. I don't fucking know, right? It's possible,' he conceded, flicking a bit of fluff off his trousers concentrating hard on the action. 'They might have got it out of him. They're real thugs.'

'What exactly did you tell him?'

'I told him we have a second home in Northumberland. I didn't mean to. We were chatting about places we'd been on holiday.'

'Well,' said Ros. 'Northumberland's huge. They'll never track you down with that information.'

'And I might have mentioned the name of the cottage.'

Ros closed her eyes. She breathed deeply trying to calm herself. 'It's a lot of mights and maybes. Without an actual real address, they're scuppered. It's not as if we're registered to vote here so my guess is they can't find us online. Look, let's think about this. We don't know who killed this Dillon person, if it is him. We don't know for sure and well, if it is, it might be nothing to do with this drug gang. It might have been an overdose.'

'He didn't do drugs.'

'OK, not an overdose then. But if he were murdered and if it was the same lot who'd threatened you, what are the chances of them finding you here? The name of the cottage alone won't help them and anyway, look outside – it's snowing like we've moved to Antarctica. It'll be fine.' Ros beamed at them both with an optimism she didn't feel.

'Do you think so? What if...?'

'Go on.'

He shook his head and motioned towards the door. 'I think someone's listening,' he mouthed.

Ros leapt up from her seat and strode to the door, pulling it open. Nothing. 'See what a guilty conscience does to you? What were you saying?'

The colour came back to his face. 'Sorry, I thought it was Mum. I don't want her to know, Ros. I mean it.'

'Yeah, you said. It would be better to tell her, though.'

He scrutinised the back of his hands. 'You're right. I mean about the gang. They wouldn't be able to find this place. I'm over-reacting.' He shook his head. 'Poor Dillon.'

Em joined in then. 'Ollie's right. I hate to agree with him as he's been such a fucking idiot but say they do know exactly where the Warren is, how would they get here in this weather? I vote we keep it to ourselves for the time being.'

'Fine,' said Ros. 'But what about the abandoned car we saw?'

'What car?' said Oliver.

Lisa opened the oven door to take out the casserole. God, she was hungry. The aroma of cumin and coriander she'd used to season the lamb tagine was appetising. The roasted vegetables were done and all she had to do now was add flaked almonds to the couscous. 'Pour us all some wine,' she said to David as she left to go upstairs.

It was quiet upstairs and Lisa hoped they weren't all asleep. She went into the bathroom and washed her hands. The water was lukewarm; they'd have to build up the logs in the Aga. On her way out, she heard Emilia say something but didn't make out the words. The tone was recognisable, though. Anger. Damn it, were they in for one of her tirades? She stood at the top of the stairs and said in a loud voice before setting off downstairs: 'Dinner's ready. I'm serving it now!'.

It was five minutes before they all appeared. Lisa had to call them twice more and wasn't pleased. They came into the room together, bringing with them an atmosphere thick with tension. Probably not the best time to tackle them about their manners so she smiled and said nothing, kicking David under the table as he opened his mouth to speak.

After ten minutes of no one saying anything, Lisa had had enough. She tried thinking of a neutral topic to bring up, but none came to mind. She'd already asked Ros if she'd slept well and got a grunt in reply. She didn't want to bring up Oliver's course work because it could so easily descend into recriminations about Cambridge from David who, whether she liked it or not, was pissed off at Ollie for being sent down. It would have to be Em; she'd ask her about her work.

'What are you working on at the moment?' she asked. 'Anything interesting?'

She almost didn't catch it – Em's quick sidelong look at her siblings. 'No.'

'Oh, come on,' said Ros. 'That article you're working on about drugs sounded fascinating. I didn't know half the stuff you were talking about.'

Something was going on. There was an edge to Ros's voice and Oliver shot her a look of dislike. What had gone on up there? Was one of them on drugs? Oliver smoked dope, had done since he was fifteen, but he'd always sworn away from anything harder. And Ros and Em were disdainful of any stimulant other than alcohol. Ros hardly drank as it was. Two glasses of wine and she was out for the count. And as for Em, well, Lisa would have said up until yesterday she was the same. But she'd turned up drunk. Was she doing drugs? No, she found it hard to believe. Emilia was such a control freak. She'd never risk getting into drugs.

Em picked up her glass and finished off her wine. 'Drugs have been done to death; an article on them would be hard to sell.' She turned to Lisa. 'I do have an idea for an article, though. About genetic sexual attraction.'

'Never heard of it,' said David, screwing up his face.

'No? My point exactly. Everyone thinks they know about drugs, but no one knows much about this. It's a much more saleable story.'

'So, tell us. What is it?' said Oliver.

'Siblings who've been separated and brought up apart falling in love when they meet.'

'What? Are you sure?' said David.

Em puffed out her cheeks, exasperated. 'Well, I can assure you it does exist. There's lots of documented cases.'

He shifted in his seat and winked at Lisa. 'Go on then, Emilia. Tell us. You're obviously dying to.'

'It sometimes happens when, for example, half siblings who didn't know about each other meet for the first time as adults or siblings who've been separated as children meet again. It can also happen between, for example, a mother or father and a child who's been adopted.'

'You're kidding, aren't you?' said David.

'No, I'm not. There are cases of people who don't know they're brother and sister, marrying and having children. It's been known about for centuries. Some people think Dorothy Wordsworth was in love with William. You only have to read her diaries to see why. She had a complete meltdown the day he got married. There are loads of instances of it in literature, too. Moll Flanders marries her brother without knowing it.'

'Yes, that's right, although he was her half-brother,' said Lisa. David looked at her in mock amazement. 'Don't look so surprised. Remember, I did English as well as Drama at university.'

'I don't get it, though. Why would you be attracted to your brother or sister?' asked Oliver.

'I'm not sure,' admitted Em. 'I think one of the theories is that we are often attracted to people who look like us or who resemble our fathers if we're a girl or mothers if we're a boy. It's called assortative mating.'

'Doesn't explain *why* we're attracted though,' said David. 'I mean, it sounds a bit suspect to me, as though it's being used as an excuse for something completely unnatural.'

'But it does happen,' said Em. 'Take Wordsworth and his sister. They were separated for years when they were children. Their mother died when William was about eight and

Dorothy seven, they were sent away to live with different relatives and didn't meet again for nine years. So, it's perfectly possible they were sexually attracted to each other. Dorothy's reaction to William's marriage was bizarre. She took to her bed. A bit strange, don't you think?'

'Maybe she didn't like who he was marrying,' said David.

'Why do you never take me seriously?' Em was working up to an argument.

Lisa stepped in. 'Tell us more about your article. Do you have a commission for it?'

'Not yet, no. But some of the classier women's magazines might be interested. I'm working on an outline at the moment.'

Lisa's intervention avoided what she thought was a brewing row until Ros interrupted with the tact of an elderly aunt asking why her gay nephew doesn't have a wife yet. 'Sounds like rubbish to me.'

Lisa held her breath but to her surprise, Em didn't flare up like she often did. 'Maybe it does, but it happens, nonetheless. Usually when an adopted child finds a long-lost parent because not only is there the chance of an abnormal parent-child relationship but the parent may have other children. And it will happen more in the future because of sperm donation.'

Time to change the subject. 'Anyone fancy a game of cards?'

Oliver jumped in as Lisa knew he would. 'Cheat,' he said.

Lisa laughed and went to fetch two packs of playing cards. Within minutes they were immersed in watching each other for clues and the atmosphere improved. Lisa couldn't help thinking she'd been played for a fool, though.

Chapter Ten

Ros JOINED in with the hilarity that always accompanied games of Cheat, but her laughter was forced. Looking at her siblings, she wished she was able to forget about the possible threat to them in the way they had. Em had out-manoeuvred her over the article she was working on, about drugs. Ros had hoped she would tell Mum and Dad the stuff she'd mentioned upstairs. Maybe it would have encouraged Oliver to 'fess up. Instead, she'd gone on about bloody Wordsworth and his sister fancying each other. Wordsworth, ugh. They'd had to learn that poem about daffodils when they were at primary school. It had taken her years to get over her dislike of the flowers.

Now she thought about it, Mum looked uncomfortable during the discussion. At the moment she was studying Emilia without her noticing, looking at her – how? Scared was the word that came to mind, but Ros couldn't imagine why, other than that Mum was worried about her becoming anorexic. If she knew about Ollie's link with drug dealers, then she'd have something to be frightened about.

Ollie was laughing as if his only care was whether the others would believe his claim of six aces.

'Cheat!' shouted Dad and triumphant, Ollie turned over the six cards to show they were all aces. A wave of dislike washed over her; he'd put them all in danger and here he was, playing cards like he had nothing to worry about. What a wanker. She rose from her seat, time to go to bed. But as she got up, she noticed Ollie's face, bleak, as he waited his turn in the game and as fast as it had come, her distaste fled. He was so young, so worried looking, why didn't the parents pick up on it? Christ, she was tired. Too tired to think about this. 'I'm off to bed,' she said.

Upstairs, she undressed and after having washed herself in the most cursory way possible, got into bed. As soon as she had, she wished she'd filled her hot water bottle. It was freezing in the bed and the sheets were so cold they felt damp. She got up again and put on a pair of socks, but it was no good. She lay there wondering whether to go and get the hot water bottle but decided against it. She was so tired she'd probably fall asleep anyway. The others were coming upstairs; she could hear their chatter as they got ready for bed: Dad telling some story, Oliver laughing, Em's voice low in the background; she sounded earnest. No sound from Mum. Why was she so quiet? It wasn't like her. Maybe she'd picked up on Ros's unease; she'd ask her tomorrow. Heavens... Tomorrow was Christmas Eve. Only another three full days and she'd be on her way home, snow permitting. She'd seek out Ian. Or maybe she wouldn't. She'd let him do the running for a change... and if he didn't, well, there was a world full of men to choose from.

Ros woke with a start. Had she been snoring and snorted herself awake? It wouldn't be the first time. The room was dark, much darker than she was used to in the city, where streetlights illuminated her flat. Here, it was different. The shadows were oppressive, closing round her like a shroud. She fumbled on her bedside table until she found her torch. She'd feel better with it on, but, shit, what was the first thing she saw? A mouse scurrying along the floor. That was it, she was wide awake now. No way was she falling asleep with a mouse in the room. She'd gone to bed without taking her watch off and she held the torch close so as to see what time it was, hoping it wouldn't be four a.m., the time when most deaths occur. Or so she had read. Was it true? How did they know? She braced herself: Twenty past five. Good. Safely past the danger zone and plenty of time to get back to sleep if she could only forget about the mouse.

God, what was that noise? Something or someone was downstairs. More mice, probably, running through the kitchen, searching for crumbs. No, *that* was the sound of something being knocked over. And now, a footstep on the stairs? She held her breath, tried to concentrate. Nothing. Her heart was pounding, and she breathed deeply to try to control herself. She had drunk too much coffee, that was what it was. All her friends had been telling her for months she needed to cut down. And she was nervous because of what Oliver had told her. There was nothing more to it. Bloody hell, that was something breaking! She sat up in bed, all senses alert. There was someone downstairs. Mum, most likely, prowling around in the early hours. But then she heard the distinctive sound of Mum's snores. Ros grabbed the torch and inched herself out of bed, trying to make as little noise as possible. She crept over to the bedroom door and opened it, her hand shaking so much she was frightened she'd drop the torch. Oliver's door was open, so she went in and shook him. He woke at once, not startled in the least. If anything, he looked annoyed.

'What is it?'

'Someone's downstairs.'

His demeanour changed immediately to one of terror. 'Are you sure?'

'There's something going on. I'm going to wake Dad.'

'No, leave it. I'll go and see who it is. You stay here.' He took the torch from her and searched for his own before handing it back to her and getting out of bed.

'Are you serious? I'm not leaving you to the mercy of whoever's down there. Do you have anything?'

'What do you mean?'

'You know, to hit him with.'

He paled. 'You think it's them then? The dealers?'

'No, I think it's the fucking bogey man,' Ros hissed. 'Who else do you think it is? How many other criminals are out to get you?'

His mouth tightened. 'No need to be like that.'

Shit, she was a real bitch at times. She squeezed his arm. 'Sorry, it's... I'm scared.'

'What's going on here?' Em stood in the doorway, her hair tangled and messy, her eyes puffy. Had she been crying?

'Ros heard something, downstairs. We're going to see what it is.'

'We should wake Dad,' Ros wanted a grown up to take responsibility. She couldn't deal with this.

Em and Ollie spoke in unison. 'No, keep them out of it as long as possible.'

Ros shrugged, defeated. 'OK. Listen, there's golf clubs in the hall cupboard. We'll creep downstairs as quietly as possible, get into the cupboard and each grab a club. There's also a sweeping brush in my room so I'll take that.'

'Then what?' asked Oliver.

'Then I'll sweep whoever it is away. I don't fucking know. Hit him... them.'

'What if it's Dad or Mum?'

'It's not,' said Ros. 'I've been listening. Each of them has their own odd way of snoring and they're both there. Whatever or whoever it is, it's not them.'

They all looked at each other; none of them wanting to admit how scared they were. It was as if they were children again and had been playing a silly game: I dare you to knock on the neighbour's door, I dare you to climb on the garage roof, I dare you to go downstairs and confront a violent criminal. Too late, Ros wished she'd stayed in bed. Or better, was back in Glasgow, safe in her flat.

'Shouldn't we call the police?' whispered Em, biting back the words as soon as she said them. 'Shit, sorry. I forgot about the power cut. And the snow.'

Oliver made a face and she snapped. 'I don't know why you're rolling your eyes, it's your bloody fault we're in this mess.'

'Sorry.'

Someone had to take control. 'Right. I'll go down first with both of you right at my back,' said Ros. 'I'll listen at the door and then we'll burst in and take him by surprise. We'll be fine. It's three against one, he hasn't a chance.'

'We don't know there's only one of them,' said Em. 'And I don't know if I *can* hit someone.'

Ros and Oliver looked at her in disbelief. 'Imagine you're nine again and fighting with one of us. I'm sure it'll all come back,' said Ros, touching a small scar on her chin.

'I'm not being much help, am I?'

Best to say nothing; they'd need all their energy for whatever it was downstairs.

There was another sound, of something falling over. 'Whoever it is, he's not scared of being heard. We have to get down there.' Ros stepped on the first stair. 'Ready?'

The other two nodded and she started her descent. It was difficult going down the steep narrow staircase with only a torch to light the way. She was used to the night lights that had been installed on the stairway. In her other hand, she held a brush. The stairs were freezing under her feet, and she cursed her stupidity in not wearing slippers. What if she tripped and fell? She stopped and handed the broom to Oliver who was right behind her.

'I can't manage this and the torch,' she whispered. 'I need a hand free to feel my way down.'

She transferred the torch to her left hand and used the right to hold on to the rail that edged the staircase. It was easier without the brush, but her progress was slow as she was frightened of alerting the intruder, It was taking forever to get anywhere. When she reached the bottom, she looked at her watch, surprised to see only five minutes had passed since she had awoken. Oliver opened the door to the hall cupboard and handed them each a club. The three of them stood in the hallway outside the kitchen door. Ros indicated to the others to stand on either side of the door and using her fingers she showed she was going to go in on the count of three. She stifled an urge to giggle. It was like being in a bad crime drama, but as soon as she thought that, she sobered up. There was a dangerous criminal in their kitchen who, by the sound of things, was destroying the place.

'Ready?' she whispered. 'Three, two, one.' They barged into the kitchen.

The back door was open. Snow had blown in and the

room was icy cold. Ros swung the club above her head ready to hit anyone who came at her but there was no one there. 'It's OK,' she said. 'Whoever it was, has gone.' She brought the candle through from the hall and lit the others ranged round the room to examine the damage.

'What the...?' said Oliver. The bin was overturned and their leftovers from last night's meal were scattered across the floor: gravy mixed up with vegetable peelings, aluminium foil with breadcrumbs, dampened kitchen towels with tangerine skins. There was a musky smell, deeply unpleasant. A male animal marking its territory.

Ros sat down on the nearest chair and laughed. 'It's a damn fox,' she said. 'Someone left the door unlocked, it's blown open and a fox has wandered in. We've been upstairs shitting ourselves over a bloody fox.'

The colour returned to Oliver's face and Em laughed. A rare event. Em was always serious. As a child she'd worried about beggars, cried herself to sleep over people dying of cancer and refused to finish meals stating she couldn't eat when there were starving children in Africa. While Ros, ever the pragmatist, had simply eaten up her sister's leftovers. Perhaps she'd been given all the selfish genes while Em had the altruistic ones. When they'd stopped laughing, Ros got up.

'I'm off to bed then.' Her siblings glanced at each other.

'What?'

'Er, maybe we should clear this up?'

''Mum'll get it in the morning.'

'Are you fucking kidding? I can't believe you said that,' said Em. 'I bet you never offer to wash up when someone makes you a meal.'

'What are dishwashers for?'

'Not everyone has one,' said Ollie. 'I don't.'

'Me neither. Seriously, Ros. You're always doing that. Walking away and leaving someone else to clear up.'

'Do I?' She was genuinely surprised. Surely, she did her fair share of chores. She had a cleaner, of course. Something she prioritised; she wasn't going to get her hands dirty. But when the family were together, she pulled her weight. She'd prepared the vegetables tonight after all. Her siblings stared at her.

Her thoughts paused on a vision of her mother washing the dishes tonight after preparing a huge meal for them all. Em had helped and her dad had dried up while Oliver cleaned the kitchen. Ros had lazed in front of the fire, painting her nails. Maybe they had a point.

'I'll get the brush.' They didn't have to look so amazed. Bastards. The mature thing was to ignore the implied criticism, so she got the sweeping brush from where she'd dropped it and started to clean up. Emilia and Oliver watched her struggle with the awful mess left behind by the fox or whatever animal had been in their kitchen. She was making it worse and judging by the glances passing between her siblings they thought the same. At last, she succumbed. 'Okay, I can see you're not impressed. Tell me what to do instead of standing there looking superior.'

'Maybe pick up the solid stuff first?' suggested Em. 'As it is, all you're doing is smearing everything everywhere. Once you've done that then use a mop to get at the gunge.'

She sounded so superior that Ros wanted to throw the brush down in a fit of pique. Why was it she couldn't do simple things like clean up without making a mess of it? But she bit her tongue and got on with it, until, at last, the others joined in, and within a few minutes, they had it completely clean. At least, it looked clean in the light of their torches. It might be otherwise once dawn came.

'Right, now I'm definitely off to b—' Ros was interrupted by the door opening. It was their mother.

Lisa wasn't sure how long she'd been half awake before the noise from downstairs filtered through to her consciousness. Muffled bumps, mumblings and the sound of a door opening and shutting. Surely, no one was up and about at this unearthly hour – she picked up her phone and saw it was not yet six o'clock. It was warm and comfortable in bed. She longed to turn over, go back to sleep and leave them to do whatever it was they were doing, but then the worries of the past two days returned. She'd been half reassured last night with the hysteria over the silly card game. But hadn't it been a little strained? Her main worry was Emilia. Ros, yes, she worried about her, too, but she had rallied round after her little temper tantrum about, what was his name? Ian, that was it. In fact, she'd shown a mature side to her. She must be growing up at last. Oliver was fine, though he had been a little off, maybe he was going down with something. She hoped it wasn't catching whatever it was.

Did there ever come a time when you stopped worrying about your children? Or was it something that stayed with you until your dying breath? She recalled David's mum dying of cancer three months after her husband had had a fatal heart attack. Marie had gripped her hand, whispering *Look after my boy, won't you?* She'd been in great pain, yet David was her main concern. Lisa had been sure that as you reached old age, other concerns would creep up on you, but it turned out she was wrong. No, you never stopped worrying about your children. Emilia, something wasn't right there. What if that was her now, downstairs being sick? Anorexia closing its cold fingers round her once more. Lisa sat up in bed, wide awake.

So, here she was in the kitchen, the three of them in front of her, cleaning up what looked to have been the most awful mess. The bin was overturned; there was a pile of rubbish beside it that had been put there neatly and presumably was about to be returned to it. The kitchen floor was newly washed.

'What's going on?' she asked.

None of them said anything but they looked guilty. She tried again.

'Someone left the door open, and a fox got in,' said Oliver.

'What?'

They all started talking at once. Lisa caught only parts of it, as if it were a badly tuned radio. *Heard a noise ... grabbed a torch ... came downstairs ... all of us ... it might be ... golf clubs ... attack first.* It was a rabble.

'One at a time, please.' Why was she talking to them as if they were naughty pupils? Easy. They weren't telling her the truth. There was something wrong with their story, they were hiding something. Oliver gabbled something about a burglar.

'Sorry, I don't understand. Why did you think there was a burglar? Here, in the middle of nowhere when we're snowed in, and nothing is moving for miles around us?'

Shifty looks between them, and out of nowhere, Ros blurted, 'I'm going to tell her. She has to know.' Has to know what? Judging by the looks Ollie and Emilia were shooting at her it wasn't good news. Her mouth was dry as she said, 'Go on, then. You'll have to tell me now.'

Chapter Eleven

Ros WISHED she'd kept her mouth shut. Oliver and Emilia were staring at her with what could only be called extreme dislike if not actual hatred. If she were asked to put her life on it, she'd bank on the latter. She tried a placatory smile, but she might well have got a warmer look from a stone as from them. Emilia sat down in a chair her face grim. Oliver looked as though he might cry.

'I'm waiting,' said her mother.

'It's um, it's not my story to tell.' She was trying to wriggle out of it, but no one was taken in. Emilia's tiny frame was rigid with fury.

'You've made it yours, by deciding to tell Mum.' She spat out the words. 'You swore you wouldn't, but you can't keep your mouth shut, can you? You've always been the same, running to mummy and daddy with tales. Is it any wonder I've never—' she turned her back to Ros.

Ros didn't know what to say. 'I'm sorry,' she tried. 'I'm sorry, Ollie, honestly, but I think it's better if they know.'

Oliver said nothing. His eyes were full, and he was very

pale. Her mother pulled out one of the kitchen chairs and sat on it. 'Let's all calm down. Emilia, make me a cup of tea, will you? I'm not going anywhere until I find out what all this is about.'

Em went over to the sink, filled the kettle and put it on top of the range. Ros looked at Oliver, her eyes pleading forgiveness, but he refused to give her eye contact. He had moved to the door, as if he were about to flee. She shrugged and gave up. Always on the outside with Emilia and Ollie, she'd done it now. They'd never trust her again. But she had one last try. 'Oliver, please tell Mum. It's not up to me to tell her and I think she'll understand.'

Lisa was in shock. This time two days ago she was desperately looking forward to coming here, couldn't wait to have the whole family together, to see them again. She'd imagined cosy meals, games of Scrabble and charades, the odd argument, maybe, especially after drink had been consumed. But she never imagined this. Here she was, freezing in the cold kitchen listening to her son tell her he'd got involved in drugs and that criminals might be out there wishing him harm. And a young man was already dead. Ros was wrong to think Lisa would understand; she didn't. Why should she? She wanted him to be the boy he was on the first night here, boasting about how he was certain to get a first, telling her how much he loved his course, and how happy he was to be doing well. Not this. Not drugs and criminals.

'Mum?' said Oliver. 'Mum? Are you alright? Say something, please.'

She said nothing. If she spoke now, it would be to say something hurtful, something she wouldn't be able to take back. She stood up, feeling every day of her fifty-four years. The cup of tea Em had made was cold now, unappetising. But even if it had been hot, she couldn't have touched it. She was scared she might throw up.

'I'm going back to bed,' she managed to say. Her voice sounded distant, as if it were coming from somewhere outside her. She didn't look at any of them as she moved to the door, but guessed from the atmosphere that there would be an argument the minute she left the room. Well, so be it. Once in the hall, she breathed deeply and made her way upstairs.

David didn't stir as she got into bed. Her feet, her hands, her whole body was icy, and she shivered uncontrollably, but whether it was with fear or cold she couldn't say. She recalled meetings she'd had with parents who'd discovered drugs in their child's possession. How the glib words had slid from her: be patient, it's natural for teenagers to experiment, try to understand. Huh. What a patronising cow she'd been. But it had caught up with her, all the rubbish she'd spouted. Her son was a dealer, involved with criminals. He had most likely brought danger to the entire family. Were they in danger or had Oliver exaggerated? She should have asked more questions, but she'd been so shocked by the revelations, so dismayed, so *ashamed*. She needed to get out of the kitchen before she said something terrible. Some years before, Em had blurted out that her friends called them the 'too good to be Truetts.' Lisa had already been aware of it, but it didn't make it better. Underlying the seemingly harmless pun, was what? Scorn? Envy? A feeling they were somewhat smug? Whatever it was, it was not affectionate.

Damn it, she wasn't getting any warmer. She moved closer to David, careful not to put her cold feet on his legs, however tempting it might be. He rolled over, leaving her feeling rejected. She moved back to her side of the bed and lay on her back. It was very dark, only seven o'clock. It wouldn't be fully light until well after eight. For a moment she thought about getting up, but she hadn't heard any of the children going back to bed and she couldn't face them. A sigh escaped; she hadn't felt like this for years, not since... well, not since she was very young. No, she wasn't going to think about what had happened then. Not now. Not ever. Lisa forced her thoughts back into the present, to the disconcerting pun on their name. It was teenagers being silly, that's all, wasn't it? Or were her own friends party to it? She hoped not. Lisa was careful not to boast, or so she'd believed. But in all conscience wasn't she a little bit too pleased with everything at times? Were there not times when she silently compared her children with those of her friends?

It was difficult not to. Her colleague Anne's son, for example, was notoriously difficult. He'd been suspended from school several times. This was hard for any parent; the system of suspension was pointless, and she'd had many arguments in the past with management, especially when they used to suspend a pupil for truancy. Thankfully, that no longer happened. But Anne was a teacher and for a teacher there was also the knowledge of how people would gossip and judge them, especially if they were in Pastoral Care. *Huh, she's always telling us how to manage pupils and she can't control her own son.* The eventual diagnosis of Asperger's Syndrome hadn't helped, as pointed comments came from less sensitive colleagues about the middle classes getting diagnoses for their maladjusted offspring. How often had Anne said to Lisa how lucky she was with her three? Lisa could have denied it and confided in her about Em's anorexia, or how Oliver had been chucked out of Cambridge or her worries about Ros's self-obsession, immaturity and need for validation by men, but she didn't, and wouldn't share these worries with her friends. Was it possible she had enjoyed this approbation too much? Perhaps anything less than perfection was never going to be acceptable to her, so she hadn't revealed her problems. It was an appropriate nickname, after all. Slowly, she warmed up, feeling life come back to her feet. With the warmth, came drowsiness, and as the sun was rising, she fell asleep once more.

It was light when she woke for the second time. David disturbed her as he was getting back into bed. He grabbed her, his hands freezing cold after his trip to the bathroom. Normally, this would have been the prelude to some not-so-early morning sex. But after the night she'd had, she wasn't in the mood. He sensed this immediately.

'Are you OK? You seem a bit distant.'

It was tempting to pretend everything was fine and keep quiet about the night's revelations – the cross examination that was sure to follow would put the Gestapo to shame. Then there would be endless family discussions – but they claimed to have no secrets, so she put him in the picture. He said nothing while she was talking but listened carefully adding the occasional 'go on' when she paused. She tried to tell the story as unemotionally as possible, but it was hard when she was so disappointed in Oliver, so angry with him. When she finished, she waited for his reaction, but he lay in bed staring at the ceiling. She gave him a few moments to collect his thoughts until it became unbearable.

'Tell me what you're thinking.'

'There's a spider up there, creeping out of that crack. Look, up there. Can you see it?'

'What!'

'A spider, by the ceiling rose.'

'I know what you said. I want to know what you're thinking.'

His sigh came from the very depths of him. 'I've been worried about something like this for months. He had too much money for a student. I mean, I know he has a job in the supermarket but it's only a few hours a week and he gets paid the minimum wage. And although we give him an allowance, it isn't enough to get him all the latest gadgets he seems to have.'

'Does he?' Lisa was surprised but then she was more or less oblivious to modern technology. For years she had accepted cast off mobile phones, usually from Ros. All three of her children were tied to expensive contracts that allowed them to update every 18 months or so.

'Haven't you noticed? The designer clothes, a new iPhone, the latest iPad, trainers costing more than all my shoes put together...'

'No, I didn't notice.' The admission shocked her. How had she missed it?

He carried on. 'It's been months now. Every time we see him, he has something new.'

'Why didn't you say something?'

He sat up and put his head in his hands. 'I did. I tackled him about it in October when he came up to Glasgow. I noticed he was wearing a Ralph Lauren jumper and joked with him about it. *How can you afford this when I have to make do with M&S?* And he told me it was a fake from a market. I asked him about the new iPhone, and he said he'd upgraded his contract. What a fool I am.'

'Maybe it was. After all, he told me he wasn't getting a lot of money for... for what he was doing.' She couldn't bring the words 'drug dealing' to her mouth.

'Oh, for heaven's sake, Lisa. Stop being so bloody naive. I

knew from the quality of the jumper – cashmere no less – that it wasn't a fake, but I chose to believe him. What an idiot I am.'

Lisa wasn't sure but thought he might be crying. She said nothing, waited for him to speak, but as he gathered himself together, it was clear he wasn't going to say anything. It was up to her to break the silence, her voice shaky. 'What are we going to do?'

He didn't answer but instead got up and started to dress. His face was set, revealing nothing. She felt guilty, as she always did when he was in a mood like this. This wasn't her fault, but somehow, he made her feel it was. Well, two could play this game. She wasn't going to say any more until he did. She got out of bed and pulled on her clothes. She ought to take a shower but there was unlikely to be enough hot water for everyone and she had showered yesterday. As always, she was faster than him to get ready and she left the room without saying anything else. No one else was up. The silence was deep, as deep as it often was in the middle of the night, but this was mid-morning, after ten o'clock and people should be getting up. She banged on each of their doors as she passed, taking her fury out on the wood. Why should they stay in bed and sleep as if they had no worries?

Ros groaned at being woken so abruptly. She pulled the duvet close round her, determined to fall asleep again. Something was niggling at her consciousness, though, telling her she ought to be worried about something, and in a flash she remembered. Damn, she had to get up; they couldn't lie around in bed while Mum was stomping round the house like a demented elephant. After she'd finally gone to bed, they'd stayed up for a further hour trying to work out what to do. She'd had to put up with half an hour of them railing at her for telling their mother. She'd stood her ground, though, and eventually they'd started coming round to her way of thinking. They hadn't come up with any plan, though, other than trying to get through to the police. But when they'd gone to bed, it had been snowing again and it didn't seem likely they'd have electricity or the means to get to somewhere where they were able to use a phone. And walking to the nearest town to find a police station was not a viable possibility as it was so far away. It was a small town, so, unlikely to have one in any case, so many had been closed in the past few years. Gradually, though, they had started to cheer up, and by the time they were tired enough to go to bed, they had convinced themselves that the dead body was not Robson, and even if it was, then the gang was most unlikely to find them here. 'After all,' Em had said, 'if we can't get out to civilisation, such as it is around here, how on earth would they manage to get to us from Newcastle?' They'd all nodded in agreement, half-drunk with fatigue and stress, and stumbled upstairs reassured.

Was she sure they were safe? There was that abandoned car for one thing. But Ros wanted to believe nothing bad was going to happen. She took a deep breath. 'Tomorrow is another day,' she said aloud in a southern states' accent, parodying the famous scene from *Gone with the Wind*. She'd grabbed the curtain, pulling it round her as Scarlett had done to make a dress. She stood at the window, which was covered in condensation, and rubbed at it so she could see outside. Snow, lots of it. How much longer? The snowman they'd built yesterday caught her eye. How magnificent it was. They'd made a brilliant job. But as the snow danced in the wind and a gap cleared, she saw there was something different about the snowman. It had something stuck in it and there was more. Her heart hammered in her chest. It couldn't be... Without stopping to put on slippers, she ran downstairs into the kitchen and past her mother who was filling the kettle. She threw open the door and ran out into the garden, ignoring her mother's protests and questions. As she raced towards the snowman, she felt her heart pounding in a terrifying way and wondered why she was running when she did not want to see what she thought was there. And sure enough, her suspicions were right. There, stuck in the broad chest of the snowman, was a knife and trickling down beneath it was something red, ketchup maybe? to represent blood. She reached a hand out to touch it.

Chapter Twelve

Rosalind pushed past Lisa and ran out into the garden.
'Close the door,' she shouted but Ros ignored her. What was
going on now? Frankly, Lisa was too tired to care. She walked
over to the door and pulled it closed, glancing into the garden
as she did. Ros had vanished.

Coffee. She needed coffee to wake her up. She took out
the packet of beans before realising there was no point; there
was no way of grinding them. Damn David and his preten-
sions. They didn't have as much as a jar of Nescafe; he
wouldn't allow it in the house. According to him it was floor
sweepings from the depth of hell. She'd have to make do
with tea.

Once she'd filled the old brown teapot, she started on
breakfast, then, flushed with irritation at Ros's behaviour,
flung open the door. As she turned the corner of the house,
she spotted her standing motionless in front of the snowman
they'd built yesterday and called out to her. No answer.
What the hell was she doing? Jesus. She had no shoes on;
she'd freeze to death. Lisa made her way towards her.

'Ros? Ros? What the hell are you doing – it's bitterly cold out here.' She touched her shoulder and Ros turned round. She was crying.

'What's wrong?'

Ros moved from her spot in front of the snowman and pointed. 'This. This is what's wrong.'

Lisa didn't take it in at first. She saw it – yes – but her mind was dulled by drink and all the emotions stirred up by the early morning revelations and she didn't process it: a knife stuck in a snowman with red stuff poured over it. She stared, disbelieving. 'Is that blood?'

'I don't know,' said Ros. 'Maybe.'

Lisa started to shake. If it was blood, where had it come from? She didn't want to touch it but had to know. She leaned in to look at it more closely. 'It's too red to be blood.'

'What is it then?'

She caught a glimpse of something lying a few yards away and walked over to it and picked it up, a half empty ketchup bottle. 'Tomato sauce. It's someone's idea of a bad joke.'

'A bad joke?' Ros's voice was strained. 'Ollie's mixed up with a bunch of criminals... what if it's one of them who's stabbed our snowman and – what? Why are you laughing, Mum?'

Lisa pulled herself together. Of course it wasn't funny, but stabbing a snowman? It was too ridiculous. No, it wasn't funny. She took Ros by the arm.

'You're right,' she said. 'It's horrible. But you have to admit...' Her voice tailed off. Ros would never see the funny side of this. 'Come inside, please. It's far too cold out here.' She shivered. It was much colder than yesterday, and the snow had frozen overnight. For the first time since it had started to snow, she was worried the freeze might go on for more than the usual two or three days. But there were other things needing her attention now. She pulled at Ros again and, at last, she yielded so they could walk back to the house. Inside, she poured them both a cup of tea, but its warmth, far from comforting her as expected, woke her up and, as it did, the full horror of what was outside, struck her. She put her cup down on the table trying to control the shaking in her hand. 'Who the hell would do something like this?'

Ros shook her head. 'You don't think it's anything to do with Ollie?

Lisa's heart went cold at the implications. She chose her words with care, trying to think it through. 'Maybe. I can't think who else would do such a thing.'

'One of the farmers?'

'I can't believe any of them would be so nasty. We're on good terms with all of them.'

'Not true. What about the nutter up at the farm?'

'Please don't use that term, Ros. It's offensive to those who have mental health problems. He's a bit of a recluse, that's all.'

Ros went on, her eyes boring into Lisa's. 'Great Aunt Mae always said he was difficult. Didn't he threaten to shoot Sam once?'

'Well, yes,' Lisa admitted. 'But it was years ago. Sam had escaped Mae, and he was frightened Sam would go for his sheep. He didn't of course, Sam would never have hurt anything, and as for old Harry, it was only the one incident. He's as harmless as Sam was.'

'But to threaten a dog with a shotgun...'

'...Is normal behaviour among farmers. Think about it, Ros. Their priority is to protect their flock. Once a dog has killed a sheep, there's no going back. No, I can't see it being Harry. And it wouldn't be any of the other farmers. So, possibly, it's the drug gang.' As Lisa said this, George came to mind, but would he do such a thing? She put the idea away to come back to later. He had been adamant they should meet, and she had ignored him. Was that enough to trigger this attack?

Ros was very pale and there were violet shadows under her eyes. Lisa patted her on the shoulder. 'We'll get through this, don't worry.' The words were lifeless, unconvincing.

'What are we going to do, Mum?'

She rubbed at a mark on the table: an ink stain. 'I don't know. Do you go to the police about something like this? It might be a sick joke. Anyway, how would we get word to them? I don't see how we can.'

'One of us could keep walking until the main road. Surely, there would be a signal there?'

'Yes, I suppose so.' There was doubt in her voice. 'Does anyone have enough battery left in their phone? I certainly don't.'

'And they might meet whoever did this, on the way. That's what you're thinking, isn't it?'

Lisa injected confidence she didn't feel into her reply. 'I don't see how it can be any of this gang. How would they get here for one thing?'

Ros stared at her; her eyes enormous in her pale face. 'When Em and I checked on my car yesterday, we passed one that had been abandoned. It's not far from here, maybe quarter of a mile, parked in one of the lanes. It's the one leading to the tarn.'

Lisa's mouth was dry. 'There was nothing there when we went looking for you.'

'Are you sure?'

She closed her eyes for a moment, trying to picture the scene. It came back to her, the swirling snow, the half-light. There were times when she couldn't see her feet, and, in any case, she'd been focused on finding Ros. A car, though? Surely, she'd have seen that. 'I don't know,' she admitted. 'We couldn't see much.'

'Shit,' said Ros. 'It must be them.'

Lisa jumped when David spoke from behind. 'What are you talking about?'

'How long have you been standing there?'

'Seconds. Now, what's up? The two of you look dreadful.'

He sat at the table as they filled him in, scraping at a dried piece of food with his nail. When they finished, he went outside coming back seconds later with the knife. 'No point in leaving a handy weapon lying around.' He put it on the table. 'Are there any others missing?'

The implications terrified Lisa. 'I don't know, I'll look.' She went over to the drawer where they kept their knives. 'I don't understand, there are no knives missing. This one isn't ours.'

They looked at each other. Ros was the first to break the silence. 'So, whose is it then?'

'I want to go home,' Lisa said. And she did. She wanted to escape the claustrophobic ambience surrounding them. All term, she'd longed for Northumberland, had dreamed of the perfect Christmas and how good it would be. Now, the quiet weighed her down so much she felt suffocated. There was never much noise here but with the snow covering the land the silence had deepened into something primitive and menacing. Half-remembered tales of evil beings in the woods came to mind. She longed for the sound of the siren of an emergency vehicle, the chatter of people as they came home from the pub, the clatter of a taxi drawing up in the street at three a.m. heralding the homecoming of their alcoholic neighbour. Even the thump, thump of the bass on next door's stereo would be welcome.

Neither David nor Ros replied. There was no point. They couldn't go home. They were stuck here.

Ros wanted to slap her mother. For months now she'd gone on about this precious family Christmas, all of them together, log fires, chestnuts roasting. A basketful of stereotypes. And they'd all gone along with it. Someone should have told her: *there is no perfect Christmas*. And she should have had the courage to stay away. Now, look at them: three adults together in a freezing kitchen – because, yes, it was fucking cold without the added electric heaters they used in an emergency – scared witless by a knife stuck in a fucking snowman.

'I'm going to wake the others,' she said. 'See what they have to say.'

'Good idea,' said Mum. 'We need to get our heads together, decide what we're going to do.'

Upstairs, she paused in front of Oliver's door. He was asleep, the occasional snore punctuating the silence. For a moment, she felt sorry for him. He was her little brother, running for help to mummy and daddy when he got into trouble. The nicer part of her told her to let him sleep. But common sense won. No fucking way, she thought. They were in this mess because of him. She banged on the door and stomped in.

'Get up,' she said, shaking him.

He looked so bewildered she almost laughed before she remembered how angry she was. 'What's wrong?' he asked.

'What's wrong? You've got mixed up with criminals, that's what's wrong. Someone's been prowling around the house while we were sleeping,' and they've left a little warning. Look!' She pulled open the curtains.

A frown crossed Oliver's usually placid face. He got up from bed and looked out. 'Fuck,' he said. 'Fucking hell.'

'See what you've done?' said Ros, joining him at the window. She looked down and gasped. She hadn't noticed it before, but someone had left a message. Stamped out in footsteps, a little way behind the snowman, were the words: *you were warned.* 'Fuck, I was hoping I was wrong.' She looked up at Oliver. His face was the colour of putty. She squeezed his hand. 'It's fine, don't worry.' But it wasn't. 'Let's get Emilia up.'

There was no answer when they banged on Em's door. Ros raised her eyes heavenwards. It was usually her who was the one who lay for hours in bed, too lazy to get up. She opened the door and went in. Em was deeply asleep, her face flushed. Ros shook her shoulder. 'Get up, twinnie.'

She turned over and groaned. 'Do I have to?'

Ros shook her. 'Come on, the parents are in a bad enough mood as it is without you lazing in bed.'

'Well, it's not my fault they're fuming. That's down to the dickhead.' She turned over as if to go back to sleep.

Ros pulled the duvet from her and dumped it in a corner of the room. 'We're all in this together. There's been a development. Get up.'

Em sat up in bed. There was a crease on her cheek where she had been lying awkwardly on her pillow. She looked exhausted. 'A development?'

'Someone's vandalised the snowman.'

'The snowman,' Em repeated in a flat tone.

'They've stabbed it, poured ketchup on it to look like blood and left a message saying *you were warned.*'

That woke her up. 'Shit,' Em got out of bed. 'Jesus, I feel awful. Give me five minutes and I'll be down.'

How much worse was it going to get? Lisa listened as Ollie told her about the warning stamped out in the snow. David went out to investigate, returning two or three minutes later.

'I've had a look at the footprints. There's only one set, so we outnumber whoever it is. And they're smaller than me, or their shoe size is, anyway. I'd estimate a size eight or nine.'

Em had come into the room as he was speaking. 'Anyone got an aspirin? My head's killing me.'

She looked awful. Lisa felt her forehead. 'Bit hot, aren't you? Let me take your temperature.'

'I'm fine, don't fuss.'

'I'm not fussing. I want to see you're all right.' She rummaged in the dresser drawer and found an ancient thermometer. Thankfully it wasn't digital; the batteries in them ran out quickly in her experience. She rinsed it under the tap and handed it to Em. 'Stick it in your mouth and shut up.'

She took it without any further argument and did as Lisa said. She removed the thermometer and squinted at it. 'Ninety-seven degrees. Not life threatening, I think.'

Lisa had found the aspirin and gave two to Em. 'Take these, anyway. Get rid of your headache.' She returned to the table where the rest of the family were digesting what David had said. She sat down. 'We need a plan.'

Ros put her head in her hands. Typical Mum, it was a wonder she ever got through a day. Everything needed to be planned. They shouldn't be wasting time planning. They should be out there, finding out who was doing this.

'Right. Let's go through the options open to us. I suggest we stop talking for five minutes and write down anything we can think of.'

Emilia stood up. 'Actually, I think I'm getting a migraine. I'm going to lie down to see if I can nip it in the bud.'

Poor Em, she got bad migraines at times that knocked her out for days. Was this going to be one of them? Ros hoped not. She settled down to try to think what to do.

For a few moments, they sat in silence. Ros had no idea what their best option was. Every bone in her body was screaming – *get the fuck out of here* – but that wasn't much help. Eventually she came up with:

1. Stay put and sit it out.
2. Get out.
3. Arm ourselves with whatever we can find and take turns to keep a vigil.
4. Ask our new neighbours for help.
5. Find a mobile signal and phone the police.

She put her pen down and waited for the others to stop writing. Oliver was the last to finish. 'Why don't you start?' asked Mum. The unspoken *seeing as you got us into this mess* lingered in the air like the smell of cabbage in school dining halls.

Oliver read out his suggestions. They were more or less identical to Ros's own. As they went round the table, reading out what they'd written, it was obvious no one had come up with anything better.

'So, what do we do now?' said Ros.

'We need to stay together,' said Mum. 'And that means staying here.'

'We're a sitting target, here though,' said Ros. She'd had enough, slammed her pen down onto the table. 'This is your fault, Ollie. Why did you get mixed up with such scumbags? I don't know what the fuck you were thinking about.'

'Fuck, what can I say? I'm sorry...' Oh shit, he was going to cry. Mum stepped in before it got out of hand.

'Recriminations aren't going to get us anywhere... and neither are tears. We know you didn't mean to bring this... catastrophe on us, Ollie. So, please, pull yourself together. If nothing else, we need to be strong. Ros, why don't you make us a cup of tea?'

Ros seethed as she went to the sink to fill the kettle. It was so like Mum to smooth things over, pretend there was nothing wrong. She could kill Ollie for this. She gazed out over the garden, trying to calm herself. It was snowing again. Was there no end to this? She watched the flakes float down, allowing herself to relax. Watching their slow dance was always comforting. Her eyes grew unfocused until all she saw was the white swirl, dizzying. But there was something else there, a dark shape not far from the house. 'Dad, quick, come and see.'

Her father was there beside her, peering into the gloom. 'What, what is it?'

Ros blinked, wondering if she'd imagined it. 'It's gone. I don't know... I don't know if it was anything. I thought I saw someone.' She felt than heard her father's sharp intake of breath. He got up from the table and ran to the door. 'I don't see anything, but we won't relax unless we know. I'm going to see for myself.'

The snow laden clouds cast a yellowish light over the land, and it looked gloomy and desolate. Ros watched as he trudged towards the spot she'd indicated, his head down as if he were looking for signs. When he reached it, he walked around for a bit before raising both hands in a thumbs up sign and calling, 'All clear.'

They returned to their seats around the table. David came back in with some wood and filled up the range. It was cosy enough in the kitchen, though the other rooms were cooling down. At this, Lisa remembered Emilia.

'I'm going to check on Em, see if she's OK.'

She crept upstairs and Lisa opened Em's door as quietly as she could. She tiptoed over to her bed. Em was asleep, her breathing regular. Lisa stared at her. She looked so vulnerable, poor thing. She'd inherited Lisa's propensity for migraines. With any luck, she'd wake in an hour feeling much better. Lisa sat down on the chair beside her, thankful to be away from the tension downstairs. It was peaceful in here and as she watched Emilia sleeping, she remembered all the evenings she'd spent trying to get one or other of them to calm down and take some much-needed rest. She looked round the room, noting a small damp patch on the ceiling. They'd have to get that looked at. More bills. It was expensive having a second home. Their house in Glasgow was a money pit. No sooner was one problem fixed than another one sprang up. And this house was turning out to be as bad. Not for the first time, she wondered about selling it, but

David was so attached to it. Most of his summers as a child had been spent here.

Lately, he'd been dropping hints about moving here when they retired. No way was she going to agree. It was too far from civilisation, the nearest shop was seven miles away. She'd never cope long term without local shops and amenities. But David muttered more and more about his guilt over having two homes. She supposed it came from his job. He was more aware of the pressures on housing, the numbers. In many ways she agreed with him, and she'd be happier with only one house, but she didn't want the Warren to be that house, much as she loved it here.

After some minutes of sitting without moving, she was restless and stood up and stretched. Her eye was caught by a notebook on the windowsill. It was pretty with a drawing of a robin on the outside. Her favourite bird. She often tried to draw them, mostly unsuccessfully, but this looked as though it was easy to copy. She picked it up. It was very effective. A simple drawing of a robin on a background of some text. She squinted at it trying to make sense of what it said:

> *The north wind doth blow, And we shall have snow,*
> *And what will poor robin do then, Poor thing?*
> *He'll sit in a barn, And keep himself warm,*
> *And hide his head under his wing, Poor thing!*

Lisa smiled at the irony, though in truth it was the east wind that had dumped all this snow on them. It was a pretty drawing, but what appealed to her most was it looked simple enough to copy. She was so engrossed in trying to work out how best to do it and whether she had the right shades of coloured pencils with her for the job that she didn't hear

Emilia get out of bed. She snatched the notebook from Lisa's hand.

'How dare you! What do you think you're doing, going through my stuff?'

Lisa pointed to the notebook that had an orange strip of elastic round it to ensure it stayed closed. 'Does it look as though I've been reading it?'

Em scrutinised it as if it might reveal Lisa's wrongdoing. 'I don't know. You tell me.'

'Well, I wasn't.' she said shortly. 'You should know me better. I liked the picture, that's all. I was thinking of trying to copy it.'

Em glared at her. Time to change the subject. There was no point in getting into an argument with Em about her privacy though what she had in fact done was pique Lisa's interest.

'Are you feeling any better?'

The fight seeped out of her. 'A little.'

Lisa raised her eyebrows.

'No,' she admitted.

'Get back into bed then. There's no point in getting up if you're not well enough. I'll bring you up a cup of tea.'

'I don't want anything.'

'I have some of my high-powered migraine tablets. You should take one of them.' Lisa's tone brooked no argument. She went downstairs slowly. Emilia's response was intriguing, and she was now desperate to know what was in the notebook. She was such an enigma. Well, there was no point in thinking about it. She wasn't going to invade Em's privacy and Em was unlikely to ever show her.

There was scuffling in the hall. The rest of the family were gathered there, putting their coats and shoes on. 'What are you doing?'

'We're going out for a walk, to see if we can get a signal to call the police.'

'What are you going to say? You could land Ollie right in it.'

'I... I don't know,' said David. 'I supposed we'd tell them we've had an intruder and about the snowman of course.'

Lisa wasn't convinced. 'We haven't had an intruder though. Not in the house.'

'But what about the missing food?' said Oliver.

'What missing food?'

'You asked me how many mince pies I'd eaten and also there was the remains of the quiche that disappeared...'

'What's this?' asked David.

She'd forgotten about the mince pies. In the end she'd put it down to her greedy family. She explained to David what had happened. 'How many did you all have?'

'I had two,' said Ros.

'Me too,' added David.

'Right. Well, Em certainly didn't eat the rest.' It was dawning on her that something was badly wrong. A fox had got into the house. Its foul scent lingered on beneath the smell of the disinfectant she'd used to clean the flagstones in the kitchen. Who had left the door open enough for that to happen? True, it hadn't been locked but the handle needed to be turned to open it. Foxes were cunning but they didn't open doors. Did they?

Damn. It couldn't be denied. Not when there was food missing, too. 'What about the quiche?' she asked.

They all denied it. Lisa's mouth dried up as she thought of someone in the house when they were asleep, someone who had stuck a knife in a snowman. They were too complacent about the solitude of this house, always leaving the door unlocked. For the first time she felt a real twinge of fear. 'And you're leaving me here alone?'

'Em's upstairs,' said Ros.

'Yes, and she's ill in bed.'

'Keep the doors locked. You'll be fine,' said Oliver.

She didn't know what he was thinking but his dismissive tone was infuriating. Lisa turned on him. 'Says the man who got us into this fucking mess.' She regretted it as soon as she saw his face crumple. 'I'm sorry, I shouldn't have said that.'

'No, you're right. I got us into this shit, and I should be the one who sorts it out. It's my problem, not yours. The rest of you will be safer if I go. If I leave—'

'Stop right there,' said David. 'You are not going out there alone. It's far too dangerous.'

Oliver, who had his hand on the doorknob, stopped. He shook his head. 'I'm so sorry for all this.'

She should have been able to tell him it was all right, but the words wouldn't come. He was her youngest, her adored son, but Lisa was furious at him for putting their family in danger.

Ros was placatory. 'Look Mum, you'll be fine. We'll only be gone an hour at most, I promise. We'll walk for thirty minutes and if we haven't found a signal by then, we'll turn back.'

Lisa wasn't convinced but nodded. They were determined to go. 'All right, then. Make sure you're back in an hour, though.'

Once they'd gone, she decided to see if anything else was missing. She'd check the larder first. She opened the door hoping there wouldn't be a mouse scurrying about inside. They kept everything loose, like oats, flour and cereal, in plastic or glass containers, but occasionally, a little spilled out and word got round to the mice. Everything was in order. She was about to close the door when she spotted the tomato ketchup. There had been a near empty bottle beside the snowman. It was highly unlikely that drug dealers from Newcastle would bring it with them and if it hadn't come from the Warren then where was it from? A knife and now the ketchup. Neither of them belonging to their household. Lisa swallowed. George. Had she been too quick to dismiss him?

Outside, it was bitterly cold. Ros, too, had a headache, though at least it wasn't a migraine. Poor Em. She had described them to Ros once and they sounded terrifying. 'I get visual disturbances,' she had said. 'The first time it happened I believed I was dying. I looked in a mirror and half my face was missing, with zigzagging lights in its place.' Ros's headache was nothing like that though it was thumping from all the emotion. She'd give anything to be in bed like Emilia was. Or for a decent cup of coffee.

The snow was less heavy than it had been earlier, but even so, it stung as it hit her cheeks. She wiped it from her face but to no avail. She trudged on; her feet weighed down by the walking boots she'd donned. Every step was an effort. Her father caught up with her. 'Let one of us go in front, then you can step in our footprints, and it won't tire you out so quickly.'

It made sense. Em would have protested; said they were being chauvinistic and would insist on leading the way. but Ros was happy to go along with it. She fell into step behind her father and brother, all the time scanning her phone for any hint of a signal. It was futile, with the snow swirling round it was hard to see more than a few yards in front of them. Her stomach twisted as she saw the copse of trees loom out of the snow-stricken landscape. It was an ideal place for someone to hide. For all she knew, they were crouching down at this very minute, hiding behind a tree waiting to ambush them. Who was the person watching her the night she'd arrived? It struck her how vulnerable she'd been. They were so complacent about the countryside around the cottage, she hadn't given a second thought about wandering around by herself. But nowhere was safe from criminals. They could be watching them now.

She had to stop thinking this way. There was the dark shape she'd seen earlier today though. What was it? It had looked like a person, but Dad said there was nothing, the snow was undisturbed. Her imagination had taken over. Come to think of it, perhaps she'd imagined the figure watching her from the copse the night she arrived. It made sense, she'd been tired and disoriented. Prone to seeing things that weren't there. But she hadn't imagined the deserted car. Em had seen it, too. And they'd pass it soon.

She stopped for a second to take a breather, calling to Dad and Ollie to wait but Dad kept walking, stopping only to turn and beckon her on. Damn it. It was hard work trudging through the snow. It might have been better to stay at home with Mum. She looked back at the house. In winter, they usually had the lights on all day as the windows were small and it was often dark inside. But candles were flickering in the windows. Mum must have lit some. She made a decision.

'Dad!' she shouted. 'Dad.'

He turned round. 'What is it?'

'I think I'll go back. It isn't fair to leave Mum on her own.'

'OK, whatever you like. See you later.'

Ros set off, telling herself she was doing this for Mum and not because she was so cold. The wind had struck up and it was icy in its intensity. Never mind, she'd soon be back inside drinking some tea. Not long now. She squinted trying to see better. A moment later she rubbed her eyes in disbelief. A figure was in view, walking towards the house. She held her breath, waiting to see if they walked past. No, they were in the garden now. Who was it? Damn this snow, who was it? Without any further ado she started to run.

Chapter Thirteen

If Lisa hadn't been happy at being left alone with Emilia, she was fuming now. Frightened, too. George was behind this – it all made sense, the knife and the tomato ketchup must have come from his house – and now she and Em were alone. Why had she let the others leave? They were safe, there were three of them. He might be watching the house at this very moment, waiting for an opportunity to break in. Was he dangerous? She didn't have to ask herself twice. He was.

She checked both entrances to the cottage to see if they were locked and the windows, too. Satisfied they were secure, she took stock of things and considered the house from the point of view of someone trying to break in. Smashing a window would make too much noise so as long as they were locked that was one less worry. The doors were a more likely target. There were bolts on the back door; those should hold but the front was more vulnerable. There was only the one lock and Lisa wasn't convinced it would hold. She had to do something about that now. A picture came into her mind of the house in Glasgow as it had been when they moved in all those years ago. The previous owners, an elderly couple, hadn't bothered with a lock for the back door, instead they had wedged a six-foot length of wood between the wall and the door. It was bizarre but highly effective, although it was inconvenient and unsightly. Lisa didn't have any wood available, but she did have stepladders. She'd lie them on their side and wedge them between the bottom of the stairs and the door. If they were long enough. She set off to find them, hoping David hadn't got round to putting them back in the shed. She didn't want to go outside.

They were in the cupboard by the back door. Thank goodness for the procrastination that defined her husband's personality. She grabbed hold of them and lugged them through to the hall. Heavens, they were heavy, no lightweight aluminium here, these were the real deal, an old wooden pair, covered in paint splashes, and strong enough to hold back ten men. All she had to do was to put them in place. She lugged them into the hall and looked at the gap between the door and the stairs. Damn. They weren't long enough. What else could she do? She carried them back to the kitchen and was manoeuvring them into position when there was a knock. Lisa almost dropped the stepladders in shock, but she managed to hold on to them somehow. She crept back out into the hall and stood at the front door. There was only a flimsy piece of wood between her and whoever was outside. She held her breath and listened. Whoever it was, sighed. It wasn't David or either of the others, they would have tried the door or shouted out and, in any case, they all had keys. Shit, she'd lit candles in the living room, thinking it made the room more welcoming. She tiptoed through to the living room and quickly blew them out before going to the window. A man with his back to her was standing by the door. She didn't get a good enough look to recognise him. It might be

154

George, but she wasn't sure. Probably not, this person looked taller or was she imagining it? She gasped; he was approaching the window. She dashed to the sofa and crouched down behind it, hardly daring to breathe. Whoever it was, they were now at the window peering in. Was she visible? Thank goodness she'd got to the candles in time and hadn't got round to lighting the fire. Anyone looking in would think the house was deserted. She risked a glance. She went back into the hall. They'd gone.

Or had they? That was the door handle being tried.

Lisa's mouth was dry with nerves. She didn't know what to do. Run upstairs and hide in Em's room, push a chest of drawers against the bedroom door? Confronting him wasn't an option, though if she had one of their heavy frying pans in hand? She dismissed the idea. Likely as not he'd wrestle it from her.

Another knock, firmer this time, followed by the sound of the flap over the letter box being lifted, no doubt to peer in. Good luck with that, matey. It was one of those draught proofing ones with a thick layer of bristles impossible to see through. To her horror, a hand groped through it, fingers searching, for what? A key on a string? Furious at this invasion, Lisa rushed forward and grabbed hold of it, pulling the fingers backwards as she yelled. 'I'll break your fucking fingers, George. Fuck off and leave me alone.'

They should never have left Mum and Em alone. Ros ran as fast as she could, her feet slipping and sliding beneath her. She fell once, hurting her wrist in the process. The same one she'd hurt before. As she struggled to get up, she heard her mother shout. Her lungs were bursting as she neared the house, conscious that if whoever it was turned round, they'd see her. She needed something to protect herself, there were logs lying near the house, but they weren't long enough. She was a few metres away now and for the first time saw the figure clearly. She stopped in disbelief. It was Ian. He had come after her. Forgetting her earlier qualms about him, she gave a cry of joy and ran towards him.

Lisa had hurt the person on the other side of the door. He let out a yelp then shouted, 'I don't know who George is but it's not me.' It wasn't George. It sounded nothing like him. She had attacked a complete stranger. The postman maybe? Dear God, there would be a walk out of the entire postal service, and it would be all her fault! She released the hand with a whispered *sorry.* and came to terms with the fact that she was going to have to open the door and apologise face to face. She turned the key and opened the door in time to see Ros hurl herself onto the stranger with a delighted scream. 'Ian, you came. I knew you would! Mum, this is Ian.'

He untangled himself from her. 'Well, at least you're pleased to see me. The same can't be said of your mother. She seems to think I'm a burglar. That's some grip you have on you, Mrs Truett.'

Lisa glared at him. 'What the hell were you doing putting your hand through the letter box? It was like a horror film.'

'I'm sorry. It's been a long journey and there didn't seem to be anyone in. I hoped there might be a key on a string or something...'

Lisa was beyond furious. She didn't know whether she was angrier with herself or with him. She hadn't wanted this man to come, had told Ros not to bring him. Had Ros not passed on the message? She must have and, yet, here he was. But any moral high ground had disappeared when she injured him. What had she been thinking? She could have broken his fingers. She was going to have to apologise profusely when she wanted to tell him to go back to wherever he came from. Or worse. But Lisa hated confrontation. It had been easy to say no when she didn't have to face him. She couldn't send him back out into the snow. At the same time, there was an advantage in having an extra man around, given the circumstances. There was nothing else for it but to swallow her pride. She held out a hand and said, 'I'm Lisa, Ros's mum. I hope I didn't hurt you too much. I don't normally behave in this way, but you gave me a fright. Maybe think twice about sticking your hand through a letter box in future. You might as well come in.' She sounded grudging but she didn't care. He'd frightened her.

He followed her into the house, apologising. 'I don't know what I was thinking. It was stupid of me. I must have had delirium from driving through a blizzard.'

Once inside, they sat down at the kitchen table. There had been so much going on no-one had lit the fire in the living room and the kitchen was the only warm place left.

'How on earth did you get here?' asked Ros. 'Aren't all the minor roads shut?'

'I have a four-wheel drive and winter tyres. I lived in Stockholm for a while, and they were mandatory there. I got used to changing them every year.'

'And you got through this?' Lisa found it hard to keep the scepticism out of her voice.

'Not all of it, no. There's a car blocking the road back there. I couldn't get past it. The road's too narrow.'

'Oh, that'll be mine,' said Ros.

Lisa shook off her bad mood. A four-wheel drive meant

they weren't as marooned as they had been, though how he'd turn it in the narrow road was another matter.

'I'm sorry, Ian, is it? We're in the middle of a bit of a crisis here.' Lisa gave him a truncated version of the story. If he were going to stay – and he would, she wasn't going to turn him away – he had a right to know he might be in danger. At the same time, it infuriated her to have to tell their business to a stranger and she glossed over Oliver's part in the story saying only that they thought someone was prowling round and had been in the house.

He was a remarkably good listener. He didn't seem at all worried, not even when they told him about the snowman.

'I can see now why you attacked me. I'm so sorry to have scared you. You must have been terrified.'

'Out of my mind,' admitted Lisa.

'So, this intruder. His name is George? Is it someone you know, then?'

A blush was blooming on her chest, spreading fast to her face. 'Er, no. We don't know who it is.'

'But I heard—'

'Yes, I heard it, too,' said Ros. 'You called him George before you shouted at him to go away. Isn't that the name of your friend who came round yesterday?'

She stifled the urge to barge in with *he's no friend of mine*. 'Oh, I was half asleep. I must have got muddled.' Ros raised her eyebrows and Lisa changed the subject before either of them asked any more questions. 'I'm so sorry about your hand. Is it OK? Do you need a painkiller?'

Ian looked down at it and flexed his fingers. 'I'll survive,' he said.

Ros made a face. 'You're bonkers, Mum. What did you think you were doing?'

'I know, but I was scared.'

Ian intervened. 'No harm done. Honestly, I'm fine. It was completely my fault. I'd have done the same. Anyway, there's no mobile signal here?'

Lisa nodded. 'No, we have a landline but the electricity's off so it's not working.'

'Ah, that explains why I couldn't reach Ros on her mobile.'

'You had a signal? Where?'

'It was after I had to stop the car. Not far. I can go and try for you if you like?'

'Did you? It's very rare to get one so near to the house,' said Lisa. 'And if you do get a signal, what would you say to the police? It's hardly an emergency, is it?' Now it came to it, she wasn't keen on dropping Oliver in it and there would be trouble. She wished she hadn't said anything to Ian, but it was too late now.

'Mum! How can you say that? These guys have already beaten up Ollie. They're dangerous.'

'Hang on, is there something you're not telling me?'

Lisa glared at Ros. 'I had hoped to keep this in the family.'

Ian held up his hands. 'None of my business. You don't have to say anything else.'

'My brother's been involved in drug dealing and has got himself into bother,' said Ros. 'What?' she said to Lisa. 'Why are you glaring at me?'

'Your mum's right. It's nothing to do with me.' Ros stuck out her bottom lip, miffed at being chastised by Ian. 'But I can see you wouldn't necessarily want the police to know.' There was no judgement in his voice. He said it in a most matter-of-fact way.

Lisa nodded, thankful she didn't have to spell it out.

'We don't need to mention the drug gang. There's the

knife in the snowman, and the threat. That's enough to report to them.'

'I don't know. It doesn't seem enough to involve the police.'

'At least let me go and see if there is a signal so we know for sure.'

'I'll come with you,' Ros said. She looked like a lioness who'd spotted a lame zebra in her sights. She was all but licking her lips.

'But what about Dad and Ollie? They'll wonder where you are.'

'No, I told them I didn't think you should be alone with Em, so they know I've come back.'

'If we can get a signal, if it wasn't a passing freak chance, we won't be long,' said Ian.

'I don't know...' she began, but they were already on their way out of the back door. Damn it. She was as good as alone again. She watched them struggle through the snow for a minute or two. She'd light a fire. It'd been out long enough, and the living room had cooled down considerably without the extra heat. It took an age to clear the grate and get a good fire going but once it was done, she was pleased she'd made the effort. She knelt back on her heels and held her hands out to warm then. Logs didn't give as good a heat as coal – she was old enough to remember a coal fire in her grandmother's house – but it was better than nothing. Her watch told her they'd been away for half an hour. They should all be back soon. What would David make of their visitor? Ros was his favourite so most likely he'd accept him without any qualms. Lisa wasn't sure though. Why would you turn up somewhere uninvited? Och well, he was nice enough and more to the point, he was here now.

She returned to the warmth of the kitchen to make a cup

of tea. She had sat down and was about to take a sip when there was a loud noise from the hallway. She put it on the worktop and grabbed the nearest frying pan only to put it down when she heard David's voice.

David was standing in the hall. He was stamping his feet to get rid of the snow on his boots.

'Long story. Get in, quick before all the heat leaves.'

He came in, leaving puddles everywhere. 'Any luck?'

'Nothing.'

'Where's Ollie?'

'I've asked him to give us some space. Is Ros likely to barge in? Or Emilia?'

'I don't think so, but—'

He interrupted her. 'Lisa, we have to talk.'

'Sounds serious,' she joked, but there was no answering smile. Was he suspicious of George after all? There had been something in his face yesterday but when he'd said nothing, she assumed it was her imagination.

They sat down at the table.

'So, what is it?'

He wouldn't look at her. He hadn't removed his coat, and his body was hunched inside it. 'I've been an idiot,' he said. 'I should have told you earlier, but I'd hoped...'

'Hoped what?' This didn't sound as though it was about George.

'Hoped I wouldn't have to tell you. But when we were out there in the snow, I realised I couldn't keep it to myself anymore. It's not fair on you or anyone else.'

'Go on.'

'You remember the conference I went to, in August?'

'The one in Verona, the "once in a lifetime opportunity" one. The one I couldn't go to?' Lisa moistened her lips. This was leading down one path only.

'Yes.'

'Look, spit it out. You had an affair, you're going to leave me, it's the same old story, middle-aged man finds younger woman.' She was surprisingly calm now it was in the open. For months she'd wondered what was wrong. Well, now she was going to find out for sure.

'It's not what you think,' he began, but she held out her hand as if she were a police officer halting a car. 'Stop right there! Don't you dare tell me "This is different, I couldn't help myself. It was in the stars..." or whatever nonsense you're working yourself up to spouting.'

'Please, let me speak.'

Lisa nodded, her arms folded, lips held tight together to hold back the stream of abuse fighting to get out. 'Go on.'

'You know there's this big bid on for the building of four new secondary schools and the renovation of several others? It's worth millions to whatever firm gets the contract.'

'I... is this to do with your work?'

He frowned. 'Yes, what else? On April 1st I was approached, or perhaps I should say, I received an email. It offered me fifty grand if I recommended a particular firm. The email didn't state which firm, it asked if I was interested. Of course, I fired back an immediate "no" and demanded to know who was asking. I got an immediate reply saying, "Ha ha, April Fool". I felt like a complete idiot, deleted it and forgot all about it.' His face was grey with stress. Lisa nibbled at her lower lip.

He went on. 'Then, when I was in Verona, a young woman approached me. Very personable, very pretty. She said she was doing a Masters in Planning and wanted some advice on what to do next. Should she do a PhD or try to get a job?' He swept his hair off his face. 'I was flattered, I suppose. She came to me when there were planning leaders from much bigger councils there, and academics, too. I didn't suspect a thing when she came to my room later to show me her CV.' Lisa raised an eyebrow. 'No, don't look like that, please.'

She smiled, more to encourage him to go on than in forgiveness. The vanity of men.

'I let her in, she asked me for a drink. I was reluctant because it was late at night, but she wheedled, and I gave in and offered her a drink from the mini bar. She insisted I have one, too, although I didn't want one and it must have been then she did it.'

'Did what?'

'She must have drugged my drink.'

'What? How did she manage? Are you sure?' There were a hundred questions to ask including: *What the fuck were you thinking?* But this wasn't the right time. He looked defeated and suddenly much older. It struck her that when you are always with someone, you don't notice the little changes: the sagging of chins, eyelids turning into crepe paper, a few more grey hairs. It was the same with your home. You don't notice the loose doorknob or the fraying carpet or those stains in the bath. They creep up unnoticed until you are forced by circumstance to see them. She saw him now through this young, attractive woman's eyes: *A pushover. He'll be so flattered to be chatted up by me. I'll have him eating out of my hand. Silly old fool.*

'I have no idea what happened. Rohypnol, probably. I woke up naked with two sheets of A4 taped to my chest. One had an extremely compromising photograph printed on it, the other a copy of the April Fool email with my supposed reply.'

Lisa was lost. 'So, it was all an April Fool's joke then?'

He ran his fingers through his hair. 'Oh, Lisa. How I wish

it was. No, in this version, I had written *yes*, in capitals, with an exclamation mark. There was an envelope on my bedside table. Inside was a note. Nothing incriminating, four little words: *We'll be in touch.*'

'You took it to the police, right? Or to the chief executive in the council?'

He shook his head. 'I didn't know what to do. The email was very incriminating as was the photo.'

'What was in the photo... no, on second thoughts, I don't want to know.' His face had gone red and then white in quick succession. It was true. She didn't want to know. She went on. 'What did you do?'

The look he gave her was one of gratitude for not pushing that line of enquiry. 'Stupidly, I carried on as normal. I don't know what I was thinking... there was the possibility it was all a joke.'

Lisa put her head in her hands. She thought of his first-class degree, the masters with distinction and his successful career. Naïve. Stupid. Foolhardy. How could he be so intelligent and so idiotic at the same time? She also was at a loss as to how this had anything to do with what they were going through here.

'And?'

'And so I carried on as per usual. There was nothing out of the ordinary. Nobody got in touch with me, and after a couple of weeks I put it down to someone's sick sense of humour.'

'No, wait, David. You can't possibly have believed it was a joke. You were drugged, photos taken of you. That's serious.'

'I know, I'm an idiot. But I thought it would all sort itself out.' This was David all over. He never faced up to problems, never got on and did things until it was absolutely essential.

'It hasn't sorted itself though, has it?' Lisa was overwhelmed with emotions. Fear, anger, sadness, disgust, and disappointment were all fighting for her attention. It was fear that was winning, though. She started to understand what was going on.

'Far from it. The meeting to decide who gets the contract is on 6th of January. Two or three weeks ago, I got a phone call. The voice was disguised, one of those funny machine robot like voices. It said, "We want to know the details of each of the bids." There are seven firms who've put in a bid for the contract so far, all the big firms except JM Crichton Construction. It must be them who's behind it. They're wanting a heads up so they can put in the best terms and get the contract.'

'Aren't they in financial trouble?' Something was coming back to her about some deal that had gone badly wrong for them. She frowned trying to remember. Got it. 'They were sued recently by another company, something about a poorly constructed block of flats.'

'Exactly,' said David. 'They had expanded into residential property. Up until recently they had only done commercial stuff – shops, car parks, an office block – that stayed empty for years waiting for the regeneration in Govan to happen. It didn't, so they joined forces with FJ Architects to build an apartment block in the West End. They built on a site near the River Kelvin, one which had been avoided for years but it had been shored up and the surveyor's report said it was fine. The flats were built, sold at premium prices because they were in the West End and had a riverside view. But not long after, when people moved in, cracks appeared everywhere. At first it was thought the surveyor's report was dodgy or that there were errors in the design. But it turned out JM Construction had cut corners everywhere: single rows of bricks where there should have been double, poor-quality materials, and so on. I don't know all the details. But the upshot is they're being sued and if they lose, they'll be bankrupt, which is why I assumed they hadn't put in a bid.'

'Surely, the council wouldn't consider them, though? It would be a huge risk. They'd never invest in a firm with dodgy finances.'

'I know, but it's more complicated than that. I heard a rumour last week they were going to declare bankruptcy before the court case. Their director is dodgy. I'm not sure but I think he may have done something similar before getting involved with JM Crichton Construction. What I think is happening, is he has gone over to a new firm, which will appear at the bidding stage with a good, appealing figure—'

'I don't see how that would fool the council. A new firm is not an appealing prospect. With no track record?'

'Sorry, I haven't made myself clear. It's an existing firm, new to him but well established. Jennings Engineers.'

'I see.' He was right, it was complicated, and she wasn't at all sure she was fully following the story. 'Go on,' she said.

'I'm getting ahead of myself. Every day for the last week there's been at least one phone call. The messages are more and more threatening. They're saying things like "We know where you live.", "You have children, don't you?". Then on Friday, I was tidying my desk before I left work and there was another one. "Look in the top drawer of your desk." There was an envelope, stuffed with banknotes.'

'Shit. What did you do?'

'Shut the drawer and locked it. So, you see, I'm not completely convinced the snowman incident isn't coming from them.'

She blinked, unable to take it in. 'I don't understand, why

pick on you?'

'Because I'm heading up this project. I'll have the final say as to which firm gets the contract.'

'So, whoever is threatening you must know this,' Lisa said. 'But how do they know so much about you, about the children... Jesus!' she stopped, her hand to her mouth.

'What is it?'

'It's Ros... I started to tell you. That bloke, the one she wanted to bring here... he's turned up.'

'What, here? Where is he?'

'They went out to search for a signal. He said he had got one when he was driving here.'

'What do you mean, driving here? There's no way he'd get through.'

'He said he has a four-wheel drive and winter tyres. David, what if he's from these people who are threatening you?'

David paled. 'How long has she known him?' Was it imagination or was his voice shaky?

'Not long, a few weeks, I think.'

'I got the first threat in November. Fuck, how does she know him? Did she say?'

'I don't know,' Lisa confessed. Why hadn't she asked? She looked at her watch. 'Oh shit. He said they'd be twenty minutes at most, and they've now been away for three quarters of an hour. You didn't see them?'

'No. Christ, what the hell is going on? Where did he leave his car? Did he say?'

'He said he couldn't get past Ros's car.'

'Fuck. I ought to have passed them on my way back. Right. You stay here and I'll go after them. If I'm not back in half an hour...' he stopped.

'What?'

'I don't know... what can we do?'

With some effort she controlled her nerves. Their imaginations were running away with them. 'David, he was a nice bloke. Didn't look the type to be involved in the sort of thing you're talking about.'

The look he gave her made the words freeze in her mouth. He was right. She had no idea whether the man with their daughter was OK or not. She'd taken him at face value, fooled by his charm and the fact that Ros was smitten with him. Without another word, David went into the hall cupboard and came out with a golf club.

'David, don't do anything foolish.' The look on his face scared her.

'If he's harmed Ros, I'll fucking kill him.' David went back out into the never-ending snow.

Jesus! It was so cold. They'd been walking now for God knows how long. It felt like hours, going round in circles, Ian holding his mobile in the air. The freezing air scalded the inside of Ros's nose as she breathed in. The tips of her fingers felt numb. 'I think we should go back,' she said.

'There was definitely a signal.'

'Honestly, Ian. It's so erratic here. Never the same two days running. Come on, I'm freezing and hungry, too.'

'Let's try for a few more minutes.'

'No!' She was desperate to get back to the house. Ian was behaving so bizarrely with his obsessive need to prove himself right and she was only too aware Ollie's criminal gang might be hiding out somewhere nearby. She shivered and moved closer to him for warmth. 'Please, can we go back now?'

'Get your fucking hands off my daughter!' Her father was advancing on them wielding a golf club.

'Dad! What the hell are you doing?'

'I mean it. Step away from her now.'

Ian gently pushed Ros away from him. She moved towards her father, her face red with indignation. 'Dad, what do you think you're doing?'

'Who are you?' Her father was shouting. 'Did those bastards send you?'

Ian had his arms open in a conciliatory gesture. 'Ian Murray,' he said. 'No one sent me. I came of my own accord because I was worried about Ros. What's all this about?'

Ros breathed more easily as her father lowered the golf club. He was on edge though, his body as taut as a violin string. 'Ros?' he said. 'Who is this and how do you know him?'

'As he said, Dad. Ian Murray. We met in the café where I work. He's a friend.'

He turned to Ian. 'And do you work in the building trade?'

Ian blinked. 'I... er, no. I can't tell one end of a brick from another.'

'So, what do you do then?'

'I'm a doctor. Accident and Emergency at the Queen Elizabeth.'

'I didn't know that!' said Ros.

Her father glared at her. 'This is a friend of yours and you don't know what he does? He could be anyone, Ros.'

'I do have proof.' Ian reached into his jacket pocket and pulled out a wallet. He handed over an NHS ID card that her father scrutinised before handing it back with a terse 'Bit faded, isn't it? Still, I suppose I owe you an apology.'

'Is that it?' said Ros. 'You accuse him of God knows what

and that's all you can say? Have you lost your mind, Dad?'

'I'll explain back at the house. I assume you haven't managed to find a signal?'

'No, I'm sorry. There was definitely one here earlier.'

The three of them walked back in silence. Ros, fuming, as she stumbled along. This was so embarrassing, but at least Ian didn't seem to be fazed by it. Dad had better come up with a good explanation.

Lisa let out a cry of relief when they all walked through the door. As soon as David had fled, she regretted having worried him. She prided herself on being a good judge of character. Ian was no thug. From the look of things though, Ros was in a real temper. She flung herself onto a seat and glowered up at David.

'Come on, then. Tell us why you have been so abominably rude to my visitor.'

David looked exhausted. The worry had obviously taken its toll. Lisa stepped in to defuse things. 'Leave it, Ros. You're safe and that's the main thing.'

'No,' said David. 'They deserve an explanation.' He opened his mouth to start on his tale when she realised. Ollie had not yet come back.

'Ollie... where did you last see him?'

'Christ, I'd forgotten him in all this fuss.' David glared at Ian as if it were his fault his son wasn't here. Fortunately, Ian didn't appear to notice.

'I'll go and look for him,' said Ian. 'He can't have gone far in this weather. Where did you last see him?'

'Near where Ros's car is abandoned. I'll come with you,' said David. 'You won't find it otherwise.'

'No,' said Ros. 'I'll go. I need to get out of here.'

'Can you believe my parents?' she said as soon as they were outside. 'I'm so sorry my dad was so rude to you.' She put her arm through his. 'Still, you're here now. I...' she hesitated. 'I'd like you to know—' 'Please don't say anything else. Ros,' Ian said as he extricated himself from her grip. 'Look. There's something I have to tell you.' He stopped and scuffed the snow with his foot. 'I'm sorry, but you seem to think there's a chance of our relationship developing into something romantic.' He turned to look at her. 'It's not going to happen.'

Ros blinked. 'There's someone else?'

'Not at the moment, no.'

Her throat tightened. 'Why did you come down here, then? You said you were worried about me. You must care.'

He walked on, not saying anything. She trudged on beside him, fighting to keep back the tears. It was tempting to turn back, leave him to get lost.

'I don't understand,' she sniffed.

'Look, it's complicated. I can't say any more at the moment.'

What did he mean, complicated? She straightened her back. 'Fine,' she said. 'No problem.'

'You're angry at me,' it wasn't a question.

She didn't answer. She wasn't angry but devastated, ashamed she'd made her need for him so clear. Eventually she said, controlling the tremor in her voice, 'Of course I'm not angry'.

He squeezed her arm. 'Good, now let's find your brother.'

David disappeared upstairs when they left, to watch them from the bedroom window. It was obvious to Lisa he didn't trust Ian. She could have gone after him, but he was in a mood and hard to engage with. Best leave it. There was nothing to be gained going over what he had told her, and anyway, she was angry with him for being so bloody naive. Stupid, stupid man. Falling for a honey trap. She breathed deeply to calm herself. She was in need of a diversion. She'd make soup from Oliver's vegetables to keep her occupied. Fortunately, there were plenty of stock cubes, as well as lentils to bulk it out. It would be an excellent lunch for when they returned. They were sure to get some kind of signal, and once the police were alerted, then there was nothing to worry about. She left out the turnip. There was some tinned haggis in the cupboard, vegetarian, and the turnip would go well with it. The freeze couldn't go on for much longer. This was Britain, for heaven's sake, not the North Pole. Thinking about the weather reminded her they hadn't listened to the radio today, so she wound it up and sat down to listen to it while she was chopping the vegetables.

There was nothing of note on the news. The north of England remained under snow. Another MP had been accused of corruption. There had been more bombing in Ukraine and Gaza. Near the end of the broadcast, the murder in Newcastle was mentioned, but only to say they hadn't yet identified the body. She wished they had. It would be better to know one way or the other.

The pile of vegetables was growing; at this rate there would be enough soup for days. She brought out the stock pan and put it on the range with some butter to melt. With the vegetables gently sweating, she ran upstairs for a quick shower. The water ought to be hot enough by now. Too bad if it wasn't; she needed to freshen up.

By the end of the shower, she felt much better. She dried herself, got into clean clothes and sauntered downstairs resisting the temptation to call in on Emilia on the way. She was better off in bed trying to shake off the migraine. Halfway down the stairs, she picked up that David was talking to someone. Lisa's spirits lifted. They must have found Ollie and returned when she was showering. But it wasn't them. David was sitting at the table opposite George. Jo was there, too, a bored expression on her face.

'George was saying he thinks he used to teach you,' David said to her.

Fuck. Lisa put on her best surprised face. 'I don't think so. You're not old enough, surely?'

George smiled but it stayed at his mouth and did not reach his eyes. They had narrowed and were focused on Lisa. She was a field mouse caught in the gaze of an eagle.

'I was a student teacher. English. September 1984, my first teaching practice. You were in my Higher English class, Lisa. We hung around a bit together. You know, out of school.'

'I didn't get to hang around much with anyone let alone teachers,' said Lisa. Out of the corner of her eye she saw that David was frowning. 'Do you remember George, David?' She prayed he didn't.

'I don't think so.' said David. 'But I wasn't in the same English class as you.'

'You must remember, Lisa. We had great fun. You and your friends.'

They'd been flattered by his interest, ripe for the picking. It was time to play her ace.

'I'm sorry. I really don't remember, George. Though, you're right. I *was* in S5 that year. God, it was so long ago. I was fifteen.'

George paled. 'No, you must have been sixteen. You were in fifth year.'

'I think I know what age I was then, George.' She couldn't keep the sarcasm out of her voice. 'I was the youngest person in my year. My birthday is on the 23rd of February, so I was definitely only fifteen. God, what a drag it was being younger than everyone else. One of the perils of the Scottish education system. You can leave school after thirteen years of education, go to university and do all sorts of things legally, yet not be old enough to vote or drink.'

The message had got through, all right. He looked as though he had found a dead mouse in his shoe. Jo, on the other hand, looked interested. 'What school did you do your teaching practice at, George?'

'Sandwood High,' he mumbled. 'It's near Tollcross.'

'Oh well, that settles it once and for all,' said David. 'We lived in the West End, Anniesland. I don't think we ever went further east than the city centre. You know what Glasgow's like; you stick to where you know.'

George gave a weak smile. 'Indeed. Sorry, I feel I've made a bit of a fool of myself. I was so sure I recognised you.'

Lisa laughed. 'Afraid not.' She put on a teasing voice, unable to resist firing the final sharp arrow. 'But what on earth were you doing, hanging round with fifteen- and sixteen-year-olds when you must have been what, in your twenties? Looking for trouble?'

She'd gone too far. Both he and Jo looked annoyed. David stepped in with an offer of coffee, which of course they couldn't fulfil, but George refused and got up from the table.

'We should go, I'm sure you have things to do.'

'Stay for lunch,' said David. 'Lisa's making soup.'

Shit, the soup. Lisa ran over to the range and lifted the lid. Thank goodness, the vegetables hadn't caught but they had well and truly sweated. She added the lentils and the three litres of stock she'd made earlier.

'Yes, please do,' said Lisa, remembering her manners now the immediate danger had passed.

George already had his hand on the door handle. Jo got up and joined him, looking a little despondent. It was a long walk back. She paused by the door. 'What happened to your snowman?'

She wasn't going to tell them. 'Oh, nothing. A silly joke of Oliver's.'

'It must be a handful at times, all those young people. A worry.' There was a wistfulness in Jo's voice.

'Yes, it is. But they're worth it.'

Jo nodded in reply but she was distracted by something. Lisa followed her gaze. She was looking at the knife that they'd left on the worktop, the one that had been stuck in the snowman.

'Is that a Sabatier knife? We've got a set too. They're excellent, aren't they? But we seem to have mislaid one. Bloody nuisance.'

George stiffened when Jo mentioned the knife. She'd swear to it. Was he behind the attack on the snowman? 'Yes,' she managed to say. 'They are good knives. I hope yours turns up soon.'

She stole a glance at George, but his face gave nothing away.

'Oh well,' said Jo. 'We'd best be off. See you soon. Boxing day, don't forget."

Lisa saw them to the door. She'd never been so glad to see the back of someone. She went back inside to start getting lunch ready but her heart sank when she saw David's face.

'We need to talk,' he said. 'Sit down.'

Chapter Fourteen

Ros was mortified. The only thing on her mind was Ian's rejection of her. What was wrong with her? There must be someone else. He was married... of course. That would explain why he often called off at the last moment or left in a hurry. No, no wife would allow herself to be left alone at Christmas. Unless... maybe he had split up with her and didn't want a relationship on the rebound. She had to find out, but how? Maybe Mum could help; she was good at getting people to talk and Ros suspected she'd taken to Ian. In spite of all her reservations, he had charmed her. Right, that's what she'd do; she'd rope Mum in to help.

The atmosphere was very still now. It had stopped snowing, and the only sound was the snow crunching underfoot. Now they'd got into the rhythm of dealing with the thick carpet, the walk was easier, and they made good progress.

'We should try calling out to Oliver,' said Ian. 'He might be within hearing distance.'

As they neared the copse, there were two sets of footprints visible. For a short time, they continued together before they separated: one going off towards the woods the other towards open fields.

'Mm, problem,' said Ian. 'Which are your father's and which are Oliver's?'

'Oliver's feet are bigger,' said Ros. She pointed to the track leading towards the woods. 'These are his footsteps.' She started to follow them.

It was dark in the woods as the trees were mainly evergreen, so the little light there was, was blocked out. With every step, it became darker and more difficult to follow the footsteps. A crow rose up in front of them with a loud caw startling Ros, so she stumbled, managing to stay upright by grabbing Ian's arm. 'Christ, scary or what?' More than scary. She was terrified. What if the intruder was lurking nearby? This would be an excellent place to hide.

She jumped again as Ian suddenly bellowed Ollie's name. 'Give me a warning next time,' she said.

'Ssh,' he said. 'Did you hear that?'

Ros stood and listened. All she could hear was their breathing and a faint rustling. Oh God, was someone else in the woods? If it was Ollie, he would have called out.

'What did you hear?' she said.

'I don't know. It was a groan or a moan or something.'

'OK, this time I'll shout and we'll both listen. Oliver!'

They waited.

'Try again,' said Ian.

'Oliver!' This time there was something, faint, but loud enough for Ros to make out her name.

'It's Ollie,' she said. 'He's over there.' She pointed to her left and started to run.

'Don't run,' said Ian. 'You'll tire yourself out. Or worse, you'll trip over a tree root and break something.'

She slowed down but called out again. 'Oliver, we're

coming. If you've got your phone, put on the torch part of it so we can see something to follow.'

The reply was barely audible. 'Will do.'

Onwards they went, until, at last, they saw a tiny pinprick of light.

'Over there,' said Ros and despite Ian's warning she ran towards it, her boots sliding on the hard snow. The last few yards took forever, then she saw Oliver lying on the ground. Why wasn't he moving? 'Are you alright?' she gasped as she reached him.

Lisa couldn't look at David. His voice when he spoke was sombre, the tone of which always foretold trouble. 'What was that all about?'

She hesitated, unsure of what to say. Her mind was foggy, but she had two choices: tell the truth or prevaricate. She chose the latter. 'What do you mean?'

'George, saying he knew you. Is it true?'

'No, of course not. He's a weirdo.'

David nodded. 'I agree. There's something off about him. But—'

'Something off about who?' Em had come into the room in her pyjamas, with her duvet wrapped round her. 'Is there anything to eat? I'm starving.'

Lisa could have hugged her she was so relieved to be interrupted. 'Oh nothing, sweetheart. Are you feeling better? I've made soup for lunch; it'll be ready soon.'

Behind her, David sighed. She hadn't heard the last of this.

Oliver pointed to his right foot. Something metal was imbedded in it. An animal trap. Ros's mouth filled with saliva. Shit, she was going to be sick. She controlled herself. Poor Ollie. His face was white, beads of sweat on his forehead. 'Dear God,' she said. 'How are we going to get you free?'

Ian knelt down beside Oliver. 'Ian Murray,' he said. 'I'm a friend of Ros. I think I know what to do but it's going to hurt. Shall I go ahead and try?'

Oliver's voice trembled. 'It couldn't be worse than it is, mate. Please, get on with it.'

'Right, let's have a look.' He peered at the contraption. 'I think it's a footlock trap. Most of them have quick releases so we should be OK. It's a question of moving the levers in the right direction.'

'I tried moving them,' said Oliver, 'but it made it worse.'

Ian looked again. 'Yup, it's a footlock, all right. What you have to do is to pull the levers towards you using one continuous motion. That should release the pressure on the jaws of the trap enough for you to pull your foot free. I'll count to three and do it. On three, start pulling your foot free. I should be able to hold it open long enough for you to get free. Ready?'

'Yes,' said Oliver.

'One, two, three.' He grasped the levers and pulled them forward. The jaws of the trap opened, and Oliver pulled his foot out. 'Christ, that hurts!"

'I bet it does. Can you stand up?'

'I don't know. I... I don't want to put any weight on this foot.'

'Right, lean on me and I'll pull you up.'

Slowly, Oliver got to his feet. He tried putting his weight on the right foot and winced. 'I can't do it. Sorry.'

'No problem, we'll support you and get you back to the house in no time at all and I'll have a look at your foot. It's good you were wearing walking boots. It looks as though they've taken a lot of the damage.'

'Doesn't feel that way, I have to say,' said Ollie. 'Foot's killing me.'

'Well, the best you can hope for is a badly bruised foot, but honestly, if you'd been wearing trainers or wellies, believe me, it would be much worse. Let's hope it hasn't broken anything.'

They started off on their walk back to the house. Their progress was slow as Oliver wasn't able to put his weight on his foot, so he had to half hop half slide, all the while leaning heavily on the others. At this rate, it would take an hour to get back, if not more. They persevered though, encouraging Oliver to keep going and at last they were out of the woods and on to the road. It was a relief to get out into more open countryside. The darkness in the forest was oppressive. The road was completely blocked with snow but at least they were able to see where they were going.

'At last,' said Ros as the Warren came into view. 'I'm beginning to like the sight of this place.'

'Ros, you go on ahead and get your parents to boil some water. This wound is going to need to be thoroughly cleaned and as soon as possible.'

Ros, who normally argued whenever she was asked to do something she hadn't suggested herself, set off at once. It was much easier to walk without the burden of Oliver and she was at the house within a few minutes.

'Did you find him? Where is he?' Her mother pounced on her as she came in through the door.

'He's OK, they're coming. Silly fool got caught in a trap.'

'What? Is he hurt?'

'Afraid so,' said Ros as she filled the kettle and put it on the range. 'It got him on his right foot. He can't bear his weight on it. He's OK though. He'll live.'

Her mother looked at her, her face stricken. 'Dear God, what else can go wrong during this holiday?'

'What the fuck are you doing here?' Em exploded as Ian came into the kitchen with Ollie.

Lisa looked at her daughter, stunned. Why was she being so rude? 'Emilia,' she snapped. 'Apologise at once.'

Em turned on her. 'Oh, don't be such a hypocrite. You told Ros not to bring him, she's moaned about it non-stop. And now look, here he is. Surely, you can see this has been stage-managed between the two of them?'

'Shut up, you!' Ros's vehemence was almost physical. Em took a step back. 'He was worried about me, don't you understand? Bugger off back to bed. Like you always do!'

Em stared at them both for a moment then left the room, slamming the door so hard the cottage shook.

Lisa was exhausted. This was worse than when they were teenagers. At the time they'd all been so worried about Em's health that for the most part, they'd avoided the tantrums that come with adolescence. But they were making up for lost time, now. 'What the hell was that about?'

Neither Ros nor Ian replied. Ros was busy filling the kettle and Ian gave her a small smile that she was unable to decipher. Lisa stared at them both. 'Well?'

Ros broke first 'I don't think she approves of the age difference. You know what she's like. It's all black and white with Em.'

Ian was avoiding eye contact. There was more to this than any of them were saying.

She'd get nothing more from them. 'I'll go and see she's all right.' Upstairs, she took a deep breath before tapping on Em's door. As expected, there was no answer. She went in. Em was fully dressed now, sitting on her bed, head in hands.

'Are you OK?' asked Lisa.

Em sighed. 'I know, I was rude, but I don't like him, and I hate the way Ros throws herself at him.'

'Well, if it's any comfort I don't think for a moment he has any designs on her.'

'Good,' she said.

'Is there any particular reason you don't like him?'

There was a pause of several seconds. 'I...' she shook her head. 'I'm sorry, Mum. You should go, look after Ollie. God knows what he's done to himself now.'

She'd been on the point of telling her something, Lisa was sure, but Em was right, she needed to see to Ollie.

Oliver was all right. He was pale and in pain. The boot wouldn't come off his foot, so Lisa found the Stanley knife and carefully cut it off. Ian was sure it didn't look as though anything was broken but the wound left from the trap was fairly deep. She and Ian worked together to clean it, apologising when Ollie winced, which was every time one of them touched it. Lisa was worried he might have damaged a tendon. 'We'll need to get you to a hospital when we can,' she said as she wrapped the foot tightly in a crepe bandage.

'Don't fuss, Mum.'

'I'm not fussing. I'm making an observation.' It was hard to keep the irritation out of her voice. It wasn't his fault he was hurt. But it did mean they had something else to worry about on top of everything else. And the advantage of having an extra body on hand had been whisked away. 'I'll get you some painkillers.'

'I'm sorry, Mum. I'm such an idiot. Getting you into all this and now getting injured on top of everything else.'

'It doesn't matter,' Lisa said. 'All that matters is that we're all OK, and we are.' For the moment, she added silently as she got up from the table.

A few minutes later she returned with the heavy-duty painkillers she kept for emergencies and handed them to Oliver. What a shame it hadn't been their intruder who got trapped. He could rot out in the forest as far as she was concerned. She banished the thought as soon as it came to her. It didn't sit kindly with Lisa's liberal conscience, but when you found yourself directly threatened, it was different. No, she told herself, don't think like that.

Oliver took two tablets. 'Thanks, Mum.'

It didn't take long for them to work and soon he was a little spaced out, his eyes unfocused. 'I think I'll go and lie down.'

Lisa tried not to feel too annoyed with him; he was badly hurt after all, but all she could think was, he had brought it on himself.

Lunch was a tense affair. Lisa tried to chat but without success. David spoke in monosyllables and Em said nothing throughout, Ros was subdued and kept throwing hurt glances at Ian, who kept his head down. He'd think twice about gate-crashing anyone's Christmas in future. Lisa didn't believe him when he said he'd been worried about Ros. Something about it didn't ring true. He'd been aloof and somewhat cool in response to Ros's enthusiastic welcome. She hoped her daughter wasn't going to get her heart broken.

When lunch was over, Lisa suggested they should talk about what to do next. Unfortunately, no one had anything new to say. They listened to the news hoping for some sign of an end to the power cuts, but apparently, they were likely to be without electricity until at least tomorrow: Christmas Day. She'd forgotten how close they were to Christmas. There was an update on the body in Newcastle. Police were now treating it as murder. Damn, she had hoped against hope that it would be an overdose. No name as of yet. She made a note to herself to tune into a more local station to see what they had to say, put her mind at rest.

'Right,' said Lisa. 'We need to get prepared for tomorrow. We'll have spaghetti bolognaise for tonight's supper, there's sauce in the fridge and I don't want it to go to waste. But it would be nice to get the potatoes peeled so we don't have to do them tomorrow and there's a mountain of sprouts to be dealt with.'

'I hate sprouts,' muttered Ros.

'So, you will enjoy peeling them,' was the answer. 'Get a knife and imagine you're torturing them for daring to be so bitter.'

No one laughed – it was a tasteless joke after all – but a dark cloud had descended over the gathering and Lisa wanted to be rid of it. 'Look,' she said, sounding more confident than she felt, 'there's six of us, one of him. We can either sit around waiting for something to happen or get on with things. We don't know for sure he's anywhere near here.'

'We don't even know who it is.'

Lisa threw Ros a sharp look. 'Well, thanks for stating the obvious.'

'Don't be sarcastic. You know what I mean.' She rubbed

at her forehead. 'Dad was about to tell us something when you conveniently remembered about Ollie.'

'It's not for me to tell you,' Lisa started to say.

'Oh, come off it. You're letting Oliver take all the blame for this, but Dad behaved like a maniac when he came after Ian. So, what's going on?'

Lisa looked at David. It wasn't her story to tell.

David sighed. 'OK, OK. They have a right to know what's going on but Lisa, you also need to think if there's anything you want to tell us.'

No one said anything while David was talking. Lisa felt the same sense of disbelief coming from them as she had when he told her.

Ros was the first to speak after he finished. 'Jeez, Dad. All these threats... it's terrible. No wonder you behaved the way you did to Ian. But why didn't you tell someone?'

The look he gave her was dark. 'I couldn't.'

'What do you mean?'

He shook his head. 'Leave it, please.'

For once, Ros appeared to know when it was best to stop, thank goodness. But Em wanted her say. 'There's something you're not telling us. Don't tell me you fell for a honey trap?'

David's face betrayed his shame. 'I don't want to talk about it.'

'But—'

'But nothing, Emilia. Dad's told you all he's going to,' said Lisa.

'Exactly. Anyway, enough about me. I need to talk to your mother. In private. Lisa?'

Lisa felt sick. She hadn't fooled him.

'It's stopped snowing,' he said. 'Shall we go outside?'

There was no option other than to follow him. There was little privacy to be had in the house and she didn't want the others to hear this conversation, so they'd have to go out into the garden. They went into the hall and put on their warmest jackets.

They walked over to the snow people they'd built less than twenty-four hours ago. The ketchup had frozen, and Lisa chipped at it with her nails until it dropped off, leaving little red blots on the ground that looked like jewels. She waited for David to speak but he was silent, watching her. She turned to face him. 'Well?'

'I'm not convinced, Lisa. That bloke, George. You do know him, don't you? Are you having an affair with him?'

This was her chance. She should tell him now but the words that came out were a denial. 'God, no.'

David stared at her. 'You're holding something back. What is it? He recognised you. He saw the resemblance between you and Emilia and you know how much the twins look like you did when you were young. There's something going on, something you're not telling me. His wife is suspicious, too. Didn't you notice her face yesterday when he was claiming he recognised you from school? Did it start then? Has it been going on all these years, or did you get together again recently?'

Lisa felt sick. She didn't have to pretend to be horrified. 'I don't know what to say, David. How could you think such a thing?'

'Did he have something to do with why you disappeared? You left without a word.' The hurt was there in his eyes. 'Why?'

'I've told you. Over and over. My parents didn't approve of us seeing each other...'

'Why didn't you warn me? You must have known the house was up for sale.'

'How many times?' Lisa fought to keep the exasperation

from her voice. 'The first I knew about any move was when the removal men turned up. My parents had rented a flat in Largs and they didn't put the house on the market until we'd moved.'

'They must have hated me.'

'They didn't much like me, either.' Lisa shuddered as she remembered what she'd gone through: how they'd effectively kept her prisoner, out of sight of everyone, locked in her room and forced to study. She was only allowed out to sit her exams at the local school. Her mother went with her, to make sure she didn't make a run for it. While Lisa was sitting her exams, her mother waited for her, sitting on a chair outside the head teacher's room, her back as rigid as it always was. Lisa had planned to ask one of the exam invigilators to help her, but when she was eventually brave enough to raise her hand, the invigilator's manner was so like her mother's, she changed her mind and asked for more paper instead. It was easy to see whose side she'd take. Lisa had never spoken about that time to anyone, not even to David. Could she tell him now, with so many other people around? No. It would have to wait. But after this holiday was over, she'd tell him then.

'David, you have no idea how awful my life was then. I don't want to talk about it. But I can assure you I have not had an affair with George, or any other man.'

He looked deep in her eyes as if searching for the truth. 'But you weren't a virgin.' He didn't wait for a reply but walked away without looking back.

Lisa called after him, but he didn't pause. Damn him, damn him for bringing up something he'd promised he'd never mention again. She leaned against the snowman and let the tears flow, wishing she'd never set eyes on George.

Chapter Fifteen

HER PARENTS HAD BEEN OUTSIDE for ages. Ros got up from her seat at the fire and stood at the window to watch them. They were at the far end of the garden, beside the snow people.

'They're arguing,' she said.

'How do you know?'

'The body language. Dad's fists are clenched and they're leaning away from each other. What do you think it's about?'

No one answered. 'Am I the only one here who thinks this is odd? There's something going on between them, I'd swear it.'

'I think Mum's been unfaithful,' said Emilia in a low voice. She sounded calm but sure of herself.

Ros whirled round to face her. 'What! I don't believe it. What on earth makes you think Mum would betray Dad?'

'Nothing, forget I said anything.' Emilia shrank back into the duvet she'd been huddled under.

'No, no, no.' Ros strode across the room and stood over

her. You can't make a statement like that and then leave it. What evidence do you have, if any?'

Em shrugged. 'I heard them earlier, talking about that creepy bloke who was here.'

'Him? That drip? No way. I don't believe it. Tell me exactly what you heard.'

'I don't know, something about Mum hanging about with him.'

'No. The woman is Mum's new DHT. She hasn't started at the school yet so how could she have met her husband?'

Em's face closed. 'I knew you wouldn't believe me. I shouldn't have mentioned it.'

Mum came into the room, her face flushed. 'Shouldn't have mentioned what?'

Emilia flashed a warning look at the others. Mum looked at them one by one. 'What? What are you hiding?'

There was a pause and then Ros laughed. 'You won't believe this, Mum. She thinks you're having an affair. Ridiculous, isn't it?'

Her mother didn't join in with the laughter. Instead, she turned to Emilia and asked, 'What makes you think that?'

Emilia shrugged. She didn't look at Lisa. Ros spoke up. 'She heard you and Dad arguing. About that creepy bloke who's been hanging around.'

Lisa looked at them all and shook her head. 'I am not having an affair. I would have thought you would have known without me having to tell you. You've got hold of the wrong end of the stick, Emilia. I'm not going to say any more now. I'm tired. I've hardly slept these past two nights and I'm going to lie down for a while. Please don't disturb me. Perhaps one of you can see to tonight's supper.'

Ros turned on her sister as soon as her mother had left the room. 'Now, see what you've done. You've insulted Mum by poking your nose into her business. I'm so fed up with you. You've been nothing but moody and grumpy since you got here and now, you're stirring things up.'

Em said nothing. She lay for a moment, looking absolutely stricken, as though Ros had physically struck her. Then without saying a word, she got up and left the room. A moment later the front door banged.

'Shit,' said Ros. 'Typical of my bloody sister. Drops a bombshell and leaves. Well, I'm not going after her.'

Ian sat in front of the fire, his knee jiggling up and down. He looked nervous, jumpy. After a few seconds, he spoke. 'Don't you think we should?'

Ros laughed, not in a kind way. 'Do you think it would help? You've no idea what she's like in a mood like this. And you're far from her favourite person. Believe me.'

Ian stood up. 'Maybe not, but we can't let her wander about on her own. We have to go after her. Didn't someone say she had a migraine? It's not alright for her to go wandering about like this when we don't know who's out there.'

Ros stared into the fire. It looked so welcoming. 'Do what you like,' she said eventually. 'I'm past caring about anything. I wish I'd stayed at home.'

Ian's knee jiggled up and down faster than ever. 'I'll go alone then,' he said. Ros stirred herself, there was nothing to be gained from staying here. At least it had stopped snowing.

Lisa had not long reached her room when she heard the door slam. She was lying in bed, the duvet doubled around her to stave off the cold, trying to sleep; the sound reverberated throughout the house. She dragged herself out of bed and watched as Emilia walked down the path. Her progress was slow; she was having trouble with the depth of the snow. She looked so frail. Lisa's heart went out to her. She'd been too hard on her. She knocked on the window but either Em didn't hear her or she ignored it. The latter, probably. Lisa stood with her nose pressed against the window and hoped she'd be all right. She'd said she was feeling better, but Lisa was worried, nonetheless. David was nowhere to be seen, sulking in the kitchen, most likely. Lisa stood there unsure of what to do. Would Em be safe out there?

The weather was no longer the threat it had been. Whereas this morning the sky had the yellowish glare of snow yet to fall, now the clouds had fled, and the sky had turned to bright winter blue at the beginning of the afternoon. She glanced at her watch. Half past two. There was an hour of light left. Then the door opened, and Ros and Ian emerged. They weren't far behind Em; they'd catch up in no time and there was safety in numbers. Someone was moving down below. David must be in the house. When she returned to bed, her urge to sleep had fled. Five minutes ago, she'd been on the point of sleep, now she was wide awake, her mind churning. She had to know what was going on with Emilia. Her family was unravelling. David suspected her of an affair and Lisa had failed to reassure him. Oliver was in deep trouble. Ros was alright but there was something off about this new man of hers. If he didn't fancy her – and he obviously didn't – why was he hanging around her? But of all the things, including the threat of physical danger, she was most worried about Emilia. Something was going on in her life, but she wasn't going to tell her mother. Restless, Lisa turned over, desperate for sleep, but it was gone. She knew what she had to do. she rose slowly from the bed and went to the window. If they were on their way back, she'd leave it. If not, then she was going to look for Emilia's diary. The only sign of them was their footprints. Lisa went out onto the landing and listened outside Ollie's door. He was snoring softly; knocked out by the painkillers. Lucky him. For a moment, she stood there hesitant. It was wrong, she should leave it. She turned to go back to bed, then changed her mind. She'd regret it but had to know what was in the notebook Em had been so keen to hide.

What a mess Em's room was: the bed unmade and clothes strewn across her open suitcase. Why did they bother with chests of drawers when nobody ever put their clothes away when they came to stay? Lisa was glad it was untidy. It meant she didn't have to be so careful about putting things back when she moved them. She tried to think where she used to hide her diary when she was younger. She had never been particularly imaginative, which is how her parents caught her out. A vision came into her mind of her mother standing in front of her flourishing a notebook Lisa used as a diary.

'What is this?'

Lisa had said nothing. Already she was regretting the poorly chosen hiding place of her underwear drawer. Her mother had already read her diary, she knew by the look on her face. Instead, she shrugged.

'Don't you dare take that attitude with me. We told you to stop seeing the Truett boy, didn't we? And yet, here is the proof you disobeyed us. You're grounded.'

She'd been forbidden to go out for a month. It was the summer holidays, a time she'd planned to spend with David. Her parents thought her relationship with David would fail to survive such a separation, but it only made their feelings stronger. She shook off the memory. Don't think about them. They were in the past, along with a good many other things and she would not allow them back into her life. She lifted the mattress. Nothing. Tried a shoebox, nothing, knelt down by her suitcase and rummaged through it, heart leaping when she felt something. But it was a book. She leaned back on her heels surveying her surroundings. And there it was, in plain view. On the windowsill, where she'd left it. Lisa got up, wincing at the twinge in her knees and went over to the window. She glanced outside but they were out of view. She grabbed the notebook and sat down on the bed.

Now it was in her hands, she was having second thoughts. It was unthinkable to betray Emilia's trust like this. It was beyond reprehensible. Em had a right to her own life. She put it back on the windowsill and sat on her hands to stop them betraying her. But they had their own momentum and after a few seconds, she picked it up again, telling herself Em was hiding something. She ignored the voice telling her she had no right to know and instead told herself it was the right thing to do. She opened the notebook. What a relief. It wasn't a diary at all but a series of book reviews. It said so on the first page.

January 1st
I'm not one for making resolutions, but this year I want to hone my reviewing skills by writing about every book I read. Last year, I had three reviews in the Herald. *Who knows, with practice and perseverance I might place more this year. That's my goal: at least six reviews in a quality newspaper.*

Lisa read on for a few pages. The reviews were excellent. One, she recognised as having been published in the *Scotsman*. She was determined to succeed, her daughter. Lisa was proud of her and ashamed of herself. She shouldn't be going through her daughter's private things. But they were so entertaining, Lisa read on. One – a review of the latest novel by one of the country's literary giants –was clearly never meant for publication.

The author has surpassed himself this time. Several of his more recent novels have been notable for their smugness as he delineates his own life in his pompous prose. They are nothing more than lightly fictionalised accounts of what he gets up to: using Tinder to sate his sexual appetite, eating in fashionable restaurants where you pay hundreds of pounds for artfully arranged food presented in a cloud of smoke, bemoaning the cost of his second home in Tuscany, whingeing about how much his ex-wives cost him. They are a litany of what has come to be known as "first world problems" and this one is no exception. At this rate, there will be no material left for his widely expected autobiography due out at the beginning of next year. Unless, of course, he chooses to reveal he has been faithful to his wife of thirty years and gives all his money to charity. Unlikely.

Lisa laughed out loud. It was so accurate. What a shame it couldn't be published, but no newspaper would take the risk and any reviews she'd read of this particular novel were sycophantic to say the least. A long-time fan of the author, Lisa had bought the book in hardback but had given up on it three chapters in. Em's review was brilliant – short and to the point. Once a novelist became established, all critical faculties fled. In addition, their novels took up most of the limited space given over to reviews whereas debut authors were lucky to get perhaps an inch or so. As for those published by small, independent presses, they prayed in vain for someone to notice them.

They had been gone ten minutes, quarter of an hour at

most. Lisa was about to put the notebook back when it fell open to a page near the end. She glimpsed the words: *I received a strange letter today and I don't know what to do about it.*

What was this? Was Em being stalked or harassed in some way. It might explain her moodiness. Lisa read on, desperate to know.

It was handwritten in an old-fashioned cursive writing, what's it called? Copperplate or something. I'd never seen anything like it in real life. 'Dear Miss Truett,' it started. I knew at once it was an old person writing. It went on, 'I hope you don't mind me writing to you like this, but I saw you'd written a review in the Herald. *I very much enjoyed it.' I thought it was a fan letter and I skimmed the rest.*

A fan letter, how nice. Lisa smiled. That would help boost Emilia's confidence. It was always nice if someone showed appreciation of what you'd done. What she read next stunned her.

I couldn't believe what it said next: 'I believe you may be my granddaughter. I recognised the name Truett immediately. My daughter, Elizabeth, married a man called David Truett. Elizabeth has been estranged from me for over thirty years. I would very much like to meet you. My hearing is not as good as it once was so I would be grateful if you would write to me at the above address to arrange a meeting.' It was signed by Arthur Paterson. I didn't know what to think. Paterson is Mum's maiden name, but her parents died when she was a teenager. In a car crash. Or at least, that's what she told us. I'm going to meet him. It might be a scam, but I have to know. I wrote back and said I'd meet him next week. He lives in a care

*home in Largs, so I've arranged to meet him there. I looked up
the name of the place online and it exists so he's unlikely to
turn out to be a serial killer or rapist.*

Lisa read the words again, disbelieving. She turned the
page dreading what she might find next. It was as bad as she
feared. One line. *He is my grandfather. My mother is a lying
bitch.* She cast the notebook aside. She was hyperventilating,
panicking, back in her teenage bedroom. Her father? Her
parents were dead to her. At the time when she needed them
most, they turned against her, but now, somehow, they were
back. No wonder Emilia was angry. Lisa knew what her
father would have told her. He would have distorted the
whole story, giving him and her mother starring roles as the
put upon parents striving to control their unruly daughter.
Lisa was overwhelmed by nausea as she thought about her
father's words poisoning her beloved daughter, telling her lies
about what had happened all those years ago.

She had not been a difficult teenager: a little headstrong,
but nothing out of the ordinary. She was in love with
David who she'd met at school. They'd started going out at
the beginning of fourth year. His parents were cool about
it, but hers were so old fashioned. They wanted her at
home every night before ten. They kept a check on her
homework diary and after excellent exam results in fourth
year, insisted she should try for a scholarship to Oxford.
Lisa had no intention of going there. She loved drama,
wanted to be an actor, and her mind was set on the Royal
Scottish Academy of Music and Drama in Glasgow. Her
only fear was she wouldn't be good enough for them.

There were a limited number of places, so it was highly competitive. David wanted to go to Glasgow University like his parents before him and she wasn't going to be separated from him. Her parents didn't like David. They thought he wasn't good enough. They told him to his face that he wasn't welcome in their home. Lisa was heartbroken, torn apart. At the time she loved them, but it wasn't long before love turned to dislike and finally hate. After what they did to her later that year, she despised them and vowed never to see them again.

Emilia called her a liar in her diary because she had told them their grandparents were dead. Em didn't understand that to Lisa they *were* dead to her. She scrabbled through the rest of the notebook looking to see if there was anything else about the meeting, anything about what he'd told her. But there was nothing but blank pages. Whatever he'd said, Emilia hadn't written about it.

She put the notebook down. This explained Emilia's attitude to her. Looking back over the past few weeks she saw how the signs were there, signs she'd chosen to ignore. All those little passive aggressive remarks, not returning her phone calls, making excuses not to meet up. It was all down to her father – back in her life when she least expected it.

Lisa had no idea how to deal with this. Tackling Emilia was out of the question. She couldn't admit to reading her notebook. Twenty minutes had passed since they left. They were due back any moment. She looked out of the window and couldn't see them. After she put the notebook back on the windowsill, she checked the room to see if she'd left anything to betray her presence. At this point, she wasn't ready for a confrontation. First, she had to discuss this with David. She'd have to tell him everything. Would he forgive her? They had loved one another for forty years. And yet...

Em was right to call her a hypocrite. The truth was, she had been deceiving him for all those years.

Lisa went downstairs, a sick feeling in her stomach, her heart beating too fast. Not for the first time, she wondered if her blood pressure was all it should be.

It was hard to see now, beneath the double chin and the skin, which had coarsened with time and drink, but George had been attractive as a young man, if you liked the geeky look. He had looked younger than his twenty-two years, so when he bumped into Lisa and her two friends on the street one night and started talking, it didn't seem odd. He had yet to fill out, his arms were skinny sticks, his torso muscle-free. He probably did shave, but he still had the odd spot. She had never found older men attractive – stories like *Bonjour Tristesse* where a young girl slept with a much older man while her father went through a series of young mistresses, repelled her – but George acted as if he were a teenager, not seven years older than her.

It happened a few times, him bumping into Lisa and her friends by accident. He spoke mainly to Lisa. Angie and Yvonne teased her about him, but she laughed it off. He was a teacher – even if he wasn't yet qualified – and out of bounds. Anyway, she had David. George stayed clear whenever David was around. Looking back, that was a warning, He was only interested in hanging out with the girls. He liked to show off. They had enjoyed his stories about university and were easily impressed, as only teenagers can be. Despite her feelings for David, Lisa was flattered.

It was a Saturday afternoon. David had what was then called a 'Saturday job'. In those days there weren't zero hours' contracts; supermarkets and shops opened from 9 until 5.30 and Sundays were deader than a graveyard. There were few part-time jobs available except bar work and restaurants, but you had to be over eighteen and so the main option was to work in a shop on a Saturday. He worked in a grocer's called Curley's, a Glasgow institution. Lisa didn't have a job; her parents had forbidden it. Nothing was to be permitted to get in the way of her Oxford scholarship so every Saturday morning she set off for the Mitchell Library for a full day's study.

It was a hot day. She would never forget it. Scotland doesn't stick to normal summer months and weather. There's more likely to be a warm day in May or September than a spell of decent weather in July where, unless it's an exceptional year, gardeners put away their hoses and rely on the heavy downpours to do their job for them. George came up behind her, made her jump when he'd said, 'Miss Paterson, such a pleasure. Some might call it serendipity.' Something about the way he'd looked at her made her feel uneasy but then he'd changed the subject to the Philip Larkin poem she was making notes on and she forgot her discomfort. He made some complimentary comments about her insights and then suggested going for a coffee.

She had been studying for two hours; she was due a break. 'OK,' she said. She should have said no.

The coffee stretched into lunch followed by a walk in the nearby Kelvingrove Park. She loved discussing poetry with him. Her friends dismissed it as 'lame' and laughed at her if she ever wanted to talk about it. Lisa was nervous the whole time, worried one of her friends might see her. It was one thing to hang about in a group, but another to be on her own with a teacher. George took her hand to help her down a steep path and held on too long. She shook him off.

'Sorry,' he said, looking downcast.

'You're my teacher,' she said. 'It might get you into trouble.' She'd been trying to spare his feelings. She should have run.

They walked on in silence for a bit, leaving the park at the Woodlands Road exit and starting to make their way back to the Mitchell library.

'My flat's over there,' he said, nodding towards the other side of the road.

Lisa thought he meant he was going to go home. Fine, she ought to get back to her studies, she'd spent too much time talking. She smiled and said, 'Well, goodbye then. Thanks for lunch.'

'Do you want to come up for a coffee? There's a critique I have of Larkin, an essay I did at university. You might find it helpful.'

Lisa hesitated. His insights on Larkin had been very helpful. For years afterwards she would think to herself: *If only. If only I had told him to bring it into school on Monday. If only I had been the dutiful daughter I pretended to be and gone back to the library to carry on studying.* Stupid, stupid fool.

She'd shrugged. 'Yeah, why not, thanks.' Had she been aware of the danger? Was there any warning of what was to come? She was sure there wasn't but nonetheless she'd never stopped blaming herself since. If she were honest, she was flattered. He was an adult; a teacher and he was interested in what she had to say. He listened attentively to her vocalising her tentative thoughts about life, the universe and everything. What an idiot. Lisa cringed at the thought of her younger self.

She never did get the promised critique.

Chapter Sixteen

It DIDN'T TAKE LONG for Ian and Ros to spot Emilia. 'Em, wait for us,' Ros called. Em slowed down long enough for them to catch up with her.

'Where are you going?' asked Ian.

'Mind your own business.'

Ros nudged her. 'Come on, Em. Don't be like that.'

Emilia put her head down and carried on. Ros walked along beside her, pleading. 'Look sis, we ought to stick together. You don't know who's out here. I think Mum is as good as alone in the house. Dad's disappeared in a huff and Ollie's no use to her with his foot the way it is. We have to get back. She could be in danger.' Emilia slowed down and Ros pushed her advantage. 'Please, Em. Think how you'd feel if anything happened.'

She'd gone too far. Emilia's pretty face was screwed up with disdain.

'Why should I feel anything? It isn't me who's caused this crisis. All of you, you're to blame.'

Ros shook her head. 'I don't understand. What have we

done? You keep hinting at things and throwing accusations about. Why not tell us?'

'I've already told you. Mum and Dad were arguing about that George guy. And Mum didn't give a straight answer when she came in a few minutes ago. And she'd been crying.'

'Are you sure? I didn't notice.'

Em came to a standstill. 'Ros, you never notice anything unrelated to you. It doesn't mean she wasn't crying. And that was because Dad had found her out.'

Ros breathed deeply, trying not to be too offended by the comment about her being self-obsessed. She'd come back to it later. What mattered now was getting Em to see some sense about Mum.

'Jesus Christ, Em. Talk about mountains and molehills. You're jumping to conclusions. Mum would never betray Dad. They've been together for ever. You know that. I mean, for fuck's sake, there's never been anyone else for either of them.'

Em set off again. 'Not true, I'm afraid.'

'What the hell do you mean?'

'You don't want to know.'

'You know what, Em. I don't. If there's something they're not telling us, then that's their business.'

'There's more to it. It's complicated.'

Ros grabbed her arm and pulled her round so they were facing each other. 'I am totally, utterly fucking fed up with you and this hinting at some dreadful secret. You've been in a foul mood since you got here: moping around, eating, not eating. Why can't you be fucking normal like the rest of us?'

The look on Em's face was frightening, a mixture of pity and triumph. Ros had never seen anything like it before. Emilia nodded at Ian. 'Do you want to tell her or shall I?'

Lisa went over to the living room window. It was single glazed and coated in a thin layer of frost. The fire had gone out again and the temperature had lowered; it must be several degrees below freezing outside. She hadn't seen frost on the window since she was a very young child. She pressed her hand against the window and watched as the ice melted leaving a hand shaped hole. The only thing visible was snow. Blinding snow. There was no sign of her family. Numb from cold and the frost in her soul, she moved away from the window. She set a fire and lit it. She wasn't going to freeze even if they did. For several minutes she sat in front of it once it was lit, watching the dancing flames. She was exhausted, drained of energy. Sleep. She had to sleep. Em had left her duvet on the sofa. Lisa fell onto it and gathered the duvet around her, relishing the warmth and allowed herself to drift off. Thinking about the past had exhausted her. She'd deal with all her worries later.

When she woke up, she couldn't think where she was. It was so dark. For a moment or two, she lay motionless as, bit by bit, the horrors of the day came back to her. She fumbled on the side table until she found the lamp hoping the electricity had come back on but no luck. Were the others here? She hoped so; it was so dark it must be after four. She listened but heard nothing. Christ, the countryside was quiet. The silence frightened her; where were the sounds of traffic, of people arguing, of music being played too loud? It was like the end of the world. She didn't want to be here alone with only Ollie, out for the count upstairs.

The fire did little to diffuse the darkness, which was dense in a way it never was in towns. In towns there are streetlamps, car headlights, discreet lamps illuminating nearby houses. At the Warren there was none of that; she was surrounded by a suffocating, velvet blackness lifted only by the flickering flames of the fire. She pushed the duvet off and stood up, stretching her arms out to feel her way over to the window, wincing as she tripped over something on the floor, a shoe? When she reached something and felt ice, she knew it was the window, but although she looked out, she saw nothing but the reflection of the fire. She'd hoped for some light from the moon, but it hadn't yet risen. Straining her eyes, there was something, a faint pinprick, perhaps a couple of hundred yards away. Someone was on their way home, led by the poor light of a mobile phone.

Thank goodness for the fire. Now she had to find the way to the kitchen where the candles and the matches were. How stupid to go to sleep without making provision for this. She should have had a torch beside her.

She walked forward, visualising the layout of the room as she did so. It wasn't a huge room but there were many obstacles to get past. Most of them lined the walls, though so it wasn't too hard to make her way to the door into the hall. Once there, she moved slowly forward, stifling a scream when she felt something soft on her hands. The coat stand rattled before falling over. Damn, now she had an extra obstacle to overcome. Come on, she told herself, it's only a few feet to the kitchen. She shuffled forward, felt the door in front of her and laughed out loud in relief. She pushed it open and went into the kitchen. On the worktop near the back door, that's where the candles were. The ones in the living room were burned down to stubs.

Her hands moved along the surface of the worktop. Ugh, something sticky. Jam probably or marmalade from breakfast. Trust Ros not to clean up properly. She wiped her hands on her jeans. Once there was light, she'd wash it off. Where

were the candles and matches? They must be here somewhere. She sighed, a sound that was immediately echoed
somewhere in the room. Perhaps Oliver had got up when she
was engrossed in Em's diary, but she'd heard him snoring
when she was out in the hallway, and anyway, he'd have said
something. Her voice trembled. 'Ollie, is that you?'

No reply. Shit. There was someone else breathing in the
room. Or was it her own breathing, louder because she was so
nervous? She held her breath and counted to ten. Nothing.
Lisa exhaled slowly. But there it was again, a snuffling noise.
Damn it. Where were those candles? Her fingers stretched
out, searching. At last! She grabbed the box. She could have
cried she was so grateful to have found them. The matches
should be nearby, but she couldn't find them. The range was
lit. If she managed to open its main door without burning
herself, she'd be able to light them. She turned round to face
where she thought the range was. The dark was disorienting,
and it was with trepidation she started on the journey across
the kitchen. The table was straight ahead, a foot or so away.
She edged round it, fingers tracing its shape, past the chairs.
Watch out! Don't trip over. She was almost there when she
sensed a presence. No, it wasn't that, it was more than
sensing someone, she smelled him. Body odour, cigarette
smoke, the stink of someone who hadn't washed for some
time. It was strong and foul, and she wasn't imagining it. She
opened her mouth and screamed.

'Now isn't the time or place, Emilia.' Ian's voice was hard, his
face unreadable.

Ros stared at him. 'What aren't you telling me?' Her
heart was battering at her chest. What a fucking idiot she

was. Em and Ian were an item, that's why Em had been so odd about him, why Ian had resisted her. 'How long?' she asked.

'How long what? What are you on about?'

''You're seeing each other, or you were. That's why you're so off with me. When did it start?'

'Oh, for fuck's sake, Rosalind. Not everything is about sex.' Em turned and started marching back to the house. Ros looked at Ian. He was pale and strained. His face immobile. 'Are you going to tell me or not?'

He shook his head. 'Not now. We need to go after her.'

It was always the same. Emilia pulling some stunt to make everyone feel guilty. Everyone dancing to her tune as usual. Ian had already set off and Ros had to jog to keep up with him. When she did draw level with him, he didn't look at her, but kept on walking, still with that unreadable expression.

They were almost at the house before they caught up with Emilia. She ignored them both, her head down. There was no welcoming glimmer of candles, which was worrying. Darkness had fallen and Ros couldn't imagine her mother sitting there with no comforting light though she consoled herself with the fact she'd said she was going to bed. But surely Dad ought to be back by now? Instinctively she quickened her pace, something wasn't right. A scream rang out in the air.

'That's Mum,' cried Em and started to run. They slipped and slithered over the snow that was now compacted in places from all the to-ing and fro-ing. Somehow, they managed to stay upright. Ros threw open the back door and pointed her phone into the kitchen. Its light was fading, and she saw nothing.

'Mum? Mum, are you alright?'

'I'm OK. I'm by the table. Bring that phone over here so we can find some matches.'

'What happened?' Her father had come into the house behind her. He pushed past Ros into the kitchen, switching on his torch as he did so. He found matches and lit some candles.

'I don't know,' said Lisa. 'I thought there was someone here. There was a stink of body odour and cigarette smoke.'

'Are you sure?' said Ros.

'Yes. You must be able to smell it?'

Ros sniffed the air as did everyone else. But there was nothing except the clean, cold smell of freshly fallen snow.

Lisa was baffled. She'd swear someone had been in the kitchen with her. There had been that smell – a horrible stench of unwashed body, the sound of someone breathing. Yet now no-one else smelled anything and she couldn't either. No-one else had seen anything. It was dark, of course, so perhaps whoever it was had slipped out past them all. David found the matches and lit several candles that he placed around the kitchen. Out in the hallway there was scuffling followed by a stream of curses from Ollie. Lisa pushed her way past the others and made her way to the hall as the front door slammed.

'Did you see him? Do you know who it is?'

Ollie looked round at her, his eyes wide with fear. 'What? Who? I didn't see anyone. Some idiot left the door open though.' His voice stalled. 'Do you think someone's been in here?'

'I don't know,' admitted Lisa. 'I was sure I smelled

someone in the kitchen, but whoever or whatever it was, it's gone. The others didn't pick up anything.'

'Should we go and look? If anyone's been sniffing around, they'll have left footprints.'

There was nothing but a mess of melted snow at the doorway. Too many people had been in and out to distinguish anything. Lisa moved out, but it was impossible to make anything out in the darkness. Wet seeped through her slippers prompting her to go back inside.

Lisa was shaking with cold and fear. Everything around her was collapsing: her son was in grave danger; one of her daughters hated her, thought she was a liar; and her husband believed she was having an affair. It was time to face up to things. They needed to talk, to get everything out in the open. She went into the kitchen to face her family.

'Tomorrow is Christmas Day,' she said, 'and I want...' She swallowed, close to tears. She started again. 'I want us to be happy and yet we're not. It's clear to me there's something badly wrong in this family. We need to talk.'

Ian stepped forward. Lisa blinked. She'd forgotten about him.

'I should go,' he said. 'There's clearly so much for you to talk about. I'm intruding. I shouldn't have come here.' His voice tailed off.

Lisa hesitated. 'How will you get back?'

He shrugged. 'The way I came I expect.'

'I can't let you go out in that.'

Lisa expected him to argue but he shrugged and said, 'Yes, you're right. It doesn't look good, does it? I'll keep out of everyone's way.'

'Yes, that would be best. You can share Ollie's room. There's a spare bed in there.'

'I think I'll go out for a while.'

'But...'

'But what?'

'Well, you know, there's an escaped criminal out there.'

'Mrs Truett, I practise martial arts, Aikido. I'll be fine. A good walk will clear my head.'

She wasn't convinced but he had his mind set on it. 'Well, we'll be eating around eight so make sure you're back by then. And, be careful.'

They made their way into the living room and sat down. David lit the candles. Before she said anything, Emilia spoke, her voice brimming with scorn.

'So, you're going to come clean at last. It's about time you told us.'

'Tell us what? Oh God, Mum you're not pregnant, are you?' This from Ros.

Lisa was reeling from the venom in Emilia's voice, but she had to deal with Ros first. 'No Rosalind, I'm not pregnant.' She looked at Emilia squinting to see her in the dim light. 'What are you talking about, Emilia?'

'What am I talking about? I'm talking about what you kept from us all these years. Guess what, folks. Mum's parents, surprise, surprise, didn't die in a car crash all those years ago.'

David looked at Lisa, bewildered. 'Is this true, Lisa?'

Lisa stumbled over to the sofa, her legs only half supporting her. Emilia couldn't be doing this. She sounded so, so *vicious*. Lisa was light-headed, as if she weren't in her body at all. She sat down, mouth open, the words of denial already there. But there was no point. Em had already met him, and, from the sound of it, he had already poisoned her mind.

'The letter from my father? You met him.'

Emilia's eyes opened wide. 'You've been going through my things?'

Lisa didn't reply. What she'd done was unforgiveable but what was done was done. But Emilia wasn't expecting a reply. 'Yes, I met him. Shall I tell them what he told me?'

Chapter Seventeen

It had been her secret for so long and now it was going to come out. Lisa was dizzy with shock, her face wet with tears. 'This is my story, Emilia. I'll tell it. You think you know everything but believe me, you don't.' The words were bitter in her mouth. She sat down on the nearest chair and fixed Emilia in her gaze. 'So, my father told you the whole story, did he? Everything?'

Emilia didn't flinch from her glare. 'If you mean the baby, then yes, he did. Unless there's more?'

Lisa felt, rather than saw, their shock. She couldn't look at them, didn't want them to see her shame. Her head lowered, voice barely audible, she began her story, ignoring the exclamations coming from Ros.

'Please, let me speak. I hoped I would never have to tell you this. There's so much you don't know.'

'And whose fault is that? You haven't exactly been honest, have you?'

Lisa ignored Emilia and carried on. 'You already know Dad and I met at school. What you don't know, is my parents didn't approve. To put it mildly. They were old, much older than the parents of my friends and very strict.' Her voice was shaky, and she paused to take a breath. 'It's pretty common today for some women to wait until they're forty or over to have their children but this was the nineteen sixties where life began at forty, once the children had grown up. My mother was forty-four when I was born, my father forty-two. I was their only child and they had little understanding of me. They were also very religious, or so they claimed. A God-fearing couple. They hated modern life, things like television and pop music. I remember when Boy George appeared for the first time. I was thirteen, thought he was wonderful. An abomination, they said, a sin against God.' She stopped for a second, remembering the row when they discovered she had bought one of his records. She'd been playing it on the old-fashioned radiogram when they were out but had forgotten to put it back in her room. Her father had snapped the disc in two. She should tell her family, but no, it was best not to digress.

'They stopped me seeing your father. The pretext was they wanted me to go to Oxford and I needed to study but in fact it was because his mother was a Catholic. Sometimes I managed to sneak away to see him.' She risked a glance at David, but his face was rigid. She guessed what he was thinking – about how they had never slept together until they met again, how the baby couldn't be his. She sighed. 'Every Saturday, I went to the Mitchell Library to study. It was pretty much the only time they allowed me out. There was this bloke, a student teacher, he used to hang around there.' David stiffened. He must be thinking about the conversation they'd had earlier.

'He talked to me as if I were an adult. I thought he was

interested in me as a person. I was flattered.' She paused before the words burst out of her. 'I was a fucking idiot!'

Ros broke the silence, her voice small. 'So, the child wasn't Dad's then?'

She shook her head. 'No. I never told anyone what happened. My parents nagged me constantly, assuming it was David's. I told them over and over it wasn't, but they didn't believe me. They wanted to press charges because I was only fifteen, but I said if they did, I'd make sure I failed all my exams so they backed off. I never managed to convince them it wasn't him.' She stopped. 'This is all... I'm finding this difficult.'

'Go on,' said David. His voice was flat, cold. It would have been better to tell him years ago, but she'd been so devastated by what had happened, each time she tried she couldn't bear to talk about it. What if he had blamed her? She would have been alone in the world. Someone once told her no good ever comes of secrets, they always come out in the end. Turns out it was true after all.

'We moved. One Saturday I awoke to find a removal van outside. They had rented a house near Largs and put our house in Glasgow up for sale without telling me. They were desperate to hide my pregnancy. When we got to Largs, I wasn't allowed to go to school.' There was a chocolate stain on the sofa cushion, someone must have dropped a piece and it had melted, then hardened again. She picked at it until it was gone, flicking the tiny pieces onto the floor.

'I was kept in my room, out of sight of everyone except the home tutors they arranged for me. My mother sat in on the lessons to ensure I didn't tell them what was going on. About the daily prayer sessions they'd forced on me, about how when I'd refused to kneel one day, she'd beaten me until my father stopped her. I was a prisoner. Only when it was exam time did I get to go out. I had to go to the local school to sit my exams. I wasn't known there. I had to endure stares and sniggers, catcalls as I walked along the road with my mother.' Lisa would never forget how it had been. Her mother's face red with fury as they went past a local park where a group of teenage girls lingered every day for as long as the exams lasted, to shout insults and jeer.

'The baby was due in July. They booked me into a private clinic for the birth and, without me knowing, contacted a private adoption agency. I begged them to think again. Times had changed – girls my age normally kept their babies with the help of their parents – but they wouldn't consider that. They wanted rid of their shame. I had no-one to support me.' Lisa closed her eyes thinking back to the endless rows, how they made her pray for forgiveness, kneeling on the floor while they berated her. 'I suppose one advantage for them of keeping me away from school, is that there was no one to report my underage pregnancy to the authorities. I had no ante-natal care, nothing. I think they hoped I'd miscarry.'

'But what about the clinic? They must have known your age there.' Oliver said.

'Money often buys discretion. As I said, it was privately run. They were kind at the clinic, or at least, one nurse was. She saw how frightened I was, comforted me throughout labour. She allowed me to see my son before he was taken away. A quick peep, one cuddle and he was gone for ever.' She stopped unable to continue. Although it happened forty years ago, the pain as she recalled that time felt like it was enough to kill her. She got up and left the room.

Ros stood up to go after her mother, but her father stopped her. 'Leave it, Ros.'

'Are you happy now?' Ros turned on Em, spitting out the words. 'How could you do that to her? Can't you see how upset she is? You're supposed to be the empathetic one. Dad, tell her. Don't let her get away with this.'

Her father was staring blankly into the fire. 'I can't believe it. Why didn't she tell me?'

'For fuck's sake! She was fifteen. Fifteen. And he was a teacher.'

He looked up. 'Yes, and he was here earlier today. He came round to say he recognised your mum and she lied when I asked her about it. She lied.'

Ros frowned at him. 'It sounds as though you're angrier with Mum than with him, Dad. He was older than her, in a position of trust. It's abuse.' She hadn't fully taken in what he'd said. 'Wait a minute, what do you mean he was here earlier?'

'Is it that guy who was here yesterday?' asked Em. 'The one who was leering at me?'

David ignored her. 'I have to talk to her. Find out exactly what happened. I was sure something had gone on between them.'

'Can someone please explain to me what's going on. I'm lost. Between whom, Dad?' said Oliver.

'That bastard, the one who was here. No wonder she didn't want him near.'

'Who are you talking about?' said Ollie.

'You were in bed,' said Em when it was clear their father wasn't going to answer. 'This couple dropped in and were having coffee with Mum and Dad and the bloke kept staring at me, said I reminded him of someone. Now I think of it, Mum looked a bit shaken.'

Ros sighed. 'You are the limit, aren't you? You've opened a can of worms here. What are you going to do now? Search out this bloke and tell him he has a son?'

'He has a right to know.'

'I think he already does.' Their mother had come back into the room.

'What makes you think that?'

She sat down and put her head in her hands. 'Things he's said in the past couple of days, insinuations. God, is it only two days?'

'Like what?'

'It doesn't matter...'

Em's mouth was tight. 'I think—'

'Well, stop then,' said Ros. 'We don't care what you think. The guy's obviously a creep. You're the one who's meant to be a feminist, to be all for women's rights. Can't you see how upset Mum is?'

Her two girls were fighting. About feminism of all things. At any other time, she would have laughed. Ros, who never had a feminist thought in her life, Em, who could tell you the details of every women's rights abuse case over the past year, who was passionate about them all. But it was Ros who was sticking up for her. Ros put her arm around her.

'Tell us what happened, Mum. You haven't told us everything, have you?'

It was time. She'd repressed this for years, most of her life. 'I was raped.'

'Raped? But you went willingly with him, you said you were flattered,' said David.

Lisa turned on him, spitting out the words. 'And that is

exactly why all these years I have denied this to myself. Yes, I went to his flat willingly but not with the intention of having sex. And yes, I was flattered, but I thought he wanted to continue our conversation.'

It was all coming back, memories overwhelming her. As she told them about what had happened, she saw her silly fifteen-year-old self, felt the excitement when he'd said, 'My flat is over there.' A teacher was taking a real interest in her. He thought she was important, clever. At one point on the way to his flat, he'd said, 'You know, I think you're the most intelligent girl I've ever met. You have an analytical mind. You'll shine at university.'

It wasn't a flat but a bedsit. It was shabbier than she'd imagined: a large room with a bed recess where there was a raised mattress with some grubby looking bedding spread across it. There was only one chair that he took so she sat on the edge of the bed, trying not to touch the filthy sheets. A smell of unwashed bodies rose from the bed as she sat down. God knows when he'd last changed the bed linen. He took out a book from his bookcase that was three short planks of wood supported on two piles of bricks and sat beside her.

She wasn't comfortable. He was too close and there was a strange smell coming from him, not body odour, but something musty. She shifted slightly and said she had to go.

'Not yet,' he said, stroking her hair. 'I'll make some coffee.'

Uneasy, she shrugged him off. 'I have to go.'

He kissed her. She was so shocked, she let him. He must have taken this as a sign because he pushed her back on the bed and climbed on top of her. She struggled. She cried. She said 'no' over and over again, but he pulled down her pants, so easily accessible because she was wearing a short skirt. It was her fault she told herself. She'd put temptation in his way, something her mother had said to her whenever she tried to leave the house wearing 'unsuitable' clothing.

Lisa stopped talking. Em looked ashamed, she noted. Well, good. Although her heart was in the right place, she was always too quick to judge.

'You were raped,' she said, subdued.

'It took me a long time to accept it, but yes, I was.'

'Why didn't you tell your parents?'

Lisa scoffed. 'I... well, let me tell you a story. Before all this happened there was a lot of talk about a local girl who was raped. Do you remember, David? It was all over the local paper. She was followed home and dragged into a little copse of trees about a hundred yards or so from her house. A knife was held to her throat, and he made her fellate him before he raped her anally. I heard my parents talking about it, all shock and horror. They had no sympathy for the girl. They went on about how awful it was for the parents, how she should have tried harder to stop him. I was horrified, started to argue with them but they were adamant. "She was only a few yards from home," my father said. "If she'd wanted to, she would have escaped and got away." Lisa regarded the shocked faces of her family with a wry smile. 'So, you see, I couldn't have told them. They didn't believe that poor girl. Can you imagine how they would have reacted to my story? I was asking for it. Where were the bruises, the cuts. Why hadn't I stopped him?'

'That's horrendous,' said Em. 'Why on earth did they think like that?'

'It was a different time, and they were a different generation from the parents of my friends. And they were religious, too. Presbyterian, all hell fire and little redemption. Rape in those days was very hard to prove. That hasn't changed. The idea that "no means no" is relatively new. It was only real rape if you were savagely beaten, preferably by a stranger. Your teacher pouncing on you in his bedsit, which you had willingly entered, did not count. Nobody would have believed me.'

'But it was statutory rape,' said Em. 'And if you'd told someone in authority, his career would have been finished before it started whether you were willing or not.'

'I didn't know that then. In those days, rape victims were shamed in the witness box. There were intrusive questions, slurs on character. Perhaps if I had more understanding parents, I might have coped but I don't know. I mean, I blamed myself for years for what happened so how could I expect anyone else to understand.'

'And the baby?' asked David.

Lisa took a deep breath. This was something she'd never spoken of to anyone. She closed her eyes so she didn't have to see their faces. 'Shortly after the baby was taken to be adopted, he died.'

Em shook her head. 'No. It's not true.'

Ros looked at her, her mouth open. 'Why don't you shut the fuck up?'

Her mother flushed deep red. She was near to tears. 'I'm afraid it is. My parents told me two weeks later. A cot death.' Her voice trembled. 'That's why I never said anything. If he had lived, I would have tried to find him. But as he had died... I didn't want to relive that part of my life. I left home as soon as I was able and cut off any contact with my parents. I never forgave them for putting my son up for adoption. I was sure he had died because he wasn't with me, his mother.'

Silence fell as everyone tried to process what they'd

heard. Ros thought she'd never seen her mother look so sad. Her father, too, looked devastated. Em sat nibbling at her fingernails, a return to her childhood years and one that showed how nervous she was. She was building up to saying something, Ros could tell. At last, she spoke.

'Mum, there's more to it than that.'

'Emilia! For heaven's sake. You heard what your mother said. Have some respect.' Her father was furious, angrier than they'd seen him for years. He moved towards their mother, as if to comfort her, but she turned away. Em half covered her face with her hands, muttering, 'I'm sorry.' Her father continued to glare at her. Ros put a comforting arm round her. Em wouldn't hurt anyone deliberately. She might do it accidentally but never, never would she mean it. Ros spoke up. 'I think we should hear what Em has to say. She obviously knows something, and we need to hear it.'

Emilia looked over at her mother. 'OK,' said Lisa. 'Go on.'

'Oh Jesus, what have I started?' Em took a shaky breath. Her voice wobbled as she started. 'Look, Mum. I'm sorry I said all those things. I've been a complete bitch.' No one disagreed. 'I, well your father contacted me after I'd written something in the *Herald*. He said he thought we might be related, and he wanted to meet me. I was excited. A grandfather I didn't know about. You know how I miss Mumps and Grumps...'

'You never said,' said her father. 'I thought you'd forgotten them.'

'No, never. I know I was only a child when they died but they were such fun... I'll never forget them.' She paused for a second before continuing. 'So anyway, I arranged to meet him. He asked if I would go down to Largs as he had difficulty travelling these days.'

'Well yes, he must be well into his nineties now if he were forty-two when Mum was born.'

'He's ninety-six, told me repeatedly. He talked a lot. He's in a care home. Apparently, his wife died last year, and he couldn't manage by himself so he moved into the home. As I said, he talked. He said you'd fallen out with them many years ago. You'd had a baby – "out of wedlock" was the term he used – and they'd found it hard to forgive you, so you left home and cut off all contact with them. He had wanted to contact you, but your mother... well, she was adamant it was up to you.'

Ros watched Mum. She flinched when Em said her mother was dead. She was pale and the little lines round her eyes had deepened, ageing her. She was struggling not to cry. How awful it must be for her, all of this. Having your past brought up in front of your children, your husband. And hearing of the death of your mother in that way, it must be painful. At least Ian wasn't here. All this dirty linen, in public. It would be too much.

Ian knocked at the door before coming in. He took in the atmosphere and started to retreat. 'I'm sorry. It looks like I'm interrupting something.'

Lisa nodded, half smiling. 'We're having a bit of a family crisis, as you know so...'

'Stay,' said Em.

'No!' said David. 'This is not something to be discussed in front of strangers. If you don't mind, Ian. It would be much better if you left.'

Ian had his hand on the doorknob. 'Of course. I... I'll be in the kitchen.' He left before anyone else said anything.

David rounded on Em. 'How stupid are you? I'm sorry Emilia. I know you're not feeling great today, but your behaviour is—'

'I know, I know. I don't know what I'm doing, I'm all over the place.' She broke down, started to sob.

Lisa jumped up and went over to her. She hugged her close. 'It's all right, darling. It's all right.'

The sobs lessened. 'Sorry, everyone.' She glanced at her mother. 'Is it OK to go on?'

Lisa patted her. 'Yes.'

Em sniffed. 'He talked a lot about how he wanted to contact you. He'd found out where we lived, knew about us, though he didn't know our names. Every so often he'd asked Sadie, your mother, if he could write but she always said no.'

Lisa nodded. 'That sounds about right. She always was the more domineering one.'

'Then she died. He was sad... they'd been married for over seventy years, but he said something they'd done kept playing on his mind. He wanted to make it right before he died.'

'Go on.'

'He said that after the baby was adopted, Sadie became obsessed about you going after him. She'd said that you'd never let him go, it would ruin your life,' Em took a deep breath. 'They lied to you when they said he was dead. They lied, Mum.'

She couldn't breathe, couldn't take this in. Someone was asking if she was alright, Rosalind? Emilia? She couldn't tell. He can't be alive, he can't. They'd been so definite. Took her into her room, sat her down and they were... they were sympathetic. As much as they could be. The adoption agency had phoned, they said. Her heart had leapt at those words, perhaps they'd changed their mind. Perhaps she was going to get her baby back. But no, the couple who'd adopted the baby had been in touch but not to say they'd changed their minds. The baby had died. They had gone into his room and found him stiff and cold in his cot. Lisa didn't cry. She wasn't going to cry in front of them. She stopped herself from saying anything at all, although what she wanted to say was, 'This is your fault'. And now, years and years later when the hardest pain had gone, when sometimes she was able to persuade herself none of this had happened, it was back. She wanted time alone to think, but first, she had a question for Emilia. 'Why didn't you tell me?'

Emilia was biting her lower lip, a tic that over the years Lisa had learned meant she was frightened or nervous. Lisa tried again. 'Why didn't you tell me?'

'Your father said he'd tried to find out what had happened to the baby. This was after your mother died. He felt it was unfinished business. But because he couldn't get out much, he wasn't getting anywhere with the search. He had intended to write to you directly but feared you'd throw the letter into the bin unread.'

'He was right,' said Lisa. What he'd done was unforgiveable.

'Then he saw my name on a by-line and wrote to me. When I met him, he told me the story and asked me to try to find out where your child had gone. I didn't want to say anything until I knew for sure he was alive.'

Somehow, she managed to say the words. 'And is he?'

Emilia swallowed. 'Yes.'

'So, I'm asking you again. Why didn't you tell me?' Lisa heard the hostility in her voice but couldn't control it.

'Oh God, I was going to tell you as soon as I found out, I swear I was. Your father knew who had adopted him, I don't know how, and the town where they lived. The family had lived near Largs, in Dalry but moved to Glasgow in 2001. It wasn't hard finding them. I narrowed it down to two possible families. Short of asking outright if their grown-up son was adopted, there was no way of finding out. But your father hadn't forgotten his date of birth, said it was stamped on his brain. So, I used 192.com, paid for a subscription and found him. The date of birth matched only one person. I was on my way to tell you. I was angry with you for keeping it secret and also because your father said it was your decision to go for adoption – he didn't say anything about having told you the baby died – but then Ros phoned me.'

'Oh great, blame me,' said Ros. 'You go in with a big stick, stir things right up and then when it goes wrong, pass the stick on to me. Typical.'

Em looked over at Ros. 'No one's blaming you. I don't know how I'm going to tell you this though.'

'Spit it out,' said Lisa. Her stomach was twisting with nerves.

'Ros phoned me. She was all excited, had dumped Dan, found herself a new boyfriend.'

Ros looked baffled. 'What's Ian got to do with it?'

'As soon as she told me his name, I knew I couldn't say anything to you.'

'Ian,' said Lisa. 'Ian is my son.' She got up from her chair and stumbled across the room. She'd been sitting so long, her knee had stiffened. She ignored the cries of *are you alright, where are you going*. She wasn't alright and had no idea where she was going but she had to get away.

Chapter Eighteen

Ros SAT motionless on the sofa. What the fuck? Ian was her half-brother. She whispered the words to herself, disbelieving, but the horrible fact didn't go away. Jesus. What had she been thinking? It was disgusting, gross. Emilia should have told her at once. God, what a fool she'd been, fawning over her *half-brother*. It was, it was... she didn't have words for it. She let out a soft groan. Em put out a hand to comfort her. The last straw. Ros turned on her.

'You are such a total fucking bitch. I don't understand you. For the past two days you've been making snide comments about everyone having secrets, and you, you've been going behind everyone's back, poking at things that don't concern you.' She shook her head. 'I don't know who you are anymore.'

Emilia drew back from her, her shocked expression showing Ros had hit the mark. Good. She deserved it.

'Sit down, Ros. This isn't the time for recriminations. You're not the only one who's shocked.'

'But, Dad, she—'

He shook his head. 'Be quiet, Ros. This is not Emilia's fault. Nor is it your mother's. That bastard...' he tailed off. Ros was unsure whether he was talking about George or her grandfather. Both had a lot to answer for.

Oliver looked up, his face pale with shock. 'What about Ian? Shouldn't we tell him?'

'I don't know. I think Mum has to decide,' said Dad. The door opened. It was Ian, his face red. 'I'm... I don't know what to say. I was in the kitchen. I heard it all. I'm sorry.'

No one said anything. Ian stood in the doorway looking lost. Oliver beckoned him in, but he hesitated. Ros frowned. 'You knew all along, didn't you?'

He came over and sat beside her. 'I'm so sorry, Ros. I didn't want to hurt you. I heard someone was making enquiries about me and I was curious. I'd always wondered about my birth parents, about contacting them, and so I wanted to find out who was poking about, if it was perhaps one of them. One of my friends works in Farfalle, and he mentioned you one night, Ros, so I decided I'd try to get to know you... as a way to the rest of the family. I didn't think for a second you'd be attracted to me.'

Ros held out her right hand, palm forward. 'Stop right there. That's over, gone. Eew, gross. Never happened.' Inwardly she was dying, mortified but she had to make a case. 'You're way too old for me.' She caught the look of sympathy in her sister's eye and glared at her, defiant.

He caught on straightaway. 'Oh shit, I'm sorry. Oh... that's me. Always socially inept, always getting the signals wrong.'

No one responded then Dad jumped in with, 'So, you got to know Ros to try to get to your mother? Why didn't you go through the normal channels?' His voice was cold. It would take time to win him round.

'Oh God, what can I say? I was desperate to know about my background. As soon as I was allowed, I looked up my adoption records. I wanted to contact Lisa straightaway but then my adoptive father died unexpectedly and my mum, well, she was devastated, and I decided it wasn't the right time.'

'That must have been years ago,' said Ros. She wasn't convinced by this. As far as she remembered, in Scotland adopted children were allowed to access their records at the age of sixteen. One of her friends had done so when they were in S5. Ian was in his late thirties now, so he'd been sixteen over twenty years ago. Why wait until now? Ian looked uncomfortable at the question, but she wasn't going to give up. 'Well?' she demanded.

Ian sighed. 'This is going to make me sound petty,' he said. 'But after my father died, I was in a bad place. I'd always known I was adopted. It was never a secret. When I told them I was going to try to find my birth parents, my dad was upset.' He paused for a second to control himself. 'I was sixteen. You know what teenagers are like, they know it all.' This last comment he directed at Ros's father, who gave a barely imperceptible nod.

He carried on. 'Dad didn't want me to look into it. I was too young, he said. He wanted me to wait. We argued. I ignored his advice and went ahead.'

'Your parents didn't support your wishes?' said Em.

'It's more complicated than that. Once they knew I was determined, they gave me their blessing. I got the records. They were a bit of a shock to be honest.'

'In what way?' David's voice wasn't any warmer. It was going to take a lot for him to come round.

'She was so young. Younger than I am now. And no father was mentioned.' He didn't say anything else.

Ros bristled. He had judged her mother, seen her as a young feckless girl or worse. Worthless. How dare he? Her temper was up but before she could say anything, Ian carried on with his tale.

'I felt awful for her. The notes said she was highly intelligent, an Oxbridge candidate. I didn't know what to do. I was torn. I desperately wanted to meet her, but how would she feel? For all I knew, she had a glittering career that could be ruined by the sudden appearance of an adopted child. I had decided to wait, but then my dad had a heart attack. He died.'

No one spoke for several seconds. Ros was first to break the silence. 'What happened then?'

'I blamed myself. We'd had many rows over my decision to look at my adoption records. I'd caused him so much stress, so I never mentioned the possibility of looking for my mother again. My adoptive mother was relieved, I think, and never brought up the subject either.'

'What does she think now?'

'She's dead. Died a year ago, from cancer.'

'I'm sorry to hear that,' said Ros's father. 'What I don't understand though, is why you came uninvited to this house.'

'I was genuinely worried about Ros. I tried phoning her mobile but couldn't get through and I thought I'd come and check she'd got here OK. The main roads were fine all the way to Bamburgh. It's only after there it gets bad.'

'Hmm.' David wasn't convinced.

'I'd hoped to be invited for Christmas because I thought, over a few days I'd get to know you all better and...' he tailed off. Ros put him out of his misery. 'OK, I'm sorry. You don't all need to pretend on my behalf. I'm an idiot but I am so over you now. So, let's get on with the story.'

Emilia took over. 'I didn't know what was going on. It

was obvious you were attracted to him. It's easy to see why. If I hadn't known, I might have made the same mistake. But I didn't trust him, I was terrified he might make a move on you, so I thought it was best if I was rude about him, hoped you might take the hint. In retrospect, I realise it would have been better to have come clean, but it wasn't my story to tell. Mum had to know first, and I didn't know how to tell her. I'm so ashamed of myself but I was angry with her for keeping such an important thing secret. I should have known better.'

Ros nodded. 'What a mess. Where are you going, Dad?'

'I'm going to make your mother a cup of tea and then I have to speak to her. Emilia isn't the only one to have messed up here. I need to sort things out.'

Lisa grabbed the first coat to hand, a large jacket of David's and shoved it on, zipping it up. One of Em's scarves was also hanging there, and she wrapped it round her neck. It was cold out here in the hall, so God knows what it would be like outside. Her walking boots were by the door. They'd be the best things for the snow. David always kept gloves in his pocket, so she hauled them out and put them on. She opened the door quietly and slipped out, not caring who might be out there waiting.

She switched on her torch. Above her, the stars were showing off, billions of them, sequins shimmering in the black velvet sky. She took a moment to find Orion, and then the Plough, tracing their outlines as she always did. Her knowledge of astronomy was limited to them, the north star and Venus. She walked down the driveway, her breath misting in the freezing air and paused at the gate to look back at the house. It looked so welcoming, candles shimmering in the window, but she wanted to be alone.

It was dangerous out here. Someone was out to get at her family, but she didn't care. In fact, she'd relish a fight. She looked round for a stick to use as a weapon. If anyone came near her, she'd whack them. But the only sticks there were, wouldn't hurt a fly. She ought to turn back, speak to her family, to her son. She stopped dead in her tracks. Dear God, he was alive? It was unbelievable and impossible to process. She'd accepted his death years ago, had stopped crying over it, had moved on and now – what? Her parents had done this unspeakable thing. It was worse than she had imagined. They were monsters, both of them. How could anyone do this to their own child? It was incomprehensible. No, she couldn't go back to the house; she had to work out what to do by herself. Her overwhelming feeling was anger. Rage at how she'd been deprived of her child for all these years. If her father were in front of her now... Well, he wasn't, she had to cope as best she could. The cold air would help her think more clearly. She pushed against the snow piled up against the gate and started to walk.

Her father had been a quiet man, never given to saying much. Lisa was surprised when Emilia said how he'd never stopped talking. Now, for the first time, she wondered why he was so quiet. Her mother probably never gave him much chance to speak. And when he did, she was quick to put him down – *stop fussing, Arthur*, she'd say if he asked her about her day at school. Lisa's education was Mother's territory, and he wasn't to interfere.

He was typically Scots in appearance. He looked a little like the actor John Laurie, the one who played Frazer in Dad's Army: tall and thin with a gaunt face filled with a large nose. He would be stooped now, his shoulders that were once so broad, hunched. Was he any happier now his wife was dead? She doubted it. He had been dour and humourless, always ready to see the worst in people, quick to judge. He professed to be a Christian, but his actions belied this. He hated Catholics with a hate born out of ignorance and nurtured in the dreich climate of the west of Scotland. He wasn't suited to being a parent. He and her mother were bemused by Lisa, the child born to them too late, twenty years after they had given up hope. Most couples would have rejoiced in this, the late fruit of their love, but no, they saw it as an affront, something sent by God to test their faith. And now he was an old man and alone in a care home. What did the workers there think about him and his lack of visitors? She was sure he wouldn't have told them he had a daughter.

And what of her mother, two years older than her father? This was an abomination to her; she had always told Lisa she was two years younger because this was the appropriate age gap for a couple. Or so she claimed. Such nonsense. Lisa had found her mother's birth certificate when she was fourteen – *Mum, it says here you were born in 1926. Are you older than Dad, then?* She hit Lisa, grabbing the birth certificate out of her hands, telling her she had been sent to try her. *Try you for what?* She asked with all the naïve cheek of a fourteen-year-old. *Lying?* She hit Lisa properly then, across her right cheek, the mark of her hand staining her face so she couldn't go out for hours.

Lisa tried to get them to love her. The only thing that ever pleased them was when she did well at school. She was clever and she worked hard, winning prizes, and with the prizes came a degree of approval, which, at times approached affection. It wasn't love. The unconditional love parents have for their children was missing.

Her mother was dead. Of course she was. She'd known it

intellectually. She would have been ninety-eight by now, and the odds had to be high that she was long gone. But it came as a shock, nonetheless. Above all, it felt unreal. Lisa said it aloud. 'Sadie Paterson is dead.' Two years gone. A long life which, no doubt, felt much longer as it was lived so joylessly. It didn't sink in. She looked down at the ground that was lit up by moonlight. There were footprints on the snow and unconsciously she had been following them. She tried to remember when she had picked them up. Not immediately, she thought. The going had been hard to begin with, she was definitely walking through virgin snow at that point. But later she had become lost in her thoughts; she didn't know when. It was impossible to remember. Lisa hesitated, considered going back, but couldn't face anyone yet. Despite the possible danger, she had to keep going.

Her mother was a woman who didn't know how to nurture, whose affection was conditional on her child doing what she wanted. Early on in, during Lisa's fumbled attempts at mothering her own children she had repeated what her mother had said to her: *You can do better than this. What's this drawing meant to be. No, you can't have a cuddle, you haven't been good today.* It didn't bear thinking about and what was worse, she didn't know what she was doing. It was David's mother who had gently pointed it out. 'Try giving them some praise. Children thrive on it. They are wonderful children, but they won't stay that way if you keep putting them down.' Lisa had been furious at the time. How dare her mother-in-law tell her what to do? But her mother-in-law was right. Lisa felt it in her gut. That evening, she cried for hours she was so ashamed. David fretted, wanting to know what was wrong but she never told him. Instead, she vowed to change. She read every book on parenting she laid her hands on. It was hard work, and for years, she caught herself on the point of comparing them unfavourably with others though she always managed to swallow the words before they could do any damage. She wondered if perhaps they'd picked up on something in those early years. She'd feared it more during the horrible years of Emilia's anorexia, reading about how it was girls who were perfectionists who became anorexic. She had been five years old before Lisa had stopped pushing her to perfection.

Last time she'd seen her mother was the day she left home. Her mother had stood over her as she packed her suitcase, her face pinched, her lips pursed in the disapproving way so typical of her.

'You'll come to no good. Mark my words. Where will you live? The streets? It's all you deserve. You're a tramp.'

Lisa had left without looking back. Every woman fears becoming their mother. And now her mother was dead. She'd been dead for two years and Lisa had hardly thought about her in that time. Surely, she must feel something, some absence. Lisa thought of her friend Anne at school whose mother had died last year. She must have given away something when consoling Anne, something must have been 'off' in what she said to her, for Anne said in a sharp voice: 'I know I was always moaning about her, about how she drove me mad, but she was my mum and I loved her to bits. And I'll never know anyone who will love and stand up for me the way she did. I'm on my own now.' Lisa stopped walking, thinking of these words. She'd never had unconditional parental love. She never would.

Chapter Nineteen

Ros WENT through to the kitchen to help her father. He was standing at the kitchen table his head lowered, his hands pressed on the table. He didn't look up.

'Are you all right, Dad?'

He was slow to respond. 'No.'

She went over to him and hugged him. 'It's all a bit of a shock, isn't it?'

He hugged her back. 'It is.'

The door opened and Ian came in. He stood by the table, looking uneasy. 'Should I try to talk to Lisa,' he said. 'Or is it best to leave it for now?'

Ros noticed her father's mouth tighten. 'I'd leave it, Ian. One of us is going to take her up a cup of tea in a few minutes.' On cue the kettle started to whistle. Ros took it off the range and looked for the teapot. 'Did you have any idea, Dad?' About what she'd been through as a teenager.'

'I knew she didn't get on with her parents. She didn't talk about them. I only met them once and they were formidable. Cold and aloof, the opposite of Mum. They found out my mother had been brought up a Catholic and they probably feared I'd infect Lisa, or Elizabeth as they called her, with popery. Both of them were very thin and austere looking. I used to call them the Paterson Goths, you know, after the Grant Wood painting?'

Em and Oliver had joined them while David was talking. 'American Gothic?' said Em. 'Yes, I know it. They didn't come after you with a pitchfork, did they?'

David laughed. 'No, but if they'd had one...'

'They sound grim,' said Ian.

'They were. I don't know what their own background was, but it couldn't have been happy. They were a miserable pair, and they didn't exactly give Lisa an easy time. After I met them, they made it very clear I wasn't good enough for her. They told her she couldn't see me, and, for a while, we met in secret, and then, without warning the whole family vanished.'

'You've never mentioned this before,' said Em. 'That must have been hard.'

'It was. But your mother made it clear she didn't want to talk about it. Ever. And I respected that.'

'So, what happened?'

'She disappeared without a word. I was hurt. Nobody knew where she'd gone. Except for the school of course, but they wouldn't tell me. It was "confidential".'

'Don't do that irritating quote marks thing, Dad,' said Ros. 'It's so last century.'

David ruffled her hair. 'OK, but only if you stop doing the Australian uprise at the end of sentences that aren't questions.'

Everyone laughed. 'It doesn't seem right to be laughing, does it?' said Ros.

'No, none of it is funny.'

Ros put out some mugs on the kitchen table. 'But she obviously reappeared at some point. At university, wasn't it? That's all she ever told me. Though I asked often enough.' She looked at Oliver and Em. 'Did she tell you anything else?'

Both of them shook their heads. 'I remember pressing her about it once,' said Em. 'All she said was that you'd been at school together and then hooked up at university.'

'Yes, we were both in first year. I was doing Geography, and she was studying English and Drama. I couldn't believe my eyes when I saw her in the library. She'd always planned to go to the Royal Academy of Music and Drama, but she decided to go to Glasgow University instead. To "keep her options open", she said. She never wanted to talk about it. She told me her parents were livid when she made it clear she wasn't going to try for Oxbridge. Instead, she left home and worked for a year to save up enough to live on at university. When I asked her about it, she said it was the worst year of her life and then clammed up.'

'That must have been hard,' said Oliver. 'For both of you.'

'Harder for Mum, I think. She had barely enough to live on but then my parents took her in at the end of first year when they realised what she meant to me. She had a part-time job all through university and insisted on giving my parents half of what she earned, even though they didn't want anything.

'That was good of them,' said Ian.

David smiled. 'They were good people. Lisa was very fragile, wouldn't talk about her parents, and they respected that, although my mother tried to persuade her to contact them. She categorically refused. it was all very difficult. And then, they died. Or so she told us.'

'How did she explain away the funeral and all the stuff

you have to do when someone dies?' asked Ros. 'I mean, when Mumps and Grumps died it took you weeks to organise everything.' Ros placed the teapot in the middle of the table.

David frowned. 'I was away at the time. On a field trip to Iceland. It lasted for two months over the summer and my parents were on holiday in Canada. They were away for over a month and your mum was left alone at home. When we came back, she told us they were dead, and she didn't want to talk about it. She told us they'd been in a car crash. Oh, and that they'd left their money to charity.' He fiddled with a mug on the table. 'My mother tried to convince her to challenge the will, but she became hysterical, said she wanted nothing from them, and, well, we never talked about it again.'

'It sounds as though Mum refused to talk about a lot of things.'

'Yes. I should have made her talk. But...'

'But what?'

'Oh, I don't know. I suppose I wanted to protect her from her past. She chose to put it behind her, and so I respected that. As did my parents. Years later, I tried to find out where she'd gone when she disappeared from school, but she became so distressed that I gave up.' He picked up the teapot and started to pour the tea, but he wasn't paying attention, and some spilled on the table. He went over to the sink to get a cloth to wipe up the mess.

'It was wrong of me to ignore it. And look where it's got us.'

'Well, you'll have to talk to her now. She must be...' Ros stopped. What must she be? Devastated? Happy? Distraught? It was impossible to imagine what she was feeling. 'Well, anyway, you have to go up and see her.'

'Yes, I will but take her up a cup of tea first. Let me know how she's doing?'

'I don't think that's a good idea. It'll be you she wants to see.'

'Please.'

Ros shrugged. She wanted to argue but he was determined. She poured out a cup of tea and set off upstairs. The hall was too dark, so she went back into the kitchen to grab a torch. That done, she edged her way up the narrow staircase. She paused outside her parents' bedroom door, praying she wouldn't interrupt her mother breaking her heart. She tapped on the door.

'Mum?' Nothing in reply. She put her ear to the door and listened. There was no sound. She tried again. When there was no reply, she opened the door quietly and crept into the room. Perhaps her mother was sleeping. She felt her way to the bed, hoping she wouldn't trip over anything. 'Mum. We've made some tea. Do you want some? Mum?'

The bed was flat; there was no one there. Ros tried the bathroom and then the other bedrooms, but her mother had vanished. She fled downstairs, bursting into the living room. 'Dad, she's not there.'

Her father raced to the hall. 'Her coat's here. She must be somewhere in the house.'

'No, I looked everywhere: in the other bedrooms, the bathroom and you can see she's not downstairs.'

David went out to the hall again, with a torch this time, and opened the door. He shone the torch on where the path would have been if it wasn't covered with snow. One lonely set of footprints showed the way to the gate. 'Shit,' he said. 'She's gone out. Alone.'

Lisa walked on in the dark, going through the events of the day in her head. Thinking about her son made her feel she was about to fall into a pit. It was too hard. Her thoughts went instead to her father, alive and wanting to see her, to make peace. She couldn't do it. The wounds, although they had been covered up for many years, persisted and they stung. The words of contempt when she discovered she was pregnant, the evenings spent going over and over the same thing: she was a slut, she had thrown away her future, David Truett should be castrated, on and on they went, broken records with no hope of repair. Lisa found saying nothing was the best idea. If she spoke back, it made things worse. One night he had hit her when she'd rashly said she'd done it to get back at them. He'd called her an ungrateful bitch and had taken his belt to her. A pregnant child. The rage was in his face, the hatred in his eyes. None of it had left her. No, she didn't want to see him again. He was from the past and he'd remain there.

The air was invigorating. They'd been inside too long, suffocating each other with the weight of their secrets. She breathed in deeply and let her mind turn to her son.

The birth had been everything it shouldn't be. Lisa was terrified. She needed someone to comfort her, she needed a mother, and instead, had this hard-faced woman who, when the nurse asked if she wanted to stay to support Lisa, had looked her up and down and said, 'I don't think so. This is her doing, and hers alone.' The nurse was shocked. 'Never mind,' she said, patting Lisa's arm as her mother left the room, 'we're better off without her.'

In spite of the midwife's warmth and encouragement, it was a long and difficult labour. She needed forceps at the end, and, to make matters worse, as if it wasn't already bad enough with her legs in stirrups like an animal about to be experimented on, a gaggle of student doctors was brought in to watch. 'You don't mind, do you?' the obstetrician asked as they gathered round. 'It's part of their course work.'

She didn't have the strength to object. She turned her face to one side and said nothing, which the doctor took for consent.

When it was over, Lisa struggled up to a seated position as they washed and weighed him. 'Can I hold my baby?'

The doctor was brusque. 'Best not.' He didn't look at her as he said this but turned to the midwife and said, 'As soon as you're done here, take him to the nursery.' So, it was a boy, no-one had said anything as he'd been born. The doctor left the room without another word.

The midwife continued to wash him. Lisa sunk back down on the bed and was crying. She'd never felt so alone in the world. She didn't hear the midwife approach the bed. 'Quick, sit up,' she whispered. 'He'll be back in a minute to do your stitches.' She handed the baby to Lisa.

'I can hold him?'

'Yes, but please be quick.'

She looked down at his face. It was red and crumpled and his head was a funny shape. The midwife must have seen the expression on her face for she said, 'Don't worry about that, it's the forceps. A couple of days and it'll be fine.'

'I won't see him then.'

The midwife squeezed Lisa's shoulder. She breathed in the new-born scent of her baby. He had dark hair, plastered to his funny shaped head by the water from being washed. His eyes opened and he looked at her. She'd heard people say of babies, 'Oh he's been here before' and had thought *what nonsense*, but now she saw what they meant. His eyes were wise as they studied her. He seemed to be saying: *Don't worry, I'll be all right, you'll be all right.* She smiled at him, and although she knew it was unlikely, he smiled back. 'I love you,' she whispered and handed him back to the midwife who had a look of panic on her face as footsteps approached. She hurried to the door and left before the doctor returned.

When Lisa was about to leave the hospital a few days later, the midwife slipped an envelope into her hand and whispered, 'Don't let them see it, whatever you do.' Back in the neat little bungalow, late that night when her parents were safely asleep, she opened the envelope. Inside was a photograph and a note: *Baby Paterson, three days old.* It stung that he had no name. She tried to tell her parents his name was Lewis, but they ignored her whenever she spoke.

She held the photograph in her hand and took in every detail. The midwife had been right, there were no marks on him, and his head was less pointy, less like an alien. She also had included a lock of his hair. Once at home Lisa sat in her room and let the tears stream down her face as she hugged the picture to her heart. Her parents didn't disturb her, except once when her mother knocked on the door and asked if she wanted a cup of tea. 'I want my baby,' she yelled, hoping someone would hear her. She should have confided in the nurse when she had the chance. She wished she'd thanked her more for her kindness, let her know how much it meant. She was the one person who had shown some humanity in the whole sorry business.

Lisa stifled a sob. These were painful memories, and now they were at the surface of her mind there was no going back. She stopped and looked around. She hadn't been paying attention and she'd walked further than she meant to. Where was she? It was cold, the jacket was keeping her body warm, but she was wearing trousers that weren't especially thick. Her legs were freezing and her feet, she couldn't feel her toes. She tried wiggling them and it was painful. Time to go home.

Chapter Twenty

'ONE of us has to go out and find her.' David looked for his coat. 'Damn, she's taken my jacket.'

'She'll be back at any minute, I'm sure she'll have gone out for some fresh air,' said Ros.

'No, she was pretty upset,' said Oliver. 'I agree with Dad, we need to find her and bring her back. You can take my jacket, Dad. I don't think I'd be much use what with my foot and everything. I'd only slow everyone down.'

'No, you stay here. I'll go,' said Ian.

'I don't think that's a good idea,' said David. 'She's emotional...'

'I can move quickly. I'm a runner—'

'You won't be able to run in this weather. You'd break your neck.'

'I'm used to it. I've done mountain climbing in conditions much worse than this. I brought crampons with me. It makes sense, you know it does.'

Ros watched as they stood eyeball to eyeball, neither one

wanting to give in. 'Why don't you both go? Neither of you is going to give in so you might as well both go.'

'But will you be safe here?'

'There's three of us, we'll be fine. Locked doors and all that.' She was desperate for them to go so she'd have time alone with her brother and sister to talk things over. They must have sensed her need because they joined in.

'Go,' said Em. 'We'll get something cooking so that we can eat when you all get back.'

At last, they went.

'I thought they'd never go,' said Oliver. He looked at his sisters. 'So, what do you make of all that?'

'Let's go into the kitchen and start preparing the evening meal,' said Ros. 'We can talk there. It'll be warmer. Oliver, make sure there's more logs on the fire, won't you? We don't want it going out. And where are the candles? We could do with some more light.'

Emilia was looking at her strangely.

'What?' said Ros.

'Oh, nothing. It's not like you to be so organised, sis.'

Ros blushed. 'Well, it's got to be done. Let's get on with it.'

In the kitchen, they all set about their tasks. There wasn't much to do, Ros put the bolognaise sauce in a saucepan and took out a pack of spaghetti. 'The sauce will only take ten minutes to heat up so we'll leave it until they come back but we should start boiling the water for the spaghetti. It takes ages,' she said. 'And didn't Mum ask us to prepare the vegetables for tomorrow? We can get the potatoes and parsnips peeled at least.'

As they busied themselves, there was silence. Em broke it first. 'Ros, I'm sorry. I'm sorry I didn't tell you.'

'Didn't tell me what?' said Ros, with a wry smile. 'You'd

met an unknown grandparent back from the dead, we have a half-brother, or you suspected me of shagging aforesaid half-brother?'

Oliver sniggered. 'Don't you start!' she rounded on him. 'You're another one, keeping things from me. Bloody secrets, look where they've got us.'

'So, what's your secret, then?' asked Em.

'Don't change the bloody subject. I don't have any secrets other than that I'm an idiot. Fancy falling for my half-brother.' She shook her head.

'I was trying to tell you,' said Em.

'Not very effectively! It was all hints and sideways swipes. All that stuff about genetic sexual attraction. And bloody Dorothy Wordsworth! Why couldn't you just say what you meant? It was like a cryptic crossword without any clues.'

'I don't know. I...' Em's voice wobbled.

'Oh shit, Em. It's not your fault.' Ros put down the potato peeler and went over to hug her. 'You've had so much to deal with and on your own, too. I wish you'd told me about Ian and you, Ollie, you confided in Em about the drugs... why didn't you tell me?'

There was a long silence. Em and Ollie busied themselves with their tasks, not looking at her. Eventually Oliver sighed. 'Look, Ros, we didn't confide in you because...' Out of the corner of her eye, Ros caught Em shaking her head warningly. 'No, Em, I'm going to say it. Frankly, Ros, you've never been there for us. You never phone. When we phone you, you talk for ages about yourself: how you can't get a proper job, how your latest boyfriend is a looker, a loser, a loony. You never ask how we are. You never, after you've droned on for hours about your concerns, say, "And how about you, Oliver.

How's your life?" You've never once asked why I was chucked out of Cambridge—'

'Now, wait a minute. It was clear Cambridge was off limits and we weren't to talk about it.'

'Em asked. She wasn't frightened.' He stared at her. 'And when she was in hospital and she was getting texts and emails on a daily basis, a daily basis, Ros, from those so-called friends of yours, where were you then?'

'What texts?' She grabbed Emilia's arm. 'What emails? You only told me about a card they'd sent.' Em glared at her brother, but he went on.

'You told your friends Em was anorexic.'

Ros flinched at his tone of voice. 'I...'

'And suicidal.'

'No! No, I've never told anyone.'

'I told you,' muttered Em. 'I said Ros wouldn't have said anything about what I did.'

'I promise you, I didn't tell them,' said Ros. 'And as for anorexia, they tricked it out of me.'

Oliver snorted. 'Yeah, right.'

Why was Ollie being so horrible? 'They did! They were all sympathy. All of them "knew someone" who'd had anorexia. They were all false empathy, and I was so worried, I had to talk to someone. But I swear, I did not mention your suicide attempt.'

'I believe you.' Em continued to prepare the Brussels sprouts. The three of them sat at the kitchen table in silence. Ros could bear it no longer. 'What did they do?'

Em's voice was emotionless. 'Like you said, false empathy. First, they sent me a card, I told you. That was bad enough, and then I started getting emails and texts. Did I know there were anorexic forums on the web? Maybe I should look at them, find other people like myself, talk to them.'

Ros frowned. 'Is that so bad? Isn't it good to talk to other people about these things?'

'You'd think so, wouldn't you? But they're lethal, these groups. The people on them encourage each other with their posts: *OMG, I'm so fat. You'll never guess. I ate a whole apple today. No food for me tomorrow.* And the others would reply: *Yeah, you're gross. You need to control yourself more.* It's horrible and it's not what you need when you're anorexic because you do honestly believe you're fat. Your ribs might be sticking out and your BMI less than 17, it doesn't matter. All you think about is how disgusting you are.'

'I didn't know, I'm sorry.'

Emilia gave her a wry grin. 'It gets worse. I ignored their constant texts, but they kept sending more. Somehow, they heard about... you know, and that was when it started. I never suspected you. One of the nurses was a friend of Olivia's mother, she might have let something slip. Anyway, it doesn't matter; they found out and they went in for the kill. They sent links to suicide sites on the web. The anorexia groups were bad, but, Christ, you should see these. People there post the most terrible things, actively encouraging each other to kill themselves. They provide details about how best to do it. They make suicide pacts. I was so stupid. I signed up for one of them and I was inundated with emails. I can tell you. I was depressed before, but after...'

'You don't need to say more if you don't want to.'

'It's OK. I was looking for support from other people who'd tried, people who had come through it, you know? Someone to say, "Yes, I've been there and I'm fine now. Here's what helped me." Instead, there were details about how to do it properly. I mean, they gave step-by-step instructions on how to do it. Nothing vague, like take a few pills, cross your heart and hope to die. No, these instructions were serious stuff.' Em's face was grim, remembering. 'And, then there was the praise for those who had done it. You have no idea how toxic it is.'

Ros put her head in her hands. The shame. All this time and she'd had no idea. Oliver's words stung. Was she as self-obsessed as they made out? She'd always imagined herself as someone kind. But was she? Yeah, sure, she gave to charity. A lot. But giving of herself, her time? That was a different matter. She didn't need Oliver and Emilia to tell her what she suspected. For Ros there had been only one important thing in life: Ros.

'Jesus, I'm sorry,' she said at last. 'You're right, I am a selfish bitch. That must have been a terrible time for you, and all I thought about was whether I was going to get into the Conservatoire and where my next boyfriend was going to come from. I am so self-obsessed.'

She sat trying not to cry. She didn't know what to say to make things better. She pushed her chair away from the table and left the room. Outside in the hall, she heard the murmur of their voices. Emilia's: *You were too harsh.* Oliver's: *She needed to hear it, she had to be told.* Oliver was right.

Lisa saw flickering lights in the distance: candles. Joanne and George's house. She liked what she'd seen of Jo, but how she'd ended up with someone like him, was beyond her. When Lisa thought of him and how he'd threatened her, how he'd tried to burst his way into her family, she wanted to scream. She looked at the lights and madness came over her. She was going to confront him. See how he liked it when someone disrupted his life. The house was 200 yards away. She increased her speed.

Outside the front door, she hesitated. She was hungry, hadn't eaten since breakfast and she was never at her best when hungry. She was about to turn around and go when the door opened. It was Jo who looked less than delighted to see her.

'Yes?' she said, making no move to let her in. Lisa was taken aback; Jo's previous friendly manner had vanished.

'Is George in?' she asked.

Jo stepped outside, shutting the door behind her. 'What do you want?' she said.

Lisa always felt guilty when faced with confrontational people. It was down to a lack of self-esteem stemming from her dreadful childhood. She was on the point of saying, 'Sorry, it's nothing, doesn't matter,' but instead she said. 'I want to see George. It's a personal matter. Nothing to do with you.'

Jo narrowed her eyes so much they were slits. 'I am his wife. It is everything to do with me, you slut.'

What on earth had he told her? Lisa pushed past her into the hall, which of course, was in complete darkness.

'George,' she shouted, 'get out here. We have unfinished business to discuss.'

'You're trespassing,' said Jo. 'Go now or—'

'Or what? You'll call the police?' mocked Lisa. 'I don't think so. No phone, no mobile signal.' She leaned in towards Jo. 'More's the pity. I would love to see the police because I've got something to say to them about your husband.'

'What on earth is all this shouting?' George was more composed than he was the last time she saw him. 'Why don't you come in and we can talk about this in a civilised manner? Jo, can you put the kettle on, please?'

Lisa stepped into the hall. Jo moved off into the kitchen and Lisa followed George into the living room. They had made changes. The Lumleys had never done much to the house, but George and his wife had wasted no time in improving it. It was hard to believe they'd only had the house for a few months. The old fitted carpet had been ripped up to reveal a stone flagged floor. A modern wood burning stove had been fitted into the fireplace, and, judging by the heat coming from it, it was much more efficient than the open hearth in their cottage. Instinctively, Lisa moved towards it.

'You must be cold,' said George. He sounded sympathetic and Lisa's resolve weakened. 'Would you like a hot drink?'

She nodded; the fight had left her. 'Coffee, please.' Might as well, get one down her while she had the chance.

'Hold on and I'll let Jo know.' He left the room.

Lisa sat down and looked round. It was smaller than the Warren, but two rooms had been knocked into one, and although it lacked the cosiness of their living room, it was chic and sophisticated. The walls were painted white, and there were several modern paintings on the wall. Lisa recognised one of them as being by a well-known Glasgow artist and wondered if it was an original or a print. She got up to look at it. It was original. She'd always wanted to own one. It was a still life, three lemons beside an apple. The colours glowed and shimmered in the candlelight. She studied the other paintings – there were four in total – and they, too, looked like originals, though none of them had the luminescence of the still life. Lisa sighed, thinking of the miserable reproductions of the Impressionists bought in the early days of her marriage, which they'd never replaced. One day, she vowed, one day. The sofas were mid-century reproductions, upholstered in a blue, which was only a tone or two away from grey, and scattered with a variety of cushions reflecting the colours in the paintings. The floor was partly covered by a huge rug that looked as though it was Persian. She reached down to stroke it. It was woven silk and must have cost thousands. Although the main colour was a dark red there was also blue in the pattern and it matched the upholstery perfectly. Lisa wondered who it was who had the good taste. Probably Jo, if her memories of George's filthy bedsit were accurate. He came back into the room.

'Please, take a seat.'

Stupidly she complied, putting herself immediately at a disadvantage when George remained standing. What she had to say was not to be said while she was sitting down, so she stood up again.

'This isn't a social call, George.'

'No? What do you want, then?'

What *did* she want? Retribution? A confession? An apology? She wasn't sure, and again, she felt wrong-footed. The man standing in front of her was pathetic, not someone to be angry with. It had been easier when he had been threatening. She decided to poke the hornet's nest. 'I've told David everything.'

But he was not to be provoked. 'Everything about what?'

Lisa shifted from one foot to the other. Her feeling of discomfort increased when Jo came into the room carrying a tray with a cafetiere of coffee, three mugs and a plateful of biscuits. Her whole demeanour had changed. The scowling, sullen woman who had greeted Lisa at the door, had vanished, to be replaced by a charming hostess. 'I wasn't sure if you wanted anything to eat but I've brought through some shortbread that I made this morning.' Immediately Lisa was suspicious.

'As I said, George. This isn't a social call. We did know

each other when I was at school. You were a student teacher when I was in S5.'

Jo reddened slightly. He put a consoling arm round her. 'Go on.'

'I was fifteen when you raped me, George.' Perhaps it was too blunt, but if she didn't say the words out loud now, she never would.

Jo moved away from him. 'What do you mean? That's not what happened.'

Lisa spoke calmly, going through the meeting with George at the Mitchell Library, how he had invited her back to his flat, but she didn't get beyond that.

George put his coffee down on the table in front of him. He grimaced. 'That's not how I remember it, Lisa.'

He and Jo stood in front of her, united in self-righteous anger. But Lisa was not going to be intimidated. 'Well, let's hear your version then.'

'You followed me home, tried to get into my flat. I had to be very firm with you.'

He was going to deny anything had happened.

He went on. 'I was very upset by it all, Lisa. But it's normal for schoolgirls to have crushes on their teachers, as you well know.'

The arrogance. Lisa chose her words with care. 'I do know but I also know I did not have a crush on you.' Jo tutted. Lisa stared at her. 'I don't know what he told you, but I was flattered by a teacher taking an interest in me and he offered to lend me a book, which is why I went to his dingy little bedsit in the first place.'

'You weren't in his room. He's not daft, you know.'

Lisa ignored the outburst. 'He pounced on me, I should have struggled more, I know, but I was fifteen.'

'George was with me,' said Jo.

'What? It's over thirty-five years ago. You can't possibly remember.'

'I kept a journal. I was there. It's in my journal about how you came whining to his door.'

This couldn't be happening. Lisa was the one who was supposed to be in control here, not them. Too late. She realised he must have spun Jo a story to explain his behaviour the other day. But then she looked at George, who probably looked as shocked as she felt. He wasn't aware of this; Jo had thought it up on her own and he looked worried. Lisa pressed her advantage.

'So, what exactly did you see?'

'I, well, I...'

'You didn't see anything, did you? Because you weren't there. Oh yes, you may have had a journal, and you might have written something there in the past day, to protect George, because you were afraid I might bring charges. But there are ways of seeing if something has been written contemporaneously or not. You've dropped yourself right in it.'

'I told you to let me deal with this.' George's face was red with fury.

She crumpled. 'But George, if what she says is true...'

He turned on her then. 'I'm telling you. It didn't happen. There's only her word against mine. Like I said, she came on to me, seduced me. She can't prove it was rape.'

'It is true, I assure you,' said Lisa. 'I was fifteen, I had a baby nine months later. The dates all check out. And of course there are DNA tests.' She'd shocked Jo. She looked as if someone had slapped her. In spite of everything, Lisa felt sorry for her. How awful to discover your husband is a rapist, that he had betrayed his trust as a teacher.

'You suspected there was a child, didn't you? That's why

all these years when we didn't conceive you were so sure of yourself, so positive it wasn't your fault.'

'Be quiet, woman!'

'And then yesterday, when I asked you if you'd slept with Lisa, you denied it with a cock-and-bull story of how she'd had a schoolgirl crush on you.'

'I'm telling you to shut up.'

'So,' said Jo slowly, 'you didn't sleep with her and yet there is a child? How does that happen then? Super strength sperm? Osmosis?'

'Yes,' said Lisa in her sweetest voice. 'How does that work?'

She'd infuriated him. He turned on her. 'There is no fucking child. You're bluffing. Shut up and get out!' He spat out the words.

His shouting galvanised her. 'You raped me, George.' She turned to face Jo. 'Believe me, Jo. I said no many, many times. I was a virgin, terrified, and George was in a position of power over me. Do you still teach, George?'

He moved towards her; his fists balled. Was he going to hit her? 'Get out! I'll fucking—'

He was interrupted by a furious banging at the door. Jo ran to open it and David and Ian burst in. Lisa was so thankful she started to tremble.

'Why are you shouting at my wife?' demanded David. His voice was quiet and measured and far more frightening than George's bluster.

David moved towards her. 'Are you all right, Lisa?'

She was silent. She'd said what she had to say. What surprised her most was the sympathy she felt for Jo. She had collapsed onto one of the sofas and was sitting with her head in her hands, dejected, defeated. 'Oh, George. It'll be the end of your career if this gets out,' she said.

'Fuck my career. I wanted to see my child, my son.'

'What makes you think the baby was a boy?'

George said nothing, enraging Lisa.

'I asked you a question.'

'Last year, I bumped into someone you were at school with. Kim something?'

'Kim Robertson, yes.'

'We chatted, I asked about you and why you'd disappeared from school, and she told me about the baby.'

She was going to collapse. 'But she couldn't have known. Nobody did.'

'Well, apparently she met someone who worked in the nursing home where you had the baby and she found out through them.'

Lisa shook her head. 'It's impossible. If she found out, the whole of Glasgow would have known. I'd have heard, David would have heard... It doesn't add up.'

George's voice was subdued. 'She didn't know about it until years later. She'd become a midwife and was working beside a nurse who'd been with you throughout labour. They were talking about difficult births and yours came up. She mentioned your hair and your mother, and Kim put two and two together.'

Lisa was too exhausted to be enraged. The plump little nurse who'd been so kind had betrayed her. What had she been thinking?

He continued. 'I wanted to know my son. I tried to trace you, but I had known you as Elizabeth Paterson. Kim knew nothing more than that you'd lived in Largs. I... I tried your father, but he wouldn't tell me anything.'

For once her father had done the right thing. David was holding her tight, realising how close she was to breaking down. She leaned in towards him, feeling the comforting warmth of his body. George carried on, oblivious to all but his need to justify himself.

'I want to know my son. We have no children. You do, Lisa. It isn't—?'

'Don't you dare say what I think you're going to. You've got a nerve,' said Lisa. 'Come on, David, Ian. We're done here.'

'Hang on a minute,' said George. He pointed at Ian. 'Who's this bloke?'

Lisa caught Ian's eye and flashed a warning. 'It's none of your business, George, but he's a friend of my daughter's.' She'd got away with it. George sat down heavily on the nearest seat and didn't reply for several seconds. 'What are you going to do?' he said, speaking directly to Lisa.

'Truthfully, I haven't decided. I know one thing though and that is I don't ever want to see you again. I want you out of my life. If it means your wife feels she can't take the DHT job, well, that's up to her. But you, you stay away from me. Don't ever try to contact me. I don't want you near me or my family.'

David stepped in. 'You will sell this place. I don't want our family holidays spoiled by the possibility of bumping into you.'

Jo was slumped on the pristine sofa. Lisa was sorry for her; she obviously had been in the dark about her husband's past. It must have been a shock to find out. Nonetheless, she had been ready to cover up what her husband had done. It was unforgiveable and she hoped Jo would decide against taking the job. It would be hard working in the same school. For George, she felt nothing. But finally, she had said what she wanted to say.

'We're finished here,' she said to David and Ian. 'Let's go home.'

Chapter Twenty-One

Ros STOOD outside the living room door, her hand on the doorknob, willing herself to go in. She would apologise. They would talk. Everything would be all right again. No doubt about it, she was genuinely sorry. She had been completely self-centered and selfish. Taking a deep breath to calm herself, she opened the door.

'You're right. I'm wrong. I'm sorry.'

Em and Ollie stared at her, saying nothing. She waited, counting the seconds in her head. At last, Em spoke. 'OK.'

It wasn't the burst of forgiveness she'd hoped for but at least it wasn't a brush off. 'So, are we cool then?'

'I suppose so.' Em couldn't have sounded less enthusiastic.

Ros's mouth was dry. 'Can we talk about... you know, Mum and Dad. Don't you think there's more going on than they're telling us?'

Em shrugged. 'Like what?'

Ros twirled a lock of hair round her finger. She needed to

take care with what she said next. 'Why do you think he was blackmailed? Sex, do you think?'

Em got up from the sofa where she was curled up like a small child. She walked across to the fireplace and put another log in the grate. For several seconds, she busied herself with poking the fire to bring it back to life. 'I don't know,' she said at last. 'But if you forced me to guess, I'd say that was most likely. Didn't you see how he reacted when I said honey trap?'

Was there a thaw in the air? 'Yes, he was mortified. I'm not surprised. It's hard to imagine Dad falling for something like that though.'

'What else could it be? It's not going to be fraud.'

'Mm. No, he's way too honest. Remember when he made me take that tenner I found to the police?'

'God, yes. I was livid. In my mind I had spent it already.'

'It was me who found it!' said Ros.

'I know, I know. But we always shared everything then.' Em looked downcast.

Ros studied her fingernails. 'When did we grow apart? Why did we? It feels like years since we had a proper conversation, the three of us.'

Neither of them answered. Tears welled up behind her eyelids. She and Emilia had been so close at one time and Ros didn't know what had gone wrong between them. No, she had to be honest with herself. She hadn't been as supportive as she should have been when Em was ill with anorexia. She had been too taken up with music and trying to get into the Conservatoire to care about anything else. It was so damn competitive. She hadn't been paying attention. She hadn't noticed Emilia picking at her food, getting thinner, refusing to eat. Later, when Em was in hospital, Ros had made the minimum number of visits necessary. Mum and Dad went every day, but Ros went once, twice a week at most. There was always something else to do – a rehearsal to go to or an additional music lesson, a new boyfriend to see. And, if she were brutally honest, wasn't there a smidgeon of resentment at all the attention given to Em? It was all *What are we going to do about Emilia? How can we help her?* By the time Em had recovered, their attention transferred to Ollie. He was in sixth year and the school suggested he try for a scholarship to Cambridge. There was extra tuition to arrange, books to be bought, mock interviews to be arranged. Ros had told herself she didn't mind but she must have. She saw that now. She'd withdrawn from them, subconsciously jealous. Oh God, what an awful person she was.

'Is it too late?' she asked.

'Too late for what?'

'To rebuild our relationship? I... I've been a fool.'

Emilia crossed the room towards her. 'Of course it's not,' she hugged her. 'You're our sister and always will be.'

Ros sniffed. 'I'd better get on with making dinner, then.'

'You sit down and compose yourself. You look a right mess. I'll get it started.'

Ros sat down. 'I'll be through in a second,' she said as she searched in her handbag for a tissue. She turned to Oliver. 'And what about you?'

Oliver nodded. 'Yeah, we're cool.'

Ros pulled at the tissue in her hand until it was in shreds. 'I had no idea about what those bitches had done. I feel terrible about it.'

Oliver didn't reply. It appeared he wasn't going to make things easy for her and who could blame him?

Ros sighed. 'I'll go and help Em. Are you coming?'

'Yeah, in a few minutes. I want to listen to the news first.'

He turned on the radio and fiddled with the dial. Ros picked up some cups lying about as she waited to hear the headlines.

'I've tuned into Radio Tyneside. They should give us more local news.'

She put the cups down again and waited. It was the second item on the news.

Police have now arrested three men in connection with the death of Dillon Robson whose body was found in Jesmond two days ago. Another man is also being questioned in relation to the murder.

Oliver turned off the radio. 'Fuck,' he said. 'Fuck. It was Dillon.'

'I'm sorry,' said Ros. 'You must have been hoping it wasn't him.'

Oliver didn't reply. His eyes were red. Eventually he said, 'I was. I couldn't believe they'd go that far, although I should have known. After all, they'd warned me. Poor sod. He was a nice guy, Ros. No real harm in him.'

Ros said nothing. She wasn't going to pass judgement on someone she didn't know, but she suspected Oliver was naïve when it came to his assessment of character. As long as they were generous with their joints, they were all right according to him. Hardly the best basis for a friendship. But what did she know about friendship? Over the years hers had fallen away as she spent so much time with whatever man she was seeing at the time. Well, those days were over. She needed to work on her relationships, and she was going to start with her siblings. 'Does this mean we can rule the drugs gang out then?'

'I think so. From what Dillon told me, there were no more than four of them and from what they said on the news, it sounds as though they're all accounted for...' He gave her a huge smile. 'It's going to be OK, isn't it?'

'Sounds like it. I'll go and tell Em. You coming?'

'Yes, I need some more painkillers though. Do you know where Mum keeps them?'

'Upstairs, in her bedside cabinet. Top drawer.'

'Thanks. Do you need one?' Ros was kneading her forehead.

'No, they're too strong for me. I'll be OK. It's all been a bit too much. All this emotion.' She lifted the cups from where she'd left them and moved towards the door.

Although the moon gave enough light for her to find her way, she ought to have brought a torch, too. The cups could have waited. Once she'd dumped them, she'd go back for her torch. When she opened the door to the kitchen, it was in darkness. It was hard to make out anything. Why had Em not lit some candles, or used her torch? She was sure she'd taken her torch with her.

'Are you there, Em?' she said. There was no reply. Ros swallowed, her mouth dry with fear. This wasn't right. Had she gone upstairs to the toilet? If so, why hadn't they heard her steps overhead. A match struck and a candle was lit. But it wasn't Em standing in front of her, holding a knife.

'Where's your fucking da?' A Glaswegian accent. Her head reeled. She'd thought they were safe. She hadn't taken her father's fears seriously. People didn't get harmed over building contracts. Or so she'd believed.

With any luck he didn't know Oliver was in the house. She prayed he wasn't going to burst in on them and said in a loud clear voice. 'Put that knife away. My father isn't here. Who the fuck are you?'

'Mind your own fucking business. Now, think again, where is he?' He let wax drip on to the table and placed the candle in the centre. There was a torch on the worktop, which he grabbed and put on, turning round so it shone on the back of the room. It was hard to make out, but Ros managed to see her sister on the floor, tied up and gagged. Ros's eyes widened in horror, and she moved towards her. 'Stay where you are.' He waved the knife at her. She stared at Em. Where was the telepathy so many people believed was part of being a twin? It was needed badly. Now.

'She told me she was alone in here. So why should I believe anything you cunts say?'

'I've already said, my father is not here.' Her loudest voice.

'So, where is he?'

Ros didn't know what to say. If she said he'd gone looking for her mother, he might go after him. She had no way of knowing if he'd found Mum and she couldn't put them in danger. Their best chance was if Oliver got out of the house and warned them. The knife moved in her direction.

'Where is he?'

She took one last chance, hoping Oliver could hear. 'I told you, I don't know.'

He was on top of her before she could move, the knife pressed to her throat. 'You want me to cut you, bitch? Is that what you want?'

She was hardly breathing; she was so frightened. A tear rolled down her cheek and into the corner of her mouth. Em was struggling frantically in the corner, bucking against her ties. There was nothing else for it; she had to tell him. 'He went out,' she whispered.

'That's better. As long as I know he isn't about to burst in on me. Get your arse on there.' He indicated one of the kitchen chairs. Ros stumbled towards it, barely able to see in the dim light. Em was no more than a shadow in the corner.

'Please, my sister. Let her go. She's not well, a migraine.'

The knife was closer. 'Aw, is that right? She's got a migraine?' He made a poor attempt to mimic her. 'Nice try, but even if she did, do I look like I fucking care?'

When Ros said nothing, he pressed the knife further into her neck. It punctured her skin; warm blood ran down her throat.

'I didn't hear your reply, bitch.'

Ros was so terrified she could barely get the word out. 'No,' she said.

'That's right. I don't give a fucking shit. At least it's not contagious,' he snorted back a snigger. 'Hands behind your back, no funny business.' He took out a length of rope and tied her hands together behind her back. Ros strained to keep her wrists as far apart as possible knowing it was her only chance. When he was finished, she moved them, thankful to find her hands were not as tightly bound as they might have been. He moved to her feet, and she tried the same thing, but it didn't work this time and he pinned them closer together. When he was finished, he gagged her with a tea towel. Christ, it was tight, and she moaned hoping he'd loosen it a little, but he cursed and pulled her off the chair pushing her into the corner with Em.

'Now we wait,' he said.

It was cold outside. A clear night with the full moon shining brightly in the east, stars glittering in the frosty night. Lisa exhaled. 'Let's get back to the cottage.'

She was thankful the confrontation with George was over. She hated rows, standing up to people. Larkin was right when he wrote about the damage parents do, and hers had done more than most. She'd always felt like an unwelcome add on to their self-righteous unit, springing up out of nowhere like a hair on an old woman's chin, something to be cut down whenever possible. As a result, although she was much better than she had been, Lisa lacked confidence at times and rarely stood up for herself. It felt good to have done it for once. They walked in silence. It wasn't uncomfortable but after a while she said. 'I'm sorry, Ian. This can't have been what you hoped for.'

'No. It wasn't as I imagined. I'm sorry. It must be dreadful having to relive that ordeal.' His eyes were full of compassion.

'It was a long time ago, Ian. Until recently I hadn't thought about the...' she faltered on the word, then made herself say it. 'I hadn't thought about the rape for many years. I decided to put it behind me. But you have to know... you were in my thoughts every day.'

They walked on, David's arm around her. She felt safe, sheltered. 'It's like a miracle finding out you're alive.'

'For years I believed you didn't want to see me and that was why you hadn't tried to contact me.'

Lisa recalled the two years after his birth, how she'd cried herself to sleep at night thinking about her poor dead baby, wondering about the child he might have become, torturing herself that it was something she'd done that led him to die when he was only a few days old. For years she gave generously to cot death charities, praying that, somehow, fewer women would have to go through what she had experienced. 'If I had known you were alive, I would have scoured the earth trying to find you.' She turned to David. 'I wanted to tell you and if I hadn't thought he was dead I would have. But as it was, it seemed best to leave the past behind. It hurt to think of it and I couldn't bring myself to talk about it. I'm sorry, I should have told you.'

For a terrible moment he said nothing, his face unreadable in the moonlight. 'David? Is everything OK?'

He nodded. 'I'm thinking about your parents, about how they did this terrible thing to you. It's not your fault, none of this is.' And then to Ian. 'And it's not your fault, either.'

They walked back slowly through the snow, watching where they put their feet, careful not to stumble and fall. On the way, Lisa asked Ian about his childhood. How thankful she was to hear he had a happy childhood. He had been cherished, loved. She'd hoped for nothing more.

They were almost at the cottage when Oliver startled them by appearing out of nowhere. He had been standing behind a tree on the side of the road, and stepped out as they were passing. Lisa stifled the scream that rose from her throat and then laughed when she realised it was him. 'Why aren't you resting your foot?'

In spite of the cold there was perspiration on his forehead. His voice shook as he told them how someone was holding her daughters captive in the kitchen.

Chapter Twenty-Two

THE FLAGSTONE FLOOR was cold and uncomfortable. They were squeezed into a corner, back-to-back with each other. Ros wished she had eye contact with Em, to see how she was doing. She stroked Em's hand with her little finger. After a few moments Em responded. Moving slowly so as not to attract attention, Ros edged a little closer to her sister, all the while keeping an eye on their captor. After he'd tied her up, he had lit several candles and placed them along one of the worktops. Now he was sitting at the kitchen table, playing with the knife and lost in thought. He looked tired. Or wired. In the dim light she couldn't tell for sure. From time to time, he ran his finger along the edge of the blade as if to test its sharpness. At least he wasn't looking at them as he did it.

She raised her hands to Em and prodded her with them, hoping she'd know what she was after. The bonds didn't feel too tight, and she was sure Em's nimble fingers would make short work of them. But Emilia was slow on the uptake. Ros nudged her with her elbow and pressed her bound wrists against those of Emilia. She kept doing it until at last Ros felt her sister's fingers on the rope, tugging and pulling to loosen the knot. Ros's heart was beating fast, and although it was cold in the kitchen, sweat stood out on her forehead. It was uncomfortable sitting in such a strange position and a muscle in her back twinged in protest. She prayed it was dark enough for their captor not to notice what they were doing. It took several minutes but at last the binding was loose enough for her to slip one of her wrists free. Immediately she got to work on Emilia's wrists. It was hard working with her hands behind her back. The intruder had trussed Emilia more tightly and Ros's fingers cramped as she worked at them. Her fingernails were long, and this helped. Her muscles strained with the effort, and she was terrified the man would look over and guess what she was doing.

Thank God, she'd managed it; the knot loosened, and Em's hands were free. Now what? She looked round the kitchen for a weapon, peering into the dark trying to remember what there was there other than knives. She dismissed the idea as too risky. Her glance came to rest on the golf club they'd brought down only the other night. It was only about thirty centimetres from her, leaning against the wall. Typical of Oliver not to put it back with the others but thank goodness for his laziness. Common sense kicked in. She might manage to grab it, true, but by the time she got to the intruder, he'd have his knife at the ready and wouldn't hesitate to use it. The scratch on her neck must have been small for the blood had already dried but it showed he meant business.

He was slumped at the table, his head in his hands. He appeared not to be paying attention, so Ros took the opportunity to move a little closer to her sister. As she did so her foot scuffed on the floor making the slightest of noises. His head whipped round, and he shone the torch into her eyes. 'You moved,' he said.

Ros dropped her eyes so he couldn't see them and shook her head. She held her breath, terrified he was going to come over and find out that they had managed to get their hands free, but he didn't move. He picked up the knife again and played with it. The blade vibrated as he thrust it into the wooden table over and over. He must have pushed it in too far for he struggled to pull it out. Ros crossed her fingers hoping he would find it impossible to remove but he got up from where he was sitting and plucked another one from the knife block. She froze, frightened he would come over, but he was diverted by a plate of mince pies that Emilia must have taken out of the fridge earlier and stood over them for several minutes as he shovelled one after another into his mouth.

'These are fucking good, so they are. I've enjoyed them over the past couple of days. Shame you can't have one. But I can't take the risk of you shouting out to warn that wanking father of yours. He should have accepted the offer...' his voice was stressed but there was nothing Ros could do to calm him. Although he had been remiss in tying her wrists tightly together, he had made up for that with the tightness of the gag. It was biting into the sides of her mouth, and she felt it near the back of her mouth. Something she'd always hated. She wished she hadn't thought about it. Immediately she felt as though she was suffocating. Her breathing quickened; her heart jumped in her chest like a hyperactive toddler. Fuck, she was going to have a panic attack. She was going to die, here in this room with her sister watching. It took all the willpower she had to calm down. She visualised a beach as she'd been taught to do when she'd had problems with stage fright. In her mind she saw the crescent shape, the white sand, the turquoise sea with its white-tipped waves. She was not in a kitchen with a criminal, she did not have a gag in her mouth, she was at peace on a beach with a large gin and tonic at her side. It was years since she'd had to use the technique, but it worked and as her breathing slowed and her heartbeat became more regular it came to her what they could do. But she had to let Em know her plan. How? The intruder settled down to playing with his knife again and Ros relaxed. She closed her eyes and thought hard... there was a game they'd played when they were about ten years old, but would Em remember?

They'd been fascinated by the story of Helen Keller, how the child who was deaf and blind had been taught to read and write. The idea of tracing letters on to the palms of each other's hand had appealed to them and they had spent hours learning both to do it and how to decipher it when it had been done. The first part was easy. There was a specific way to do it. You did not 'write' the word on the other person's palm. Instead, each letter was traced separately, one on top of the other and a pause was left at the end of each word. Each letter had to be traced in a certain way so as not to confuse it with any others. It was more difficult to decipher, and they'd had fits of giggles at the things they thought they'd said to each other when 'misreading' one letter changed the whole meaning of a sentence. Em had called her a 'cold fish' once, which Ros mistranslated as 'goldfish'. The insult passed unnoticed in the laughter that followed.

Ros brought the letters to mind, trying to remember exactly how to write them. She traced E on to Em's palm, the vertical line in a down stroke followed by three horizontals top to bottom. She then traced M, starting at the bottom left of the letter and writing the letter with one stroke. She paused, holding her breath... then Em started on her palm. She felt her sister's finger move down the palm of her hand, followed by one that was curved at first then moved diagonally to the bottom – R. She spelled out Ros and Ros, grateful that she remembered, squeezed her sister's hand hard. Em tried another word. OUCH, deciphered Ros. If she hadn't been gagged, she would have laughed. Taking a deep breath, she started to write out her plan on her sister's hand.

Lisa started to run but she'd only covered a few yards when her feet slipped on the snow, and she landed face down with her arms splayed out on either side. It was as if she were doing a snow angel, but on her front not her back. For several seconds she lay there, stunned.

'Lisa, are you alright?' David was at her side.

She took a moment before pulling herself up to a standing position. The breath had been knocked out of her but otherwise she was fine.

'We have to get back to the cottage,' she said as she started off. There was no running for her now. Her ankle, already a little weak from the fall two days ago, was throbbing and she felt a twinge in her knee. 'Come on!'

Oliver came to her side. 'Wait, Mum. We need to think what to do. He has a knife.'

'Are you sure?'

'Yes, Ros was talking very loudly and mentioned it. She was trying to warn me. I was in the hall about to go into the kitchen and heard her. I had to get out and warn you.'

He was right. They needed to plan their next steps carefully and not go barging in. She stopped. 'Tell us everything you heard.'

'It was definitely someone after you, Dad. We listened to the news and the drug gang have been picked up.' He continued with his story and when he finished David spoke up.

'Right, this is what we do. We go back to the house as fast as we can. On the way, look out for anything you can use as a weapon. A decent sized branch would be good for a start. He's bound to be in the kitchen because he won't risk leaving the girls where he can't see them. We can look in through the window to gather what's going on then we'll attack.'

'How?' asked Ian.

'We'll be the main players if that's OK with all of you.' He looked round at them all. 'Oliver can't move quickly so he can be back up, and you Lisa...'

'He has my daughters tied up at knifepoint. I'm going to cut his fucking balls off.'

David gave her a warning look. 'No heroics. The aim is to disarm him. So, you are going to knock on the window to distract him while I get ready at your signal to charge in through the back door and Ian goes in through the front. Oliver, I want you right at my back ready to take over if he manages to get at me somehow.'

Lisa interrupted. 'You don't think we should try to get help?'

'Where from? George?'

'No!'

'Where then? This has been the problem all along, no access to police.'

'You're right. Sorry, I'm being an idiot.' Lisa had been terrified when David mentioned something happening to him. He'd put himself in the front line. He'd be first to be attacked. He was right to do so, of course, but it didn't stop her worrying. David went on. 'If he does attack me, it will put him off kilter. And remember it will be three to one. Four, if we include you. You follow Ian, there's a cricket bat in the cupboard under the stairs. Use it.'

Lisa nodded. It made sense... and she'd carry it through. She'd kill the bastard if she had to.

Em traced the words 'got it' in response to Ros's final question of, 'Do you understand?' Ros edged a few inches towards the golf club getting herself within easy reach. She scrutinised the intruder but couldn't see if he were watching her.

'Move again and I'll slash you,' he said. 'Understand?'

Ros nodded. He bent over the table intent on carving something on the wooden surface. Mum would be furious. She waited a few minutes until he appeared to be more relaxed and nudged Em. It was time to act.

Em immediately started to make retching noises.

'What the fuck!' He jumped up from his seat and ran across. Thank God, he'd not picked up the knife. Em rolled over on to her back to disguise the fact that her hands were no longer tied. Her head to one side, she continued to heave as if she were going to be sick. Ros watched as the man bent over her, trying to unfasten the gag. She had to do something now before he realised Emilia was acting. She leaned across and grabbed the club, but she'd been spotted.

'You cunt,' he roared. 'Give that to me.' But he was too late, Ros swung it with as much strength as she could muster, given she was in a sitting position and her legs were still tied together. She winced as it slammed into his face, the crunching noise telling her she'd most likely broken his nose.

They reached the house within fifteen minutes. Lisa walked carefully so as not to fall again. Her heart was beating so fast she feared a heart attack. Adrenalin, she told herself, that's all it is. Use it to save your girls. There was no light from the living room, the candles must have blown out, but a glimmer at the kitchen window told them they hadn't moved from the kitchen. They moved silently through the garden. David and Ian had broken branches off trees on their way. They were a good size, heavy enough to daze someone but not so large that they were unwieldy. David placed himself at the back door with Oliver right behind him while Ian moved round to the front door that Oliver had left off the latch. He was going to let himself in as quietly as possible and wait at the kitchen door while Lisa watched at the window. Lisa crept towards it, heart thumping. She knelt beneath it. She comforted herself that whoever the intruder was, he was unlikely to be looking towards the window. She peered inside in time to see Ros hit a stocky little man with a golf club. There was no need to give the signal to David, the unearthly noise coming from the kitchen was enough for him to barge through the door. Forgetting the plan, Lisa ran to the back door to follow him and Oliver inside.

The look on his face was terrifying and Ros was paralysed by it. After hitting him she had struggled to her feet, and she felt her legs buckle beneath her. Only with a supreme effort of will did she manage to stay upright. He was threshing about, red with fury, and she feared that if he managed to get the knife then both she and Emilia would die. She couldn't run because her legs were still tied together. But focused as he was in coming for her, he didn't see Em stand up, hop over to the cooker and grab the frying pan. She raised it above him and brought it down hard on his head. At the same time, the door opened, and her father charged in, followed by Ollie and her mother, just as the door from the hall opened and Ian barged into the room. As the man collapsed unconscious in a heap in front of her, Ros allowed herself a little smile. She and Em had defeated him; together they could do anything.

Lisa didn't believe her eyes. Her gentle twin girls who had never hurt a fly (well, apart from the times when they were little and had fought with their brother and each other) had got themselves out of the worst possible situation. 'Are you OK?' she managed to ask them before collapsing on the nearest chair, tears streaming down her face.

It was all too much. All the emotions of the past few days hit her with the strength of a ball hammer. She sat there, half laughing, half crying, wondering if Emilia had killed a man and what they were going to do about it. Luckily David was much more proactive. He was leaning over him, checking his pulse.

'He's alive,' he said. 'Best tie him up before he comes round.'

'Do you recognise him?'

David shone his torch onto the man's face. 'I'm not sure. No, wait a minute. He used to work for the council.' He closed his eyes for a moment. 'Got it. He was a computer technician. Ryan something. I haven't seen him for a while. Shit, they must have used him to get at my email...'

Lisa nodded. She had been going to suggest not tying him up – he was injured after all – but then she pictured her daughters being threatened with a knife and her heart hardened. She pointed to a corner of the kitchen. 'There's the rope he used on Ros and Em. Make sure the knots are tight.'

Ros leaned against the toilet bowl; would she ever stop vomiting? Every time she closed her eyes, she saw that man coming towards her in a rage. If Em hadn't hit him... She shuddered. Christ, it was so awful. She fingered the wound on her neck, it was only a surface scratch after all, but she had seen the look in his eyes when he'd attacked her. There was a knock on the bathroom door.

'Give me a minute,' she managed.

'Are you OK in there?' It was her mother. Ros made herself get up. She flushed the toilet, rinsed out her mouth and opened the door.

'I feel terrible,' she admitted.

'Come here,' her mother gathered her into her arms. 'My brave, brave girl.'

Ros sank into the welcome warmth. It felt good to be hugged. Behind them Em said, 'Is this a private party or can anyone join in?'

'Come here, you,' Ros grabbed her. 'You saved my life.'

'No,' said Emilia. 'You saved mine. Who knows what would have happened if you hadn't hatched that plan.'

'It wasn't all that good, as it turned out.'

Em stared at her. 'You have no idea, do you? I was so passive, accepting it all. I couldn't think what to do. But you, you came up with that brilliant idea.'

Ros blushed. 'Don't exaggerate.'

Mum smiled at them. 'How did you do it anyway?'

Ros let Emilia tell the story. She was worn out by the terror of the past hour. She zoned out as Em went into details of the system they'd used to communicate, trying not to think of what might have happened if it had all gone wrong. Em traced out some letters on Mum's hand, making her close her eyes to try to guess what she was spelling. Ros watched as they laughed and joked, joining in at times but keeping herself apart. She felt as though she was outside her own body. She closed her eyes.

'Ros, what's wrong?' Mum's voice was gentle.

'I... we could have died. I didn't know what he was going to do. It was horrible.'

Em hugged her. 'You were so brave.' She paused before going on in a shaky voice, 'I didn't know how much I wanted to live until I saw that knife.'

Ros blinked back tears. She felt exactly the same way. She'd heard of people facing death and escaping it and how they felt as though they'd been reborn. She was ready for anything the world had to fling at her. 'What happens now?'

'Well,' said their mother. 'That bastard is tied up. It's safe to go downstairs.'

'We don't have to see him, do we?'

Mum shook her head. 'He's in the utility room. It's probably best to stay away from there because I imagine he'll have a very sore face and head when he wakes up. We'll leave Dad and Ian to deal with him.'

Was there a hint of pride as she said Ian's name? 'Mum...' She stopped, unsure what to say.

'What?'

'I wanted to say how sorry I am about what happened. You know, when you were young. It sounds awful and we'll support you whatever you decide to do.'

Her mother smiled and drew her back in for another hug. 'Thank you. I'm hoping Ian will become part of our family. George, I think has been dealt with. I went to confront him and I'm sure it'll be the last we see of him. They'll be selling the house.'

'You're not serious? It must have been some confrontation,' said Ros.

'It was,' said Lisa. 'I'll tell you about it another time.'

'I can't imagine how hard this must be for you,' said Emilia. 'And I've been such a bitch about it all. All those horrible remarks. I'm so sorry.'

Lisa shook her head. 'Emilia, you weren't to know. I should have spoken about it years ago. I should have told Dad about it when we got together again but I was too raw, too traumatised by my loss to talk about it. I was afraid of not being believed, of all the questions people would ask. The years passed, and once you've kept something quiet for so long, it's hard to bring it up. It would have been different if I'd known Ian was alive...'

'What do you think you'll do about your father?'

'Honestly? I don't know. My parents have been dead to me for many years, so it's not as though there's a gap in my life needing to be filled. And he told me my child was dead. I don't know if I can forgive him.'

'He did seem sorry,' said Em. 'There were tears in his eyes when he was talking about you.'

Lisa shuddered. 'Can we talk about it another time? We ought to go and find out what's happening with our unwelcome guest.' Lisa set off downstairs.

Ros nudged Emilia as they watched their mother leave. 'You should have left it. I think you've upset her.'

'I know. I should have kept my mouth shut, but you didn't see him. He was a pathetic old man, all alone. I felt sorry for him. Although now, I don't know. What he and his wife did was horrendous. They must have been nasty, horrible people.'

Lisa couldn't get away from the girls quick enough. She didn't want them to see her crying and to think Em had hurt her. The truth was, it was tearing her apart. One part of her wanted to see him, to hear his side of the story. Perhaps it had been her mother behind it all, and he was a willing participant. Another side of her wanted revenge, to scream at him, deride him in the way he had done to her. She'd flaunt her family in his face. *See what you're missing, old man.* But she wouldn't go through with it. Either she'd choose not to see him, or, if she did, it would be to hear him out. She drew her hand across her face to wipe away the tears before going in to see what was happening. It would be a difficult decision, one of the hardest she would ever make. For now, though, she had to see what was happening with their prisoner.

'We have to get help for him.' David looked worried. 'We don't want him dying on us.'

'He's not going to die. But yes, we do need to get help. Any suggestions?'

We all looked at each other in dismay. This whole holiday had been about trying to get help. How many times had they tried to get a mobile signal with no success?

'I'll check him over,' said Ian.

Despite her feelings of animosity, Lisa didn't want this Ryan character to die so she was relieved Ian was going to examine him. It only took a few minutes to see how he was.

'He's beginning to come round,' he said when he came back. 'He appears to be fine. I don't see any symptoms of concussion, but he'll have to be checked out properly at hospital. I've given him some painkillers.'

'Do we have to keep him tied up?' Despite everything, Lisa hated the idea.

Ian sighed. 'I think it's best. He's saying all sorts of things in there. I'm not sure we'd be safe if we let him go.'

This problem wasn't going to go away. More than ever, she wished they had some way of contacting the outside world.

Lisa went through to the kitchen to prepare the evening meal. She put the radio on to hear the news. What she heard had her rushing through to the living room. 'David, try the landline. They've fixed the telephone lines.'

He picked up the phone immediately. 'Yes, police and ambulance please.' They put him through to the ambulance service first. Lisa listened as he outlined what had happened.

'We have a doctor here, perhaps it would be best to speak to him?' He handed the phone to Ian who said little other than that he didn't think he was concussed. When he'd finished, he handed the phone back to David. 'They're transferring you to the police now. And an ambulance will be with us as soon as possible.'

David explained to the police what had happened. 'Yes, he tied up my daughters at knife point and threatened them. They managed to escape, and it was then he was wounded.' He stopped speaking to listen. 'How long will you be?' A pause. 'Oh, has it? I hadn't noticed. Well, the road here is blocked with two cars. We'll move them now. Thank you, we'll see you then.' He hung up.

'It's raining apparently. Has been for the past half hour. There's a thaw underway. Ian, can you come with me, and we'll try to move the two cars. Otherwise, they won't get through. They're hoping to get to us within two hours.'

While David and Ian were away, Lisa dished up the meal to the others. She herself had little appetite and pushed the food around the plate. Ros noticed. 'Are you OK, Mum?'

Lisa looked at her plate. God, she hated spaghetti bolognaise. 'What are we going to tell the police?'

'The truth,' said Em. 'Dad was being blackmailed and they used us to try to get at him.'

Lisa thought of the compromising photos, of them somehow getting out. What would they do if that happened? How would David cope? How would she cope? 'I wish it were as simple as that.'

'It is as simple as that,' said Ros. 'Blackmail is a crime. Having a photo taken of you in a compromising situation when you're drugged or whatever, isn't. Who cares what people say?'

Lisa gave her a shaky smile. 'But we're the "too-good-to-be-Truetts".'

'We're not, though. Are we? We have our faults like everyone else.' Ros gathered the plates together and stacked them by the dishwasher. She started to load it. 'It's true, Mum. I've heard your friends praise you for your perfect family, tell you how lucky you are.'

Lisa opened her mouth to protest.

'I know, I know,' said Ros. 'You always pass it off as a joke – *oh, you don't know the half of it* – but you never told them there were real problems, did you?'

Oliver joined in. 'You didn't tell them I was chucked out of Cambridge. I bumped into your friend Anne in town and had to listen to her going on about how sweet it was that I'd left Cambridge to be nearer my family. It was embarrassing, Mum.'

They were right. Lisa bent her head so they couldn't see her tears.

Oliver pressed on. 'If we don't tell the police then the problem will never go away. From what Dad said, this is a large company with lots of money and they'll keep going until they get what they want.'

He was right, they all were. She only hoped David could be persuaded as well. He and Ian arrived back not long after. They had to persuade him to tell the police everything. 'David, about our statements to the police. We all think—'

Her father held up his hand. 'Ian and I have discussed this on the way to the car. I'm going to tell them everything. We'll never be shot of these thugs otherwise.'

Lisa closed her eyes in relief. 'Exactly what I was going to say.'

Now they had to wait and see what happened. The emergency service had estimated it would be two hours before they arrived. One hour had already passed. The lights went on, bringing with them a sense of normality, of hope, even. Lisa went back into the kitchen to warm up some food for David and Ian. The intruder, who was locked in the utility room, heard her and started mouthing off.

'I'd like to carve up that daughter of yours,' he sneered. 'Not the skinny one, the other one. She's lush. I could screw her all night long. I should have taken her while I could. Up her arse, up her cunt. Fuck, it would be good.'

How dare he? A seething mass of rage was rising within her and she fought to keep herself calm. She wasn't going to give him the satisfaction of seeing her lose control, but neither was she letting him get away with those foul words. Lisa picked out her largest knife and the knife sharpener and opened the door to the utility room. She stood in front of him sharpening the knife. The sneer left his face, she thought he was going to be sick.

She gave him her coldest look. 'You know, we're very isolated here. Nearest neighbours half a mile away. No one to hear you scream.' Her tone was conversational. 'But then you knew that when you tied up my daughters...' She went on. 'Do you know, I've always thought this was the perfect place for a murder. Dark, dark nights, plenty of places to bury a body. We even have a cess pit. Ideal.' He was silent, his eyes on the knife. 'I'm sorry, were you saying something there? I didn't quite catch it.'

He shook his head.

'Oh, OK then. Well, I have things to be getting on with.' She closed the door and smiled when she heard the whimper coming from the utility room.

Chapter Twenty-Three

It wasn't long before the emergency services turned up. Two paramedics and two police officers. The police officers introduced themselves as Sergeant Sharif and PC Bowes. The sergeant took the lead. 'Can you take us to the intruder? We'll deal with him first.'

Lisa led them through to the kitchen. 'He's in the utility room through in the back here. We tied him up.'

He raised an immaculately groomed eyebrow and she guessed he didn't approve. Too bad. He hadn't had to imagine what the bastard might have done.

As soon as she opened the door, the threats and swearing started. 'She's a fucking loony, threatened to kill me and throw me into their cesspit. You need to arrest her.'

Sergeant Sharif turned to Lisa. 'Any comment?'

Lisa rolled her eyes. 'We don't have a cesspit.'

'Good. Jim, would you untie this man please.'

Once he was free, the paramedics checked him over. He made a fuss, groaning every time they touched him. When they were finished, one said, 'He's fine but we should prob-ably get him checked out at the hospital.'

'From what I've seen he doesn't have concussion,' said Ian.

'And you are?'

'Ian Murray, I'm a doctor. Friend of the family.'

'Best to take him to hospital anyway. PC Bowes, you stay with him and don't let him out of sight when you get to the Infirmary.' He turned to the older paramedic. 'Is it safe to handcuff him?'

'Yes.'

'It's her there you should be cuffing, not me. She threat-ened me with a knife—'

Lisa interrupted him. 'Inspector, one of my daughters has a wound on her neck where he cut her, would you like to see?'

He nodded. 'The paramedics will check her out.' He turned to the intruder. 'Name, please.'

'Ryan Neilson,' he muttered, glowering at Lisa.

'Ryan Neilson, you are under arrest for breaking and entering this house and the unlawful imprisonment of Emilia and Rosalind Truett. You do not have to say anything. But it may harm your defence if you do not mention when ques-tioned something that you later rely on in court. Anything you do say may be given in evidence.'

'Fuck off. It's them should be arrested not me.'

'Noted,' said Sharif. 'Right, you can take him away now.'

Thank God. Lisa was relieved to get him out of the house. Before they left, the paramedics cleaned the scratch on Rosalind's neck and put an Elastoplast on it. They also checked Oliver's foot and put a fresh dressing on it.

Once Sharif had seen them off the premises, he came into the living room and said he was going to take their statements. Lisa caught David's eye; they were all exhausted.

'I think we're all a bit tired, Sergeant. Can it be done some other time?'

He frowned. 'It would be better to do it now, while it's all fresh in your minds.'

They gave in, not wanting to annoy him.

He took out a notebook. 'Just tell us in your own words what happened.'

David took the lead and went through the whole story starting with the email on April Fool's Day. It took longer than they thought because the sergeant was interrupted by a lengthy phone call.

'Sorry about that,' he said when he was finished. 'Shouldn't be too much longer now.'

He took statements from the others, but it was Ros and Em who he questioned the most thoroughly. Lisa shook while Ros and Em described how he'd attacked them in the kitchen.

'And he put a knife to your throat?'

Ros nodded. 'I know it's only a scratch, but he broke the skin and I honestly thought he was going to kill me.'

'Can you describe exactly how you were tied up and how you managed to get free?'

Em explained and he nodded.

'And the ropes he used, where are they?'

David replied. 'We used them to tie him up.'

'OK, good. We'll be able to examine them for skin cells etc from your daughters.' He closed his notebook and rose to go.

'What happens now?' asked Lisa.

'Well, it's quite complicated as there are two crimes involved. There's the blackmailing and his role in it but it'll be up to Police Scotland to pursue that. Then there's the incident here today. If he is charged with that, he'll stand trial here in England. But we'll liaise with Police Scotland either way.' He paused. 'You might need to prepare yourself.'

'What for?' said David.

'He may raise a complaint against your daughters – of assault.'

'You're kidding, right?' said Lisa.

'I'm not, I'm afraid. The thing is, I've just heard from my colleague, PC Bowes. Apparently, Robertson was very aggressive in the ambulance. He claims he came to the door and was attacked without warning by Rosalind and Emilia. He says they tied him up, not the other way round, He wants to press charges.'

Lisa felt bile rise to her throat. 'I don't believe this.'

'Well, forensics will be round as soon as possible. Please don't clean any surfaces. We need to get evidence that he was in parts of the house that he says he wasn't, if you see what I mean.'

'Not really.'

'He's saying he was attacked at the door, knocked out, tied up and locked in your utility room. If that was the case, there would be no fingerprints anywhere else in the house. You said he stole food, boasted of it to your daughters. If he did, there will be evidence to support that.'

'If he did?' Lisa was pleased to see him blush.

'I'm sorry. I thought I ought to warn you.'

Once he'd gone, they all sat around the fire in the living room, mulling over what had happened. Lisa zoned out while they talked, gazed at them all: her lovely daughters, her flawed son, her long-lost son and her husband. Only three days ago, she had been complacent, her only worries a stupid parental complaint that came in on the last day of term and a silly fallout with Ros. Now, their lives had changed forever. Some things were better. Her first-born child was alive. She was both elated and terrified at the thought of getting to know a grown-up child. They had so much catching up to do. How would he fit into their family with all its idiosyncrasies and imperfections? It wasn't going to be easy, but, oh, dear God it was the happiest moment of her life when she found out he wasn't dead after all.

Her relationship with Ros had changed. Ros had grown up fast over these last few days and was becoming the woman she ought to be. The tension between her and the others had lessened. Lisa sensed they'd said some hard words to her about her selfishness, Em especially. But she was proud of how she'd coped with the attack, how resourceful she had been. She was proud of both of them.

Other things were not so good. She had no idea what to do about her father but suspected she'd always regret it if she refused to meet him. She didn't want him in her life but perhaps she ought to allow him to tell his side of the story. She could always walk out. She only had to see him once. Gradually she was coming round to the idea that it was something she was going to have to do. The sooner the better.

And Oliver. It was hard to admit but he was weak, and they had ignored this for years. They should have stamped on the cannabis use when they had the chance instead of being so damned liberal. It would be best if he left Newcastle and went to another university. This called for some tough love and there were difficult times ahead.

Finally, David. He was lying back on the sofa, his eyes closed. He looked exhausted. This had fallen upon them because they hadn't been honest with one another. If he'd told Lisa about that email, she would have advised him to go to his section head with it at once. Planning officers were always at risk of being compromised. He'd been too quick to dismiss it as a joke.

Lisa sipped her wine and thought about some of the things that had been said over the past few days. How instead of facing up and admitting their problems, they had sought to hide them. She needed to share more of her troubles with her friends, let them know they weren't the perfect family after all. She'd start by letting Anne know about what had passed here. She'd phone her tomorrow now the landline was working again. She looked at her watch. Tomorrow was already here; it was long past midnight. Christmas Day.

Em got up and looked out of the window. 'The snow's gone. It won't be a white Christmas after all.'

'Doesn't matter,' said Lisa. 'We're all together and safe, that's what's important.' She raised her glass. 'Happy Christmas, everyone.'

Epilogue

IMAGINE A GLOBE. Made of glass. One with snow that falls when you shake it. Except the snow has vanished leaving only what lies beneath: the truth. The cottage is lit up with the family inside, all safe and warm. Take a last look. Lisa is glowing, her long-lost son returned to her. Oliver is relieved to have shaken off his attempt at a criminal life; perhaps he can get on with the job of getting a decent degree now. The twins are embarrassed. Em, because she's jumped to so many wrong conclusions, and Ros, well, imagine how you'd feel if you found out you'd fancied your half-brother. David is quiet, mulling over the day's events. What is he thinking?

Then there's me, the prodigal son returned. Except I'm not. I'm the cuckoo in the nest. It's a comfortable nest, better than I ever imagined and I have no intention of giving it up.

I hadn't known Ian Murray for long. He was a casual acquaintance; someone I'd see from time to time in the hospital where I worked. He was a doctor, I was a porter, but he was one of the less prickish docs, always acknowledged me when we bumped into each other in the corridors unlike most of the stuck-up twats who worked there. I don't recall the exact details of how we got talking that night in the pub last October. He was looking glum I remember, his mouth downturned instead of his customary smile.

I sat down at the table where he was sitting alone and said, 'Mind if I join you?'

He shrugged.

'You OK?'

'Suppose so.'

'If you don't mind me saying, you don't look it.'

He took a long drink from his pint finishing it off. I took his glass and stood up. 'Same again?'

'Thanks.' The effort of speaking took a lot out of him.

After the third pint he revealed he owed money. 'Bloody Charlie,' he said.

'You owe money to Charlie?' I asked. Charlie was a lab technician. I couldn't imagine why one of the doctors was borrowing money off him.

He cracked a smile at that. 'No, his name's Drew. No, I owe it because of cocaine. Charlie.'

The error made me feel a bit of a dick. I opened the crisps I'd bought in an attempt to cover my embarrassment. 'Of course,' I murmured as I stuffed half a packet in my mouth in the hope of lining my stomach. I've never been a heavy drinker and I was reaching my limit.

'I thought I'd got shot of him but now I hear someone's been "making enquiries".' He sighed, it came out as more of a groan. 'I'm adopted you know.'

I didn't know. Lucky bastard. How many times had I wished someone would adopt me. But I'd been too old by the time my social worker decided my mother was too feckless to look after me. Twelve, a difficult age. Three fostering attempts followed before social work gave up on me and dumped me in a children's home where I learned to look out for myself.

'I'm sorry, I don't understand,' I said. 'What's that got to do with what you owe?'

He told me. A tale of how he hoped it might be his birth family looking for him but thought it more likely to be thugs.

'Why don't you look for your family yourself?'

'My mother got pregnant at fifteen. I got my adoption papers when I was sixteen as I wanted to find her then, against my adoptive parents' wishes. No father's name on my birth certificate. My parents persuaded me to forget it and I did. "Leave it to her," they said. "If she wants to find you, she will." That was over twenty years ago.'

'So, why can't you find out who it is looking for you? Someone must have told you.'

'I'll be back in a second,' he said, getting up from his seat. 'Need a slash.'

I waited for him to return, mulling over what he'd told me. I understood the longing he had to discover his birth family. I'd gone through something similar a few years back when my mother contacted me. I was thrilled. For years I'd longed for a reunion, imagining a welcome fire, roast chicken dinners, a tearful mother apologising for years of neglect. What a fool. She was drunk when we met, the smell from her breath was rank with stale gin and beer. All she wanted was money. I gave her what I had to get rid of her and refused to answer the door for the next month until she took the hint and stopped trying.

Ian returned and sat down. 'Jimmy told me a young

woman was asking about me. Some bird with red hair. Too young to be my mother, but I thought...'

'... Your mother had sent someone on her behalf.' I finished the sentence for him.

'Yup. But the thing is, the guy I owe money to has a girl-friend, with red hair. How do I know it's not her? Casing the joint, so to speak.'

'Can't you just give him the money?'

The look he gave me was bleak. 'It's thousands, mate. Don't have it. Ex-wife screwed me over in the divorce deal.'

I didn't know what to say. The thought of owing thou-sands made me ill. Another doctor from the hospital joined us then so the talk turned to other things and gradually he cheered up. I didn't stop thinking about his dilemma for the rest of the evening.

———

I didn't sleep that night. For one thing, I was consumed with jealousy. Ian Murray had had everything I hadn't: loving parents, albeit adoptive, and a medical degree. Oh, how I had wanted to be a doctor when I was a child but that was never going to happen. Do you know the statistics on educational outcomes for young people in care? Well, let's start with school leaving age. Three quarters of those who leave school at sixteen are in care or 'looked after' as they like to call it. If you look at Highers, the qualification needed to get into university, you're more than four times more likely to get one Higher if you are living with a parent than if you are in care. The odds are stacked against such children.

Ian Murray had it all. And he was throwing it away on drugs. I never touched them. I was one of those who left school at sixteen with no formal qualifications. I counted myself lucky to have a job, I wasn't going to risk it for a few hours of pleasure. I wanted to help him and so I found myself approaching him at work.

'Hey, Ian. How's it going?'

His face was grey with worry. 'Not good mate, not good.'

'I've been thinking,' I said. 'What about if I try to find out if it's your mother behind this or the drug dealers.'

'Ssh,' he said, looking round to check no one was listening. 'Don't mention that here.' He looked at his watch. 'I'm off shift in half an hour, I'll meet you in the usual place.'

I waited for him in the pub, hoping no one else would come in. He was late, by three quarters of an hour. There was an emergency, apparently. He works in A and E, so it was hardly surprising. After passing over a pint to me he said, 'Right, what's this idea then?'

'How did you find out someone was looking for you?'

'A mate, Jimmy, who works in a pub on Byres Road. The woman was in there last week asking if anyone knew Ian Murray. It's a right bugger because it's somewhere I like to drink and now it's off limits in case it is someone from the drug dealer. Everyone knows not to say anything to her.'

'Right, tell me where and I'll pop in to see if I can find out more. I mean, what if it is someone from your birth family and you miss out?'

'Why are you doing this for me? I haven't got any money. I can't pay you.'

I was offended but tried not to show it. 'Let's say I'm a sucker for happy endings.'

His last comment changed my opinion of him. I'd been treating him as someone who could become a friend, but it appeared he didn't think the same way. If a friend offers to do something for you, you don't immediately assume they're doing it for money, like he did.

Anyway, I went to the pub and Jimmy pointed out the 'bird' that had been asking about Ian. 'Has she asked about Ian again?' I glanced across the pub to see a young woman with long red hair sitting on her own at a table. The first thing that struck me was how much she looked like Ian. Apart from the hair, that is. His was a very dark brown. Maybe she was his half-sister. She was very pretty if a bit gaunt for my taste.

He passed me a pint, on the house, he said and shook his head. 'Don't think so, but it's worse than I thought. She's a journalist. I heard she's doing a story on drugs and doctors. Can you imagine the scandal? Murray's not the only medic who likes his nose candy.' He stiffened. 'Don't look now but she's coming to the bar.' Jimmy sidled along the bar to where she was standing.

'All right, darling? What can I get you?'

The glare she shot him would have felled a thousand soldiers. 'I'm not your darling.'

I tried to listen in. Jimmy was defensive. 'Sorry love, I'm only doing my job.'

She sniffed at the 'love' but didn't say anything other than, 'Has Ian Murray been in tonight?'

'Sorry, love. Don't know who you're talking about.'

She looked less sure of herself then.

'Why are you after him? You're not up the duff, are you?' Jimmy was pulling her strings but if he'd hoped for another stuck-up reaction, he was disappointed. She walked back to her table without another glance.

'Do you know what her name is?' I asked Kyle.

'What, you going to ask her out?'

'No, I've got a girlfriend,' I lied. 'I was going to look her up and see what sort of things she writes.'

'Good idea.'

I pressed my point. 'I mean, she might not be a journalist. Maybe it's a cover for the drug dealer. It's worth checking, don't you think?'

'Right enough. Don't know her name though, sorry. And between you and me, I think she's a lezzer. Did you see that look she gave me?'

I refrained from telling him he deserved it, bought another pint and settled down in a seat not far from her. It was crowded in the pub now and she'd been joined by a group of friends. They were drinking hard and were pretty much pissed by ten o'clock. She'd hung her handbag over her chair. I sank my pint, walked past her table, bent down to tie my shoelace and while I was down there, I dipped my hand in to search for her purse. It took two seconds for me to find it and another three to leave the pub.

On the bus home I looked through her purse. She was a journalist. Emilia Truett, according to her NUJ card. A good name. There weren't going to be hundreds of them to sift through. I waited until I was home before I started a google search.

It's astonishing what you can find online: links to articles she'd written, her professional details, prizes she'd won. She came from a family of high achievers. An article in a Sunday supplement told me more about this gifted family. I read it through.

That the three Truett children are talented, there can be

no doubt. Twins Emilia and Rosalind play the oboe and violin respectively and passed grade eight at the age of twelve. Rosalind told me she hoped to study at the Conservatoire, but Emilia's hopes lie in literature.

"I'd like to be a writer," she said. "To write about social injustice. Our society is very unequal, and I'd like to do something about that," she said with a maturity belying her fourteen years. Yet, as if this is not enough, Oliver has astonished everyone with his top-grade A in Advanced Higher Applied Maths at the age of eleven.

Yes, that's right, eleven. He wanted to be an astrophysicist, he said. I'm wondering now what happened to that ambition. Drifted off into the ether like the smoke rings from the dope he consumed, no doubt.

The title of the piece was *Three Gifted Children Reach For The Stars!* I broke off reading this nauseating stuff to study the photographs. There were two. One was of Oliver alone. I studied it. I could have been looking at a photo of a young Ian Murray. The other photo had been taken in the garden. The two girls standing with their instruments, Oliver seated, with a cello the size of himself between his legs. All concentrating on the music stands in front of them. Behind them stood a massive house. Well, massive to me, anyway. The article referred to a 'second home' in Northumberland. My stomach churned with envy that Ian Murray could be part of this. I wanted it for myself. More than anything. With that thought, the idea of passing myself off as Ian took root.

I told Ian it definitely was the drug dealer looking for him. 'He's out for blood. Best keep out of pubs for the time being,' I said. In the meantime, I set about getting to know the family. It didn't take me long to track down Rosalind. Her LinkedIn profile told me she was trying to get a permanent job in an orchestra. In between gigs with various orchestras, she was working in a restaurant called Farfalle. It was easy enough to pinch Murray's lanyard, so I had something to prove my identity. A few runs through the washing machine and the photo was blurry enough to be anyone. The rest is history, as they say.

I hadn't factored in Ros falling for me. I could have had a bit of fun, but I was in it for the long game, and I reckoned it was best not to seduce my supposed half-sister. But I'd forgotten about her sister. Emilia's antipathy to me could have blown it.

There are hard times ahead. It's a shame I had to use Ian's lanyard to prove my identity to David. How will I get out of being a doctor, I wonder? I'll need to give it some thought. A wish to find myself perhaps? A sudden phobia of blood? Professional misconduct? It's a hard one but a solution will come to me. I need this family. First thing I'll do is change my name legally to Ian Truett. After all, I've told my new family my adoptive parents are dead. Isn't it fitting that I should do this so as to show I belong? I'll have to watch my step with David though. He's not as accepting as Lisa. And Emilia, we got off to a bad start. I'm sure it'll work out fine in the end. One thing the children's home taught me was how to think on my feet. It's not much but I'm good at it.

THE END

Acknowledgments

My thanks are owed to many people. Rebecca Collins and Adrian Hobart, thank you for taking a chance on me and publishing my books. If anyone had told me in 2022 that I would have had four books published in two years I would have asked them if they were hallucinating. But here we are. Thank you to the whole Hobeck family.

I'd also like to thank Alex Shaw for the highly professional job he did copyediting the book. I am always totally amazed by the skills of copyediting and by the level of detail that goes into their work. Thanks also to Miranda Saintey for proofreading *What Lies Beneath*. I am very grateful. Jayne Mapp has designed the cover and it's exactly as I wanted it to be.

Bloggers play an enormous part in the promotion of books, particularly those from small, independent publishers. I have been so lucky to have had my books reviewed by bloggers and I am so thankful for their support.

I am so lucky to have many wonderful writing friends: Ailsa Crum, Alison Irvine, Alison Miller, Ann Mackinnon, Bert Thomson, Clare Morrison, Emily Munro, Emma Lennox Miller, Griz Gordon, Heather Mackay, Natalie Whittle and Les Wood. In particular, Ailsa Crum, Alison Miller and Ann Mackinnon all read earlier complete drafts of *What Lies Beneath,* so long ago they may not even remember. Their comments and observations were invaluable.

Geraldine Smyth, a friend for over fifty years, has been a

great support in my writing, and has enthusiastically recommended them.

My family is as supportive as always, especially my husband, Martin.

Finally, if you have read this book, thank you very much. Writers without readers are nothing and we are grateful to every one of you for taking the time to read our work. If you have the time, please do post a review. It means so much.

MAUREEN MYANT

About the Author

Maureen worked for over 25 years as an educational psychologist but has also worked as a teacher and an Open University Associate Lecturer. She is a graduate of the prestigious University of Glasgow MLitt in Creative Writing course where she was taught by Janice Galloway, Liz Lochhead, James Kelman, Alasdair Gray and Tom Leonard among others. She also has a PhD in Creative Writing. Her first novel *The Search* was published by Alma Books and was translated into Spanish, Dutch and Turkish. It was longlisted for the Waverton Good Read Award and was one of the books chosen to be read for the Festival du premier roman de Chambéry. Her second novel, *The Confession*, was published by Hobeck Books in 2022 and introduces DI Alex Scrimgeour and DS Mark Nicholson. In an earlier incarnation it was shortlisted for a Crime Writers' Association Debut Dagger. *The Confession* has been followed by *The Deception* and *The Shame*.

Maureen has been a voracious reader since the age of six when, fed up with her mum reading Noddy stories to her, she picked up her older brother's copy of Enid Blyton's *The Valley of Adventure* and devoured it in an evening. She hasn't stopped reading since and loves literary fiction, historical fiction, crime fiction, psychological thrillers and contemporary fiction but not necessarily in that order. Her favourite book is *The Secret History* by Donna Tartt and go-to comfort read is *Anne of Green Gables*.

Maureen lives in Glasgow with her husband. She has three grownup children and six grandchildren who love to beat her at Bananagrams.

Hobeck Books - the home of great stories

We hope you've enjoyed reading this novel by Maureen Myant. To keep up to date on Maureen's fiction writing please do follow her on Twitter.

Hobeck Books offers a number of short stories and novellas, including *You Can't Trust Anyone These Days* by Maureen Myant, free for subscribers in the compilation *Crime Bites*.

- *Echo Rock* by Robert Daws
- *Old Dogs, Old Tricks* by AB Morgan
- *The Silence of the Rabbit* by Wendy Turbin
- *Never Mind the Baubles: An Anthology of Twisted Winter Tales* by the Hobeck Team (including many of the Hobeck authors and Hobeck's two publishers)
- *The Clarice Cliff Vase* by Linda Huber
- *Here She Lies* by Kerena Swan
- *The Macnab Principle* by R.D. Nixon
- *Fatal Beginnings* by Brian Price
- *A Defining Moment* by Lin Le Versha
- *Saviour* by Jennie Ensor
- *You Can't Trust Anyone These Days* by Maureen Myant

Also please visit the Hobeck Books website for details of our other superb authors and their books, and if you would like to get in touch, we would love to hear from you.

Hobeck Books also presents a weekly podcast, the Hobcast, where founders Adrian Hobart and Rebecca Collins discuss all things book related, key issues from each week, including the ups and downs of running a creative business. Each episode includes an interview with one of the people who make Hobeck possible: the editors, the authors, the cover designers. These are the people who help Hobeck bring great stories to life. Without them, Hobeck wouldn't exist. The Hobcast can be listened to from all the usual platforms but it can also be found on the Hobeck website: **www. hobeck.net/hobcast**.

Also by Maureen Myant

The Glasgow Southside crime series

The Confession

The Deception

The Shame

All three books in the series available to buy from Amazon or Hobeck Books.

The Search

In Czechoslovakia, 1942, Jan's father has been summarily executed by the Nazis. His mother and his older sister Maria have disappeared, and his younger sister Lena has been removed to a remote farm in the German countryside. With Europe in the throes of war, the ten-year-old boy embarks on a personal journey to reunite the family he has been violently torn from. The experiences he goes through and the horror he faces during this desperate quest will change his life for ever. While examining the devastating effects of war on ordinary families, *The Search* provides an exploration of fear and loss, and of the bond between parents and children. Riveting, moving, at times disturbing, Maureen Myant's debut novel will haunt its readers for a long time after they have put it down.

Available from Amazon.